Country Pleasures

'I asked you a question, earlier,' Maddock said to Janie. 'Did it turn you on, watching me and your friend?'

Sally folded her arms crossly around her knees. Since Janie had unexpectedly burst in, both the rugged farmer and her friend seemed to have forgotten she was in the same room.

'And I would like to ask *you* a question,' said Janie. 'When would you like to leave? Right now or in one minute's time?'

'My question was, did you enjoy watching us?' Maddock persisted.

'A bit difficult to avoid watching, seeing as how you just strolled in and started shagging my friend on the floor.' Janie still had one foot in the hall, as if she was contemplating her escape. 'Now, I really don't want to hold you up any longer. Don't you have to be somewhere?'

'His Lordship and the lads can get the pints in,' said Maddock. 'I want to know . . . did you enjoy it? Looks like something's flicked your switch.'

'Yeah. Don't pretend to be so uptight, Janie,' goaded Sally. 'Admit it, you were turned on just then, weren't you? Sex in the sitting room on a rainy night with a bit of rough. What could be a better way to pass the time?'

Maddock kept his eyes on Janie, unflinching at Sally's description of him. 'And that was just the warm up,' he said.

Country Pleasures
Primula Bond

BLACK LACE

Black Lace books contain sexual fantasies.
In real life, always practise safe sex.

First published in 2003 by
Black Lace
Thames Wharf Studios
Rainville Road
London W6 9HA

Design by Smith & Gilmour, London
Printed and bound by Mackays of Chatham PLC

ISBN 0 352 33810 5

1

Rain spattered on the windows. It drenched the old thatch and tried to seep under the doors. The wind yanked at any loose timbers it could find and howled round corners before giving way to more bursts of rain.

Janie couldn't believe it. It was July, for God's sake. Tucked away in the shallow hills of South Devon, this place was meant to be a summer retreat. It looked more like a witch's cottage, covered with poison ivy and crawling roses, and it was invisible from all the surrounding roads. Perfect for a hideout. They were meant to be lolling around naked in the garden, concealed from view by the wild trees and bushes, sipping home-made Cosmopolitans and skinny-dipping in the sea at sunset. It should have been an opportunity to sort out their lives, and generally chill until it was time to rejoin the rat race. Instead of which . . .

'Are there logs we can chop to get a fire going?' asked Sally as they sat in the beamed sitting room. 'And while we're at it, are there any hot-water bottles? I'm losing the feeling in my toes and I've only been here a couple of hours.'

Janie turned from the window seat, where she had been watching the dog roses lose their petals under the weight of rain.

Sally was hunched in front of the empty fireplace, listening to one of the handful of jazz and classical CDs they'd found stacked beside the hi fi, and contemplating the demise of her career. She was nursing a bruised ego after taking on the might of yet another City tribunal and, yet again, losing.

As usual, Janie had waded in with a rest cure. At least, that was what it was supposed to be. She turned back to the window and frowned at the rain. The slightest discomfort in these supposedly idyllic surroundings would be bound to tip Sally into a foul temper, she thought.

Ever since they were at school, Janie had been Sally's unofficial therapist. She worked like a kind of escape valve. The pair were total opposites, which was probably why their friendship worked. Janie was bohemian and dreamy and, for all her friend's braying confidence and skimpy business suits, Sally depended on Janie, rather than her brash City mates, to get her back on track after a crisis. By the same token, Janie's own life was brightened by the drama and chaos that accompanied Sally wherever she went. When life and limb were restored and Sally had hurtled back to reality, Janie's world always seemed, for a while at least, much too quiet.

'I can cut it, Janie, whatever they say about me,' Sally had insisted a week earlier, as she jabbed at the financial pages spread all over the café table in Portobello Road. They were sitting in the sunshine and had forced themselves to read the sniggering reports about Sally, the 'petite blonde' trying to take the markets by storm. 'It's just that this time they had one over me. I didn't see it coming. Those jerks hijacked my deals. Particularly that bloody Jonathan Dart. I only hired him six months ago, and yet, before I could blink, he'd wheedled his way into my knickers and then shafted me. And not the kind of shafting you're thinking of. Now a bit more of that I *would* have enjoyed.'

'That's it.' Janie chucked the newspapers onto the pavement and slapped her hand over Sally's complaining mouth. 'Enough. *Verboten*. No more talk of office politics or shafting or Jonathans or any of that stuff. Off the menu from now on.'

'I didn't mind that,' continued Sally after unpeeling Janie's hand from her face. 'You know, the knickers bit. I was really getting the taste for it, but then it turned out I was sleeping with the enemy. Just out of the blue.'

'I said stop! Men are off the menu.'

'Even hunks in pinstripe suits with big lunch boxes?'

'Especially them. Now listen, you're out of a job, right?'

'No need to rub it in,' Sally grumbled as she reached for her handbag. 'Where's my lipstick?'

'So, you have some free time. A bit of redundancy pay came out of all that, didn't it?'

'Quite a lot, actually.' Sally smirked, her lips painted red again. She raised her voice and pinned her shoulders back as the waiter edged past the table. 'Enough to send me to the Caribbean for a few weeks, anyway. Get away from this shit hole. Could we have the bill, please?'

'Forget the Caribbean.' Janie coughed as a motorbike backfired along the traffic-heavy street. 'Come to Ben's cottage with me. I'm going down there anyway. I said I'd do some painting for him in return for a freebie, practice some of my designing skills while he's away, cast my eyes over some of the other properties in the area that might need tarting up.'

'Not more work,' sighed Sally, gazing up as the waiter returned, and holding tight to a fiver so that he had to prize it, very slowly, from her extended fingers. She had already scribbled her mobile phone number on the back of the bill. 'I refuse to get my head round any more business.'

'You don't have to. You can just laze about, lick your wounds, prepare the odd salad, open the odd bottle of wine. I could do with the company. It's very quiet down there, especially since the cross-eyed neighbours across the field sold up or died of the plague or whatever. Anyway, they left. No one to flash your tits at, Sally. Sally!'

Sally wound her tongue back in and turned to Janie with a mock batting of her eyelashes.

'Yes, yes, I'm listening. Therapeutic rest cure in the middle of nowhere? No shops, no bars, no men? Darling, it's a lovely idea.' Sally scraped the iron chair back to stand up. She rested one foot on the seat and raised her arms to cram her messy hair into a comb. Her frayed miniskirt rode up her thigh, until the denim was drawn tight over the twin curves of her bum. The crease where the plump cheeks met the tops of her legs parted and closed as she jigged about, fiddling with her hair. In the shadow cast by her skirt it was possible to catch a glimpse of Sally's golden pubes, her pussy-lips parting with the movement of her leg to reveal a delicate magenta sliver of flesh before vanishing again. Several heads in the café snapped round, and over at the counter the waiter slammed the till shut.

'By the way, what knickers?' Janie yanked at Sally's tiny denim skirt to grab her attention, then began to gather her own belongings. 'You said that chap Jonathan got into your knickers.'

'And?' Sally brought her foot down slowly, not bothering to adjust her skirt. The hem rested cheekily halfway up her crotch. She leaned across Janie to lift her bag; the little skirt may as well have given up and gone home. Sally's white buttocks were totally on display, and a defiant yellow curl of her bare bush brushed against the sharp edge of the table, catching croissant crumbs in its blonde hairs.

'*And* . . . you never wear knickers!'

Sally's mobile phone trilled as the girls giggled. She flicked it open, listened, then glanced across at the waiter, who was leaning in the doorway of the café, talking on his own mobile. Her tongue slid out again and ran across her wide mouth.

'I'll see you in Devon,' she said, winking at Janie and bumping her hip against the chair to shift it out of the way. Sally's skirt rose higher still. She sauntered through the audience of swivelling heads and drooling mouths towards her waiting admirer.

Now Sally was hunched, as promised, on one of the deep flowery sofas in the cottage sitting room, books and magazines strewn across the old carpet, rubbing her hands together as if they were sitting in a gale, and blowing into a cup of tea.

'Here, put this on if you're cold,' urged Janie, chucking a bulky sweater across the room. 'I found loads of Ben's jumpers in the cupboard upstairs.'

'Lovely,' croaked Sally, before blowing her nose. 'Let's have a rummage through his drawers. Such huge, manly jumpers he wears. They smell all soapy and woolly. I expect you were always borrowing them when you were a kid.'

'Fat chance. I was the annoying little distant cousin who wouldn't go away when he and his ugly friend Jack wanted to play cowboys and Indians. He always said I wasn't distant enough.'

'Cowboys and Indians, eh? Kinky. Bet they would have used you as the squaw in their game if you'd all had more imagination.' Sally tilted her chin and threw her arm towards the window. 'They'd have caught you stalking them and tied you up with your own lassoo to the totem pole. Ah, the ultimate phallic symbol. They'd have erected their great big totem pole right out there, in the garden, hidden from view by that big beech tree so the parents couldn't see. The pair of them, whooping round you, waving their tomahawks, offering up bloody sacrifices to the gods, then sparing you from execution, untying you and dragging you into the tepee – Big Chief Throbbing Dick and his sidekick Flicking Tongue!'

'You're so wrong!' spluttered Janie, laughing at the idiocy of it. 'Our childhood was all Enid Blyton, not Linda Lovelace.'

'Sod that. Consider the potential.' Sally kneeled up and waved her arms around to sketch the imaginary scenario. 'Just think, there you are, bound with your own ropes, being tumbled naked onto the bearskins – at least they'd have had a fire going in the wigwam, unlike this apology of an inglenook.'

'I'll complain to the management.'

'And then both of them are crouching over your supple young body, one starting at your head and one starting at your feet. They are new to this, as well, and they're taking it in turns: exploring you, working on you with their hands and mouths then, using teeth and tongues, groping every inch of you, stroking your skin, nibbling slowly up your thighs –'

'Still thinking of roasting me in the pot?' asked Janie.

'Silly! And all the while you're squirming and wriggling away on the bearskin, struggling to keep your legs crossed to hide what little modesty you have left, yet at the same time you're straining to be free of the leather cords.'

'Stop!' Janie threw a magazine at Sally. She was blushing at the vivid picture: the two boys and her, tangled up together inside the secret wigwam. 'Nothing like that ever happened.'

'Well, if you don't want the fantasy, I'll keep it for myself.' Sally sniffed.

'It's just that we were scrawny kids. The boys were far more interested in drawing blood from each other than using me as some kind of sex toy. Thank God neither of them knew what a desperate crush I had on them both.'

Janie moved round to the fireplace and stared at her reflection, indistinct in the enormous tarnished mirror. She twisted long strands of hair into two plaits and stood up straight.

'What good's a crush when nothing comes of it, Mini Ha-Ha?' remarked Sally. 'You have to pounce on men you fancy; at least let them know you've got the hots for them. That's what I do. It's what comes of having no one to play with when you're little. But you've never been a brazen slut like me, have you? You look just the part now, all tall and solemn, with that dark-red hair, the way your eyes slant up at the corners. All we need is the feather headdress, the buffalo-skin tunic –'

'You can laugh,' said Janie, trying to bring Sally back down to earth. 'Dressing up may be our only entertainment until we can get the TV fixed. Now, get off your arse and help me look.'

Sally made a face and had an exaggerated fit of coughing. 'Look for what?' she asked.

'Logs, electric heaters, Monopoly, a pack of cards –'

'Vibrators?'

'Like an eligible single man would have vibrators in his weekend retreat!'

'You're always very defensive about him, aren't you?' sniffed Sally, hobbling to her feet like an old lady. 'Won't hear a word against him.'

'I'm just saying, about the vibrators –'

'Don't tell me, he's a walking, talking vibrator! So well hung his girlfriends would have no need of any ... *aids* for their pleasure.'

'I wouldn't know about his love life,' Janie said primly. 'We used to see each other a lot, when all the rellies used to troop down here to visit his family in their holiday home, but now it's usually by phone or email. I haven't seen him for ages.'

Janie wandered out into the chilly hall and yanked open the cupboard under the stairs.

'But he's happy to let you come here while he's away?' said Sally as she followed her friend and crouched next to her.

'Yes, keeps it occupied, and anyway, look at the place: it needs more than just a lick of paint. He can't have touched it in ten years. I had a good snoop round before you got here. It needs complete redecoration.'

'Not going to be much fun for me if you're slaving away over a hot paintbrush all holiday.'

'I told you, you're to relax. In any case, I won't be able to do the whole thing. Not on my own, anyway. I'll have to talk to him about getting some builders in.'

Sally pushed Janie aside and burrowed into the cupboard.

'Look at all this!' she exclaimed. 'It's like something out of a Noel Coward play: tennis racquets, croquet hoops, parasols. What's this contraption?'

A pile of metal poles and rods clattered out of a bag.

'I think it's a swing-seat for the garden,' Janie said, pushing it all back in the bag. 'You'd think from this stuff that the sun always shines down here.'

Sally wandered down the hall and into another little room at the back of the house.

'Not necessarily,' she called. 'He's got a neat little office set-up here. You could spend all winter in this place, holed up with plenty of food and booze, working away on some big business deal or writing a book.'

'Ben never sits still, though,' said Janie, joining her friend who was busy snooping round the office space. 'I'm surprised to see all these computers and stuff. I don't think he's here more than two or three times a year.'

'He might be your hero, Mini Ha-Ha, but there must be loads you don't know about him. Perhaps he runs some kind of racket from here, far away from the prying eyes of Interpol or the Inland Revenue.'

Janie shut the cupboard door and brushed cobwebs out of her hair. 'You're right, there is loads I don't know. I don't even really know what he looks like these days.'

'What happened to his ugly mate?' asked Sally, as she climbed the stairs with her bag.

'Jack? Haven't a clue. I last saw him crouching half-way up the cliffs, shooting at seagulls and narrowly missing my head. We must have been about fifteen. Oi!'

Janie spotted Sally on the landing, and bounded up the stairs, two at a time, to catch her.

'Bags I the master bedroom.' Sally giggled and pushed her shoulder against the first bedroom door.

'Too late.' Janie barred the way into Ben's bedroom. 'I'm in here. I'm likely to be here all summer if he wants me to blitz the house, so I get first choice.'

'But I'm supposed to be your guest.'

'Your room is very sweet. Look.'

They trooped into the smaller bedroom, which had a

bowed wooden floor and a vast Victorian brass bed covered in lace cushions.

'It's cute: a real love nest. But who chose the décor, his mum?'

They both looked round. The muslin curtains wafted gently in the draught. Outside was a tiny balcony.

'Very likely. Or his sister. I guess she still comes here sometimes. It's not very masculine in here, I admit.'

'Perhaps he puts his girlfriends in here, and visits them for a shag late at night.'

'Do you ever stop thinking about sex?' Janie asked.

'Nope. It's twenty-four seven for me, girl. Are you sure you want to spend two whole weeks with me?'

'Well, I'm beginning to wonder,' mocked Janie.

'Because I'm not sure I'd want to spend two weeks with me in the horny frustrated state I'll be in by the end of it.'

'That's not why you're here, and you know it. You're here to put the world to rights, and I'm here to help you.'

'I'll try my best not to behave.' Sally lunged at Janie to get past her. 'Now, let me see the master's chamber.'

'Later. I haven't settled in yet. Now I'm the one who's freezing,' said Janie, turning to go back down the stairs. 'We've got to get some heat going in this house.'

'Ooh, look up here! *This* is going to be my room!'

Sally had vanished up a little spiral staircase in the corner of the landing. So Ben had been doing *some* work to the house. This was all new. Janie climbed up into what was once the attic, and found Sally clattering around under the eaves. The room had been transformed into a hideout. The walls were painted dark red, the timbers were all exposed, and an enormous dormer window had been set into the thatched roof to look seawards. A telescope rested on a tripod, and was aimed at the sky.

'This used to be just full of clutter. I wonder when he converted it,' said Janie.

'Think what larks you could have had hiding up here. Especially with that telescope.' Sally peered through the lens, shook it a bit, then gave up. She threw her bag down on the patchwork quilt that covered the low bed, which looked like a raft made out of driftwood. 'It's very homely, all these little signs of cousin Ben everywhere. But I can't get rid of the feeling that we're trespassing.'

'He knows we're here, silly.'

'Yes, but what does he do on his own here? Have orgies, do you think? Plenty of room, after all!'

Janie took Sally's arm and led her back down the spiral staircase. 'He relaxes; chills out. Now stop asking questions.'

The wind gave an extra loud howl through the front door as they came down, as if to reiterate its unseasonal violence. With much grunting and heaving, the two girls dragged a couple of electric heaters and some picnic rugs out of the cupboard, along with a dusty box of Trivial Pursuit and a chessboard.

'Phew, it's like the mummy's tomb in here now.' Sally screwed up her nose as the warming heaters gave off the smell of scorched dust. 'I take it our Ben doesn't have a Mrs Mop, like my Mrs Mop in London. You can see your entire reflection in the shower door-handle when she's finished at my flat.'

'Welcome to the good life, *mademoiselle*,' commented Janie, holding her hands over the heater for a moment and surveying the room, which at least looked cosy now that it was more cluttered. 'No domestic help, no cook, no bottle washer. Just *moi*. Now, does the ambience, if not the temperature, meet with your approval?'

Sally wrapped her arms around herself, her hands invisible beneath the long sweater-sleeves. She jogged up and down on the spot for a few seconds, then sat down on the sofa that she had now earmarked as her own. 'Absolutely,' she said. 'It's adorable once it's lived in, isn't it?'

'So that means I don't have to go out into this infernal storm, hunting for logs?'

'Maybe later. You're excused for the moment, but the fireplace does look kind of bleak without a fire going, doesn't it?'

Janie changed the CD and enjoyed the few moments' silence.

'Trivial Pursuit?' she asked eventually.

They both shook their heads.

'Draughts?'

'Too many draughts in here already.'

The wind rattled the window in agreement.

'I'll tell you what'll warm the cockles and cheer us up.' Janie leaned over the squashy sofa and rapped her knuckles on the top of her friend's head. Sally blew her nose into a bright-pink handkerchief and looked round eagerly.

'You've dreamed up Big Chief Hard-on. You've planned the big surprise. Any minute now, Ben and some hunky mates are going to roll up in an enormous black four-by-four, loincloths akimbo, armed with tomahawks and baying for our bodies.'

'Guess again. I told you, this is a man-free zone. Anyway, Ben's overseas, working in Amsterdam or somewhere. He'd go running straight back there if he knew a harlot like you had designs on him. Ben needs protecting.'

'You mean you want him for yourself,' said Sally.

'Don't be silly. I'm going to put the kettle on.'

'Kettle?'

'OK, I'm going to open some of that Chardonnay you brought,' Janie corrected. 'You must have spent your entire redundancy cheque on those cases of food and wine. And then, for this evening's entertainment, you're going to tell me what happened with that waiter.'

'What waiter?' asked Sally, feigning innocence.

'Come on, you haven't said a word about that particular close encounter since I left you creaming yourself at the café last Sunday.'

Sally laughed and wriggled herself back into the soft cushions.

'Oh, right, him. I haven't had a chance to tell you, and anyway, I'm still recovering from the experience.'

'I don't believe you,' said Janie. 'You can take all comers.' She wandered into the kitchen to fetch the wine, and decided that the cupboards would look good painted a misty blue.

'Too right I can, but I thought you had declared this a man-free zone,' called Sally.

'That doesn't include telling stories about them,' Janie said returning to the room with the wine, two glasses and an assortment of savoury snacks. 'At least, not for today. Come on, you can start with, "it was a dark, dark night ..."'

'Well, if you insist. And if you're sitting comfortably, I'll begin. Except that, as you know, it wasn't a dark, dark night. It was a boiling hot afternoon, not seven days ago, although the welts and bruises are still there to remind me.' Sally's voice went husky with remembered lust. 'Now then, what you're about to hear makes cowboys and Indians look like child's play.'

'I'll be the judge of that,' said Janie, pulling out the cork with a pop just as a clap of thunder exploded over the cottage.

'Well, for a start, it turned out that he wasn't a waiter at all. He owns the bloody joint! I recognised his name from the financials when he told me. Rod Mastov. He owns a whole chain of cafés and bars.'

'Good name, Rod. Especially if he turned out to be the sex dog you thought he was. Or perhaps a sugar daddy?' said Janie, crossing her legs under her on the floor and scooping up a handful of peanuts.

'Nothing daddy-ish about him. Admittedly he's older than he looked when he was strutting about in those tight black jeans taking orders, but he's still fit as a flea. We were jumping into a taxi before you could say Marco Pierre.'

'Haven't lost your touch, then,' murmured Janie, easing a peanut from her tooth with her tongue.

'I was on a roll. After this knock-back at work, I needed a good seeing to. It's what I always need when I'm stressed, and that's why I cast my beady eye over him.'

'I didn't even notice him,' said Janie.

'That's because you're never on the lookout. Wake up and smell the coffee, Janie. You never know what or who is out there. And it's usually where you least expect it.'

Janie laughed and pulled a couple of cushions off the sofa: one to sit on and one to hug. The wind rattled the latch on the door and she shivered.

'I don't care if Antonio Banderas is out there today,

imploring me to come out and play,' she said. 'I'm staying put!'

'That's why you'll never have adventures like I do,' mocked Sally.

'No, poor old me. I'll just have to get my kicks out of hearing about yours.'

'We'll see about that. Now, where was I?'

'Zooming through London in a cab with a shady tycoon.'

Sally picked up the thread. 'It turned out we could have walked. He only lives round the corner. But there's something about cabs, isn't there? Very dangerous and exciting being in a cab with a strange man.'

'And you couldn't have walked more than a couple of yards in those shag-me shoes, anyway.'

'I know. Daft. And those taxis have plastic seats, don't they, and my thighs kept sticking with sweat because it was so hot in there. Every time I crossed my legs, the skin squeaked, and that little skirt just rode up higher. Very unsophisticated. But he just looked at me, and after a while I couldn't help wondering –'

'That there might not be anything lurking inside those tight black jeans, after all?' Janie cut in.

They both laughed.

'Yes, in a way, except that he was so *cool*, you know? A kind of Bryan Ferry type. You could just *tell*. And all of a sudden his fingers brushed down my arm and I jumped like a scalded cat.'

'Oh, Sal, even *I've* had more than a brush on the arm to write home about,' yawned Janie, sipping from her glass and absent-mindedly stroking the velvet cushion.

'Yeah, but we're talking *starved* here, Janie. I hadn't had more than a handshake from another human being since Jonathan and I got naked on that business trip to Paris, and that was ages ago ... well, two months.'

'You'll have to tell me about that in our next story-telling session. Tomorrow, in fact, if the weather keeps up.'

'Oh, it'll be your turn tomorrow,' corrected Sally. 'My Paris story will have to wait. It's a corker, though – Jonathan has the biggest dick you've ever seen. Stands right away from his stomach when it's erect, all proud and stiff, like some kind of a –'

'*Gendarme*'s truncheon?'

Sally grinned lasciviously. 'You said it. Just like that. It has to be seen to be believed. It's a wonder we got any work done on that trip. Humping away we were. Paris in the spring, or early summer, it was, right on the hotel balcony overlooking the Champs Elysées, those posh shoppers trotting up and down below with their designer bags, all unaware of him taking me from behind, bent over the railings a couple of floors above them, the Eiffel Tower just a few blocks away –'

'I thought you were going to save it,' said Janie.

'I'm going to have to, otherwise I'm going to explode just thinking about it. I'm just trying to explain to you why I was so sensitive, sitting in the taxi next to Mastov, after all that dreary celibacy. Like I said, a flick of the fingernail, right on my sunburn, was all it took.'

'I'm not spending my evening hearing a rampant tale of one man and his fingernail now, am I?'

Janie glanced over at the velvet curtains. The wind outside was strong enough to lift the heavy fabric in lazy ripples. Sally was brilliant at talking about herself, and Janie enjoyed listening but, even so, she did wonder how on earth she was going to keep her randy friend amused for two whole weeks.

'Janie.'

Janie jolted round to find Sally studying her intensely. 'If you're totally honest, that must be how it is for you, only ten times over. If you haven't had sex in months, or even years, I don't know, how could you not be fizzing for it every minute of the day?'

'I can't answer that,' Janie admitted. 'I don't know. I guess if you don't think about it, the urge sort of goes away.'

'I don't go for that theory. I think desire is lurking just under the surface, for all of us. Unless you're like me, who's gagging for it all of the time.'

'Even now?' enquired Janie with a playful smirk.

'Even now, given the chance. Talking comes a poor second, but it's keeping us happy, isn't it? I promise you, all it would take would be one tiny touch. Maybe even the whiff of a particular aftershave, or even a look in some guy's eyes, and you'd be off – going like a train.'

'I'd forgotten how you like to instruct people.' Janie laughed and swallowed some more wine.

'Listen and learn, girl, listen and learn. Which is why I'm telling you that all Mastov had to do was look at me with those incredible eyes. First, he looked at my feet, then my legs, then my tits – which wasn't difficult as they were practically hanging out of that strappy white vest.'

'Half of West London knows you weren't wearing a bra that day,' Janie pointed out, in between sips of wine. 'But then you're lucky, you don't need a bra, unlike some of us.'

'People are never happy with their tits, are they?' said Sally. 'You know I've always envied your big boobs, Janie. You always try to hide them under those glorious flowing shirts, but it's no good. It's still perfectly easy to see what they're like under there. Blokes must be trying to take a peak all the time. I wouldn't fancy walking past a building site if I were you!'

Janie shrugged, blushing. 'What about you, tarting about in your little mini skirt?' she countered.

'Don't play the innocent with me. If it hasn't happened already, one day some bloke is going to want to tear your shirt off and get his muzzle right in there.'

Janie giggled into her wine glass. Her breasts started to tingle beneath her dark-red linen shirt at the thought of a bristly face nuzzling to get inside her hidden cleavage; a man's nose and mouth, breath warm and tongue wet on her white skin. She started to dream about whose face it might be, then crossed her arms defiantly to stop the encroaching thought.

'You see? You know it really. You just need to lose your inhibitions.'

'We're not talking about me at the moment, though, are we?'

'Why not? We can if you want. There's loads we could talk about.'

'No, I don't want. I just want to get pissed, and get warm, and hear about Mr Mastov.'

'You are a curious creature, Janie. You can't live vicariously for ever, you know. I will make it my mission to find you someone to teach you all they know. Maybe I'll even introduce you to Mastov.'

'But I don't know where he's been!'

'Oh, but you're about to find out, girl. Listen to this. He had the weirdest chat up technique. He put his mouth right up by my ear and said, "I won't eat you, whatever you may have heard about me. But I might lick you."'

'What a sleazy line!' cried Janie, squeezing her arms across her chest to soothe her still-tingling breasts. 'What on earth *had* you heard about him?'

'Well, he has a reputation of being a bit of a wolf, so it all fitted, really.'

'So what did you say back?'

'My lips were too dry to say anything. I just banged my knees together awkwardly like a schoolgirl and got this picture of his tongue, glistening and red, probing like an animal's under my tight skirt. I imagined it slithering up the insides of my thighs, higher and higher, getting closer to my – I mean, remember I wasn't wearing any knickers.'

'Whoa, cowgirl, spare us the nooks and crannies.'

Janie rearranged herself on the floor, tucking one of the cushions tight between her legs. An insistent twitching had started somewhere inside her knickers in an echo of what Sally was describing. Tiny tremors fussed across the surface of her pubes. It was the image of someone – the one that had been between her breasts – now probing higher and higher, getting closer and closer to her.

The thunder rumbled away over the sea, the rain hissed and dribbled on the windows outside and an early dusk began to fall.

'I was really squirming on the seat, I can tell you,' Sally went on. 'I put on a silly voice and squeaked, "Oh, grandmother, what a big tongue you have!"'

'Not your usual banter, then. Normally, you say –'

'Get your dick out!'

They spluttered into their wineglasses.

'So, let me guess,' choked Janie. 'He said, "All the better to taste you with, my dear."'

'Yes! That's exactly what he said! And to make it even funnier, I caught the eye of the cab driver in the mirror. He'd heard every word. I could see he was interested, his eyes were all glittery.'

'Perhaps he was part of the plan?' Janie said, then

pulled her knees up to her chin, her legs squeezing the cushion as she started to rock. The cushion rubbed back and forth underneath her, pressing into her crotch. 'Mastov's partner in crime. Perhaps he was going to stop the car, leap over the seat, shove Mastov aside and push your little skirt up before Mastov had a chance, let Mastov watch you at it.'

'You're getting the hang of this, aren't you? Was it all that talk of threesomes in the tepee, perhaps?'

'You put the idea into my head, remember!'

The cushion was heating up under her. Janie stopped rocking. An invisible, untouchable part of her was aching. She crossed her legs the other way and started to wind her long hair into another plait. Now she was back in the rickety tent made out of bamboo shoots and an old blanket, which the boys had built in the copse behind the cottage. In fact, she'd never been allowed into the copse, or the wigwam. But in her mind she was barging her way inside to find Ben and Jack huddled together, rubbing sticks to make a fire and muttering made-up curses. Her entrance made their mouths round and dark with surprise. Jack was squinting through the gloom at her and Ben was frowning. They weren't quite the kids of her childhood in this fantasy, and not quite men either. She was pushing them off their haunches so that they toppled sideways onto the grassy floor and she was standing over them, long legs stretching up to the tattered buffalo-skin wrapped tightly round her body and fastened with safety pins. She was not being dragged in there at all. On the contrary, she was the one in charge. She was her grown-up self, staring down her nose as she started to unhook each pin. Strips of animal skin were dropping one by one onto the floor as the boys clutched their bows and arrows and watched. Each smooth curve was revealed, little by little, in the weak daylight filtering from the smoke hole at the top of the tent.

Then only the last pin was left, the one bending under the strain of her breasts, and she was yanking her shoulders back so that the pin flew off its moorings. Her squaw outfit disintegrated and her breasts bounced out for the boys to see.

'Are you listening to me, squaw?' Sally was wiggling her empty glass under Janie's nose like smelling salts.

'Er, sure.' Janie took the glass but didn't refill it. 'I was just wondering how far you'd got with the taxi driver?'

'Liar. You were getting down to business inside that wigwam, weren't you?'

'I hadn't got that far, actually. I was just standing over them, teasing them.'

'That's my girl. Go on, tell me more, get further into it.'

Janie got up off the floor. The cushion dropped from between her knees, and her legs were shaking from the effort of grasping it.

'I was teasing them, that's all, letting my squaw outfit drop away so that they'd get their first ever eyeful, and it would be me who would show them a real woman's body; me who'd be their teacher.'

'You're doing so well. Let those inhibitions go. Get those boys eating out of your hand!'

'I can't.' The heat that bubbled up in the spot where the cushion had been rubbing was too sudden and too strong. 'I'm not like you, Sal.'

'Tell you what,' Sally said, 'when I've told you my story, my challenge for the week is for you to match it with your own. Ideally it has to be a true one. You have these next two weeks either to recall something that has actually happened to you, or to make something happen before I go back to London.'

Janie staggered into the kitchen and swished the glasses noisily under the tap, gazing at the thick branches of violet wisteria drooping over the window.

'That's some challenge,' she called. 'Do you realise just how quiet it is down here? There isn't even a shop, or a pub, or a bus stop, for at least a mile.'

'Like I keep saying, there are men and boys every-where, if you just open your eyes. Honestly, Janie, do I have to do it all for you?'

'For now, yes.' Janie came back into the room and switched on one of the lamps. There was still some greyish light outside, but it didn't penetrate further than the windows. She decided against pulling the curtains.

'And at the end of two weeks, if there really isn't anyone or anything with a decently proportioned, fully operational willy between here and John o'Groats, I'll make you tell me the wigwam story.'

'Deal,' conceded Janie, then she started to giggle.

'What?'

'You and your way with words. Now I can't get this picture out of my head. Rows and rows of them, penis after penis, all lined up along a kind of yellow brick road with a signpost at the end.'

'Honey, ain't no good if they're not attached to anything!'

Janie poured two fresh glasses of wine, still giggling.

'What was his house like?' she asked.

'Whose? John o'Groats?'

They laughed some more.

'Oh, it was one of those big pastel houses in Holland Park. Vast inside, with black and white marble walls and floors, and echoing rooms. He's obviously too busy ruling his catering empire to bother with personal trimmings. Definitely no woman's touch.'

Janie handed Sally a fresh glass of wine and sat down again, this time on one of the armchairs. She grabbed the cushion and stuffed it between her legs once more and immediately she felt the heat seep through her again.

'So you felt perfectly safe alone with him in there?' asked Janie, trying to ignore the rush of excitement she was secretly experiencing.

'I just kept going over his share offers I'd read about in the *FT*. I knew that if he turned nasty I could always just name him and shame him.'

'So why don't you?' enquired Janie with a wicked glint in her eye. 'That would put you back on the map, too. Think of all those City jerks who would sit up and take notice. You could do a centre spread: MY NIGHT WITH MASSIVE MASTOV. You'd make a fortune.'

'I can't do it, because he didn't turn nasty, and anyway, it would confirm what they are all saying about me: that I just slept my way to a good story.'

Sally grew silent for a moment. Janie kicked her.

'Can't have you turning into Goody Two-Shoes! So what was it that kept you in Blue Beard's castle?'

'Simple. Presents. The sight of a designer box tied with ribbon always brings me to my senses. Suddenly he was just another older man, flattering me into bed. Putty in my hands, or so I reckoned. I thought it was time to explore upstairs, but Mastov chased after me to stop me peering into the other rooms.'

'Why? What was he hiding? White slave girls locked up in there, shackled in chains?'

Sally laughed and kicked her leg over the arm of the sofa. 'I could ask you the same thing. What's hidden in the master's chamber upstairs, I'd like to know?

Perhaps you have someone tied to the bed, who you're not going to share? The master himself?'

'I wish,' murmured Janie. 'The bed's certainly big enough, but, no. Sorry, no shackled men, no vibrators, nothing upstairs except a white cotton duvet and some very prim pyjamas.'

'Oh, I almost forgot,' shrieked Sally, suddenly animated again. 'Talking of games, we could dress up!'

'What are you on about now?'

'The present in the box I was telling you about; the gift from Mastov. It was a long white negligee, with spaghetti straps and made of semi-transparent chiffon, so thin you could thread it through a needle. I've brought it with me.'

'So did you put it on?'

'Yes. He took me into this room, which was totally dominated by a huge Chinese opium bed, all dragons in black and gold lacquer twining round each other. And then he grabbed me from behind and bit my neck. I'm not talking adolescent love bites, either. Look.'

Sally pulled down the collar of Ben's big jumper. There were two little red points in her neck, just below her ear. Janie looked on in astonishment.

'Hmm, so the story's changed from Little Red Riding Hood to Dracula.'

'I didn't mind, because it was a really sexy kind of vicious pain. Like electric shocks shooting through me. And what was even better was that, at the same time, he was wedging a rock-hard erection into my buttocks.'

Janie jumped as some last minute thunder, trailing behind the crowd, gave a dying growl over the cottage.

Sally laughed at her as the rain renewed its attack. 'This is perfect story-telling weather,' she said. 'And Mastov is just like Dracula. His room was cold, too. I was starting to shiver. So what does he do? Starts taking my clothes off.'

'Makes sense,' remarked Janie, sarcastically.

'I was ready for the famous probing tongue, I can tell you. I wanted it to start with the licking he'd promised me. My clothes were off, goose bumps on the skin, nipples out like corks ... but he just said he wanted to look.'

'After all that?' Janie sat up in her chair, unable to disguise her disappointment.

'I was furious, I can tell you,' continued Sally. 'I hadn't come all that way just to be gawped at.'

'Maybe men of his age can't get it up or something.'

'Well, I nearly bottled it then and there, but then he held out the negligee and told me to put it on. I decided to give it one last go. Apart from anything else, I needed warming up. I went into the bathroom and I could see in the mirror that there was already this mark on my neck, and it spooked me.'

'I'm not surprised,' Janie agreed. 'You do hear of real-life vampires who live off human blood.'

'But a business tycoon in modern day London? I told myself not to be stupid and dropped the negligee on over my head. In fact, you should try it on, Janie. You'd look gorgeous in it. It's long, and see-through.'

'But he gave it to you.'

'It would suit you far better. It was too long for me, anyway, but I have to say, draped in all that white silk, I did look like a vestal virgin. Just suitable fodder for a vampire.'

'Like you could pass for a virgin!'

'Enticing thought, though, eh? A bit like you being offered up as a sacrifice to your two Indian chiefs.'

The two women stretched in their chairs, glancing round the cosy room. They felt totally cut off from civilisation, with only their gathering fantasies for company.

Sally was eager to continue with her story. 'When I came out of the bathroom, there was music playing, so I decided to dance. I was going to sock it to him. I was going to pretend I was stepping out on stage, like in one of those those dance shows we used to do at the holiday clubs, do you remember?'

'How could I forget? I was the one wandering round the audience, trying to sell programmes and ignoring the sniggers.'

'Ever the faithful friend, Janie. But it was a laugh, wasn't it? Me and the Kicker Girls? I should have kept on my career as a dancer, rather than ending up a failed stockbroker.'

'Knicker Girls, more like. Now then, no self-pity allowed around here. Tell me, what sort of music did Mastov put on?'

'It was like ... hang on, let's see if Ben's got something similar in his collection here.'

Sally shuffled off the sofa and crawled across to the CD player. She flicked through the selection and put on some dance jazz with a wailing saxophone accompanied by a low, hypnotic bass beat.

They listened for a moment, nodding their heads in rhythm, then Sally jumped to her feet. 'Imagine this jumper is a long, white negligee,' she said, and Janie laughed.

'And I'll be Mastov.' Janie stood up as well, and leaned moodily against the fireplace.

Sally stretched the jumper down, which in any case reached down to her knees. She kicked her legs out like a pony and then started to pace up and down the carpet in her socks, glaring into the mirror.

'You look furious, not sexy,' Janie pointed out.

'I *was* furious!'

Sally tilted her chin so that the glare became seductive rather than sulky, then shook her hair round her face.

'Your hair's gone all frizzy in this damp air,' Janie remarked, unable to prevent herself chortling.

'Unlike your smooth mane, lucky cow,' said Sally. 'You look like a thoroughbred that's been groomed for a race, even when you've just got out of bed!'

They both ran their hands through their hair. It was true – the moisture in the air was making Sally's frizz up, while Janie's fell straight down her back in two glossy plaits.

'Now, pay attention,' Sally said, letting the music direct her. She closed her eyes and rotated her neck so that it looked like her head would spin full circle.

Janie recognised the movement. She'd forgotten just how supple Sally was, and silently agreed that it was a shame her friend hadn't made it as a dancer. Sally was a born performer.

'This is one of the routines we didn't get to perform in public.' Sally's hands edged up her thighs, wrinkling the jumper up towards her hips. 'Imagine this is the white slip, pulling up slowly from my ankles to reveal my legs, and then my thighs,' she crooned.

Sally paused, hooked her fingers into the jumper, stepping her feet apart and then together, and then she dropped the hem to let her fingers run over her ribcage. She fluttered her eyes at Janie, and then into the mirror, covering her face in a pretence of coyness. Her hands wandered down her neck and over her shoulders, to trace the outline of her small tits where they pushed against the thick jumper. She ran her hands down between them, squeezed them briefly together, then flickered on over her stomach and down to her crotch, clutching her mound hard for a moment. She closed her eyes and let her mouth snap open as if in surprise, then slid her hands along her legs and pushed her thighs and knees open and closed.

The music grew louder and Janie's hip bumped against the chimney breast in time to the rhythm. Sally accelerated her knee movements, bending and straightening them, and sliding her legs further and further apart each time.

'It felt different, doing it in front of him,' she gasped, testing her muscles before edging towards the splits. 'I was turning myself on with the movement, and wearing that dress made it all the more exciting. Dancing never made me feel like that before. My hands kept creeping round to play with myself. They wouldn't leave it alone. I guess I wanted him to keep looking.'

Sally demonstrated, pausing halfway down in the splits and cupping the secret slit between her thighs in both hands as if she was balancing herself off the ground, before springing upright again.

Janie's face was hot, but still she wanted Sally to go on dancing.

Sally bent herself at the waist as if touching her toes. Her fingers pulled at the hem of the jumper again and crept under it, exploring the inside of her thighs. She straightened, and her fingers climbed higher, lifting the jumper up to her waist. She pushed her pelvis towards the mantelpiece again, one hand bunching the knitted wool over her flat stomach, the other hand sweeping down her body towards her triangle of golden hair.

'I don't remember you doing a stripper routine with the Kicker Girls,' Janie remarked, but Sally was not to be distracted. She continued to sweep her hands over her body.

'We made up several routines, but our dance teacher

never knew about it,' she said, panting slightly with either exertion or excitement. 'This was one of my favourites, one I choreographed for the troupe.'

'And what did Mastov make of it?' asked Janie with a grin.

'I couldn't make out any response. So I revved up the action.'

Sally swivelled her hips round and around, clenching her bottom and thrusting herself forwards in a violently sexy move. Her fingers splayed across her crotch as if parting the sex lips to show him what was inside, and Janie remembered the dark pink slit which everyone had seen at the café last week. Then Sally whipped her hand away and dropped the hem, but still she managed to look as if she was on fire. Her eyes were blazing, and she had the fixed grin of a can-can dancer on her face. She twirled in crazy circles away from Janie towards the sofa and bent over it, falling onto her elbows and presenting her buttocks to her friend.

'You see monkeys do that, don't you?' mused Janie, as she flopped back onto her chair and stuffed the cushion between her legs again. 'In mating rituals, they show each other their bottoms.'

'Thanks for lowering the tone, Janie. But you can't put me off my stroke now. As the audience, you're there to encourage me.'

Still offering her bum to the world, Sally hitched the jumper back up her legs and swayed slowly from side to side, in time with the sensuous music. She was well into it now; she looked as if she could easily forget that Janie was even there. She lay on her front and moved both hands back between her legs to play up and down the crack of her raised butt, parting the cheeks as she wriggled provocatively.

'Your dance teacher would have had kittens if she'd seen this!' yelped Janie, fiddling with the cushion.

'Yeah. I should have showed her,' Sally answered breathlessly, bent double and eyeing Janie from between her legs. 'The Kicker Girls never got the chance to perform really suggestive stripper routines. I was chucked out of the troupe for being too short and dumpy, if you remember, but I know I was the sexiest dancer. Dancing is so exhilarating. I'd forgotten. We'll do some dancing, Janie, if this weather goes on.'

'You know I can't dance for toffee. That's why I was the one selling ice-creams. But, come on, what did Mastov make of your stripper routine?'

'Not a flicker. You're supposed to be standing by the wall, by the way, if you're being him, not wriggling about. Do you want to go to the loo? Oh well, sit down and shag the cushion if you must. But I reckoned I needed to go one step further, and in any case,' said Sally, returning to her story, 'I don't think I could have stopped myself even if I'd wanted to. There I was – remember this sofa is the bed – spread open with my fanny in the air, and it was reaction time! So I got to work with the old finger.'

'Sally, stop –'

'You asked me to tell you, so I'm telling you.'

'Yeah, but do you have to give it to me with both barrels?'

Sally rolled her eyes and, for a moment, Janie thought there was going to be a hissy fit.

'Of course I do. You asked me what happened, and I can't tell you without giving you every gory detail. Anyway, I'm enjoying it. I'm getting all revved up telling you. It's exactly how it was and, believe me, you ain't heard nothing yet. Do you really want me to stop?'

'Well . . .'

'And what do you suggest we talk about if I do stop? The coming harvest? Muck-spreading?'

Janie shook her head. 'You and I can always find something to talk about, and I don't know anything about muck-spreading. No, Sal. I'm just being –'

'A prude? You spend too many weekends down here, planting out your cabbages or whatever you do, and not enough time trawling the hot spots of London with me. In any case, I have to get this off my chest now I've started, even if you don't want to hear it.'

Janie tossed a bag of crisps at her friend. The bag landed on the small of her back, which was still bent over. The kitchen door creaked, and she heard one of the flower baskets banging outside, but she didn't dare say anything. She *was* being a prude.

'Go on, Sally. I like having you here. Go on.'

'I don't want to shock my little milkmaid,' Sally ridiculed. 'OK, remember, I was making it up as I was going along. I started with the friction, like this, like you see in those movies, and I just kept on going. It was like I was alone in my little game, my hips kept swaying to the music and my finger, all my fingers, kept . . . exploring, so that he could see what I was doing.'

'So did you get your reaction?'

'Did I? The man's into slapping and bondage, as it turns out – both things I've never tried before. I'm bent forwards, like this, my nose in the bed, my fingers all over the place, totally engrossed in my game, when suddenly he's crept up behind me and, before I can open my mouth, he's slapped my rump. It stung, and was hot, and then, like the bite, it was a nice pain, sizzling through me. Mastov started stroking the spot but I wanted him to do it again; I wanted the shock of the slap itself, and the lovely afterglow you get. It was weird; I'd always scoffed at people who like spanking.'

'He obviously knew a willing victim when he saw one.' Janie stretched her leg out and poked her toe into the dead ashes in the grate. She peered into the empty fireplace to see if there was any kindling or firelighters, but there were none. 'I'm getting colder by the minute,' she said.

'I'm not, I can still feel that slap now. You should try it. All the blood and heat concentrates in one place. One moment my buttock was hot from the slap, the next minute it was cold from the air in the room, and then he smacked my other cheek hard and this time the heat was reaching everywhere. It was like fingers prodding me all over, inside and out. I could feel addiction coming on. I reckoned if straightforward fucking wasn't on offer, then this would do fine. After all, penetration's something I can do for myself – as could you, Janie.'

Janie was still poking her toe around the grate. 'What?'

Sally attempted a mid-air spin and landed on the sofa.

'If you're determined to be a spinster, you have to learn the art of self-penetration, like I was doing, right there with my fingers in front of him.'

'I'll have to get logs later,' said Janie, purposefully ignoring her friend. 'It's too cold.' She turned and saw Sally shaking her head at her. Janie curled her arms around her knees. 'I heard you, Sal. The art of penetration. I couldn't, not in front of someone else . . . and I'm not determined to be a spinster.'

'Prove it. Or else you're doomed to use the vibrator forever and ever.'

Janie shifted on her chair and picked up her glass.

She felt hurt by her friend's comments but did her best to hide it.

'A man would be nicer, obviously,' she muttered.

Sally got her breath back from the dancing, and took a slug of wine. They both looked out of the window. It was still gloomy out there, even though the rain had eased off slightly and it was not yet tea-time.

'Where does Ben-baby keep his ties?' she asked.

'No idea, Sal. We really should leave his things alone.'

But Sally had already skipped out of the room and up the stairs before Janie could stop her. She heard the floorboards crack and complain above her head as Sally scampered about. She could see the ceiling bend slightly in the middle. Let her rummage, she thought. It was keeping her amused, and in any case Sally's story was having an extraordinary effect on Janie, whether she liked it or not. Where those early tremors had been, tickling and fussing round Janie's pussy, there was now a low pulse inside her, throbbing like the regular ticking of a clock.

Suddenly Sally was in the doorway, a collection of silk ties draped over her arm. She selected one, rolled one end round her hand, then cracked it in the air like a whip. The sound sent a shock down Janie's spine, and Sally's face lit up.

'This was his next trick,' said Sally excitedly. 'Penetration wasn't on the agenda yet. I could demonstrate the whipping technique on you, if you like?'

'No thanks.'

'Well, we'll use this poor cushion, then. The sound of the tie cracking tells you a lot about how it feels. He just brushed the tie over the backs of my knees and down to the soles of my feet while I waited for the next hit. Then he flicked the tie across both my buttocks. It left a red stripe of heat burning – doesn't quite sound the same across a plump cushion, I know – then he raised his arms and brought both ties down once, twice, three times, like this, like this, like this, each time on an untouched area. I expected it to hurt every time, but it just . . . sizzled . . . electrifying.'

Sally cracked the ties a couple more times, like a circus master, then collapsed onto the sofa, laughing and out of breath.

'Did he have any other tricks with the ties?' Janie asked as she leaned down to put another CD into the machine.

Sally leaped up again, now fizzing with energy. She started to raise her shoulders, pulling at the neck of the jumper so that it stretched wide enough to slip down her arms to her wrists. Then she wriggled until the jumper slid down her like a sheath.

'Imagine that I'm now standing in a puddle of white chiffon, with absolutely nothing else on.'

'OK, I'm imagining,' Jane humoured.

Sally parted her legs again. Her haunches swayed to the music and she let her fingers stray down over her stomach, then fan out to grab at herself again. Feebly she made as if to knock her fingers away, but her pelvis only tilted to push itself against the flattened palms of her hands.

'You're looking more heated than he did, Janie. But then, at last, as I was standing there starkers, I glanced at the tight black jeans and saw a nice big bulge. So I kept on jerking my hips, swaying, threatening to start the fingering again.'

Janie's body was reacting to Sally's words and actions. Her cushion was clamped up hard against her crotch, her own pussy convulsing whenever Sally mentioned touching hers.

'And then he was right in front of me and had my whole bush in his hand, still holding me at arm's length with the other, and every one of his fingers was up inside me, probing like – well, like I'd imagined his tongue might do.'

Janie's sex gave a restless spasm as Sally paused. She ground herself into the cushion to try and ease the growing excitement.

'What happened then? Was that it?' Janie asked impatiently. The rain was running down the windows now instead of bashing at them, and the wind seemed to have eased a little.

'He was just keeping the engine running. I wanted to do something for him, feel him up, touch him . . .'

'But you'd already given him a floor show to remember.' Janie spoke faintly, feeling moisture seep through her trousers onto the palm of her hand.

'You're right, but still he was in no hurry. It was like he was measuring me or something, because he whipped his hand away and then he hitched me up the bed and tied my hands to the wooden rail at the head. Then he produced the ribbon that had tied up the gift box. To be honest, by now I didn't care what he did so long as it felt good. He slid the ribbon round me like this – I'm going to demonstrate on you.'

Sally brought one tie round behind Janie's shoulder blades and tied it in a tight bow over her breasts. Janie gasped as the tie drew them tightly together so that they were constricted in a kind of harness that cut straight across the nipples.

'It looks far more sensational on you, because your tits are so much bigger,' Sally remarked, pulling the tie tighter. Janie felt her breasts swell under the restraint. 'Really titillating, don't you think? They kind of struggle against the tie, but love it at the same time.'

Janie couldn't speak.

'I haven't tied it as hard as he did. Imagine it: your tits should be straining now against the tie but they're totally trapped so that they seem to grow larger every time you take a breath. My nipples escaped over the edge of the tie and poked straight up into the air. It was like wearing a tiny corset. Then he selected another tie, and started playing with it down here, like this.'

Sally started working the tie between her legs, rubbing it back and forth along her pussy and down between her buttocks, gyrating over and around it like a stripper using her stockings or feather boa for a prop. Janie could see that the tie was actually making contact with the crotch of Sally's jeans as it ran back and forth, and the tip of Sally's tongue came out and flicked across her mouth.

'The friction was unbearable, rough and sweet at the same time, like rubbing flint on flint to make a fire,' she gasped, still moving with the tie.

'Like my boys making their fire in the wigwam,' Janie murmured weakly, swaying unconsciously in a mirror of Sally's movements. Her breasts began to throb heavily.

'One thing the tie round my tits did do was make me breathless. Are you finding that? I could only take in short gasps of breath because it had pulled my ribs in as well. I was almost hyperventilating, though I could still control it, and my head was light with oxygen. I suppose that's what getting high is like, sniffing hairspray or whatever. Anyway, everything you are seeing and feeling becomes bright and exaggerated, like a cartoon. And then it all stopped with the tie, as if he was switching me off like a machine. Except that I had to keep on going, although my wrists were tied up, I had to keep rubbing myself against the sheets to keep the feeling.'

Sally jerked to a standstill, hooked one finger inside her fanny and tugged at the crotch of her jeans, which had ridden up right inside her crack.

'Ben would never wear that tie again if he knew what was going on now!' Janie said. She reached down to pull her trousers away from herself, and found that the crotch was soaking. She hoped it was hidden behind the damp cushion.

'You should make a special point of selecting it for him,' Sally cackled, 'and point out the wet patch while you're at it!'

She bounced back onto the sofa, smoothing her hand a few more times over her fanny. Then she shook her hair back, grabbed her wine glass and drained it. Her eyes gleamed across at Janie.

'Oh, yes, I almost forgot,' added Sally matter-of-factly. 'Then Mastov showed me his hard-on.'

'I thought it was never going to happen!'

'There I was, tied to the bed, and he lowered himself down over me, and got his dick out: it wasn't long, but it was thick, and throbbing.'

They both squealed with laughter. Janie was sure she would give herself away any moment. Her knickers were sticky and she was breathless with mentally enacting Sally's story. As Sally kept reminding her, she hadn't been with a man for years. She couldn't even remember when she had last felt remotely aroused. Sally always said it was because Janie was too romantic, expecting a knight to come galloping along on a white horse waving his sword, instead of a real sweaty man rolling up in an Aston Martin waving his hard-on. But until now, Janie had refused to worry about it. She was perfectly happy in her world of friends and paints and the odd flirtation but, if that was the case, why was she so turned on now? Perhaps it was the cottage, the rain, the weird twilight falling over the afternoon, or Sally's way with words. Whatever it was, she had virtually creamed herself in the chair and she was utterly confused.

'So much for your man-free zone,' Sally said, waving the wine bottle around. 'I've brought Mastov right into the room, haven't I? By the way, you can unleash the tits now, unless you're happy like that!'

'I wondered why I was feeling so light-headed.' Janie chuckled, flushing. As she undid the bow and loosened the tie, her breasts bounced forwards heavily. They seemed to expand with the freedom, but the tingling ache inside them only increased. She wanted to be alone, to hold and massage them or, better still, to have someone else caress them.

'Don't look so serious!' Sally exclaimed, as she made to refill Janie's glass. Janie put her hand over it to stop her. 'You've enjoyed every minute, don't deny it. Look at you. Colour in your cheeks at last. I think I'll stop there for today.'

'You can't stop,' Janie protested. 'What about Mastov's tongue? You got the teeth, but what about the tongue he promised you?'

Sally started to laugh.

'The secret of good story-telling: get them engrossed, then leave them in suspense!'

Janie uncurled her long limbs from the chair to stand up. She was shaking. She put her glass on the mantelpiece and once again looked at herself in the mirror. There was a hectic flush along her cheekbones, her mouth was hanging open and there was a knot just behind her navel which felt as if it was unravelling, strands of unaccustomed excitement trailing down through her stomach towards her groin.

'Yeah. It's a good story. I guess you could say it's woken me up a bit,' she said slowly, tugging her shirt down and looking at her friend in the mirror behind her as if for the first time. 'We're old mates, but I don't know what you get up to in bed, and you know I don't get up to anything. It was so graphic. Is it always like that?'

'Darling, I'd forgotten how naïve you are.' Sally chuckled. 'I know you're not a virgin, but you may as well be. You're too happy to adore people from afar. There are so many men out there, and every one of them is different, and there's so little time!'

'But you'd do it all again? With a stranger, I mean?' Janie persisted, hands gripping the mantel.

'With the slapping and the ties? Oh, yes, if I ever see Mastov again. He certainly showed me a thing or two. I'm obviously not as much a woman of the world as I thought.'

'So are strangers always the best?'

'Not necessarily. They just allow you to be more outrageous.'

'There's so much to discover, isn't there?' Janie murmured, looking again at her reflection, and still shaking. She was breathing fast, and standing up made it worse. The strands of excitement had twirled down to her groin, reaching through her like fierce tentacles hooking onto her sex and tugging at it, parting the soft lips. Sally's description and dancing had conjured up the same sensations inside Janie that she knew her friend had experienced. Delicious sensations. She wanted to keep hold of them, bottle them, build on them if she was alone in her bedroom, perhaps. But now wasn't the time.

The two women listened to the rain for a moment, Janie staring down at Sally, Sally lying back on the cushions with her eyes shut.

'Remember, it was you who asked me to spill the beans, and with the beans all sorts of sexy thoughts have spilled out as well, haven't they? Admit it,' said Sally, suddenly opening her eyes and staring questioningly at her friend. 'You're feeling all horny after what I've told you. But we're here in sunny Devon to commune with nature, get away from it all, banish all thoughts of big warm hands, flat hairy stomachs, hot throbbing dicks, wet tongues, all that caper. So there's no need to tell you the rest of the story ... right?'

Janie pushed herself away from the mirror and faced Sally.

'Right. I mean it. No hot throbbing anythings. We won't find them down here, anyway. Let's leave Mastov and his tie collection in Holland Park, shall we? For the next two weeks, it's just going to be the two of us.'

'Absolutely, sergeant major, whatever you say. And now it's my turn to bark orders. If we're forbidden the real thing, you can be the man about the house, and go and get some logs.'

2

It was still raining, and much darker by the time Janie got herself psyched up for going outside. She shrugged on one of the enormous hooded raincoats that hung in the hall, making a big deal of undoing the latch and clucking at the appalling weather.

'No dithering,' Sally warned from the relative cosiness of the sitting room. 'I'm going to find another bottle of wine.'

'Keep it on ice then, will you?' Janie said. 'I'm feeling kind of restless. I could do with a stiff walk.'

'Horny, you mean! God, I should talk dirty to you more often.'

'I won't be long,' Janie said, ignoring the truth of Sally's comment. She put on a wholesome air. 'Here I go, into the wind and rain, hunting and gathering.'

Sally waggled her fingers dismissively and sprawled out on the sofa again, one leg hooked over the arm. Her petite hand slid down the front of her jeans as she absently stroked her stomach and started to doze. She had switched off already and was probably dreaming up another colourful scenario, but Janie was as jumpy as a sack of fleas.

First, she searched outside the cottage but, as she suspected, there were no logs to be seen. Ben might own this little place, but he was the most impractical person she knew. She walked on down the uneven garden path and opened the gate. An enormous willow leaned over, brushing her face with its long silvery leaves and sending drops of rainwater down her neck as she passed. The garden was so overgrown that a passer-by would never know there was a cottage there unless they looked really hard, which was how Ben liked it. The gate led straight onto a pitted driveway, which in turn led up onto the narrow road that ran up from the sea towards the nearest town.

Instead of making her way along the road, Janie walked straight across the drive in her huge borrowed gumboots. She felt through the thorns and found the gap in the hedge where she and her cousin used to punch and scrabble their way through to the farmer's land. It would take forty minutes or so to go round by road, and only about ten minutes across the field. No one would see her. She'd be there and back with some logs in no time. And if not, they'd have to go down to the beach tomorrow and gather driftwood.

The wine was making her ears sing, and Sally's adventure threaded through her brain, words and images popping like bubbles in front of her eyes. Chasing up behind the words and images was a new, sharp hunger that pierced and twisted in Janie's consciousness. As usual, Sally was right. This must be sheer frustration for her friend, she thought. She supposed this strong feeling was usually dormant or non-existent, but now it was so acute that it hurt.

She started to stride round the edge of the field towards the farm. There were no crops planted there this year, only tufts of tall meadow grass and clumps of mud. The owners were letting the farm go to ruin. Janie looked down at her boots as she walked, her friend's erotic play re-enactment still vivid in her mind. Sally was sex-mad, they'd always joked about that, but seeing her dancing and showing what went on between her legs was like peering through a keyhole and being unable to tiptoe away. Rushing away from the cottage made no difference. She could still visualise the steamy scene in the London flat, the silk ties flicking like whips over Sally's supine body while she bent over the bed. Janie could go further than that. She could see herself lying on the black sheets, her own legs spread open, her own naked breasts tied up, her own nipples singing with the excitement and the cold while a stranger stood over her, unbuttoning his trousers.

Sally was rocking the boat by introducing all that sex. Janie had been planning a long quiet summer with no drama and no hassle. But then again, she should have known better than to expect a quiet life once that little she-cat was at large.

She was glad that the rain lashed hard to distract her, as it swept in from the nearby sea. Janie was forced to bend against the wind as she got closer to the ramshackle buildings of the neighbouring farm. She thought she could hear the rattle of a Land Rover engine over to her left, approaching the cottage, but that wasn't so unusual. The road was accessed by all the nearby fields and was the only route to town from the sea.

She took the short cut into the old farm by scrambling over the broken fence beside the pig sheds, and landed up to her ankles in thick mud. She had to tug her knee with both hands to get her foot out and plant it on the concrete yard. Near the farmhouse a couple of wheelbarrows had been left, and a bright yellow digger was parked with its claws resting against what used to be the old dairy. But there was no sign of life.

Janie had no desire to inspect the rest of the farm tonight, although as kids she, Ben and Jack would have been unable to resist clambering all over the abandoned digger, trying to start it up. She glanced over to the other side of the yard and sure enough there was a pile of logs, just as she remembered, stacked tight under the eaves of the biggest barn so that most of them were still dry. She looked around. The whole place really was falling down, and was creepy in the dark wet evening light, even without the ancient farmer with his squint and missing teeth jumping out at her. She hurried over to the logs and stretched until she could reach to pull the top ones off the pile, and chucked them into her basket.

'What do you think you're doing?'

Janie straightened so sharply that she cracked her head hard against a metal rafter, knocking the hood over her eyes and dropping a log on her toe. Someone equally hooded and dripping wet had materialised round the corner of the barn and was standing a couple of feet away. She could barely see through the curtain of raindrops, but he was extremely tall, extremely broad, and extremely armed with a shovel.

'Nothing. Well, alright, I'm looking for logs,' Janie croaked, hopping about and biting back yelps of pain. 'We're cold in our cottage and I want to make a fire. There's nobody here to mind.'

'Oh, but there is. Me.'

The figure stepped closer and Janie dodged against the wall. The man wore a tweed cap under the hood of his jacket, which he tipped up to take a better look at her. All Janie could see was an unshaven chin, a grimly set mouth, and a pair of black eyes that glinted behind a pair of understated tortoiseshell spectacles. The two soaked figures glared at each other for a moment.

'I thought you were a bloke, until you started speaking,' he said.

'Not this time.'

'So I'll ask you again: what do you think you're doing?'

'I thought the place was sold, thought the old man had gone,' Janie muttered, rubbing her head to try and remove the stars that danced in front of her eyes. 'I didn't think anyone would be here. The logs will only get wet if they're not used.'

'It has been sold, and the old man died a while ago. The new owner thought he was buying an old farm in the quietest corner of England he could find, and he'd be extremely pissed off if he thought thieves were at work the minute he takes possession.'

'He's not here, is he, and we're only talking about a couple of old logs.' Her head was banging painfully, and she started to sway.

'Are you all right? I can see a cut,' the farmer said, sounding suddenly concerned. He put one hand on the clapboard wall beside her and leaned forwards to examine her forehead. He raised his other hand towards her face, and Janie flinched, knocking the hood off her head.

'Relax! Jesus, a guilty conscience, or what? I just want to take a look.'

'What are you, a paramedic as well as a poacher?' Janie asked.

'As it happens, I do know what I'm doing. Now look, you're bleeding,' he said. He turned his hands inside out like a conjuror to show that there was no weapon, then lifted her wet hair off her forehead. 'Not much, but it's trickling from your scalp, just here.'

He held out the tip of his finger, and they both stared at the blood.

'Come in here. It's the only place with a roof,' he said, guiding her backwards into the barn. He propped the door shut with his shovel.

Outside, the wind ripped at pieces of tarpaulin and loose sheets of corrugated iron, but this corner of the barn was sheltered and the straw was dry. Janie sat down on a hay bale and bent her head between her knees for a moment. She'd never been good with blood. The sight of it made her sweat. Still with her eyes closed, she tugged off her drenched coat and shook her hair in wet ropes down her back.

'I was rude,' she said into the floor. 'If we're going to be closeted away in here until the rain stops, I should say I'm sorry. But I wasn't expecting to bump into anyone. It's been derelict up here for years.'

'I know. It's going to take a lot of work to sort this place out. I'm sorry, too, for alarming you.' He tried the light switch, but nothing happened. Then she heard his feet rustling through the straw. The dry scent of old hay wafted into her nostrils. He stopped. 'The natural light's not very good, but I wonder if there's something familiar about you.'

His voice was right up by her face, tickling her ear. The hay bale wobbled as he sat down next to her.

'What?'

Janie lifted her head. It felt better. *She* felt better. This was the first moment since Sally's descent on the cottage with her fizzing urban energy and her teasing, tormenting tales, that Janie had felt some calm. The heat was still there, resting in her veins, but it made her limbs languid. She was so calm that she was pinned to her hay bale like a butterfly.

'That dark-red hair of yours, colour of claret. I've seen hair like this before. Never got close enough to smell it, though, in the old days. Tell me, what is that smell? Rain, mixed with nervous female heat and what? Marigolds?'

Janie's mouth dropped open. In the dull light his

specs were like blank screens. Behind them she could just make out his eyes, fixed like beads.

'How would you know that?' she asked. 'As it happens, you're exactly right. It's my shampoo. It has marigolds in it.'

'I told you. It's either the smell or the colour that's familiar. And so are you, though I can't put a finger on it yet.'

'You're mistaken. I'm not from round here.'

'Nor am I, but you knew this farm was derelict.'

'We used to visit, and play around here as kids. My cousin and his friend. We used to think old Maddock and his sons were evil trolls. They used to chase us with their pitchforks. Once the whole tribe came after us with a gun.'

'I don't blame him,' said the stranger. 'You were probably ruining the harvest and frightening the livestock.'

'Yes, we were pains in the arse, but nobody could say I was frightening the livestock today.'

'You frightened me.'

Janie laughed. He smiled back, his glasses glinting. He slid off the bale and squatted down in front of her, then balanced his hands on either side of her thighs. His oilskin jacket creaked across his shoulders as he sniffed at her again like a gun dog.

'I ought to call you Marigold,' he said.

'And I ought to call it a day,' replied Janie, swallowing her laughter and pulling back. She glanced towards the door, where the rain was bucketing down. There was no light out there, not even a sickle moon. She had no idea what time it was.

'You can't, not yet, you have been injured. Head injuries need rest, and relaxation.'

'Head injury? It's a tiny cut from a rafter!' protested Janie.

'A rusting metal rafter. You can't be too careful. And this storm is doing nothing to clear the air, is it?' The stranger wiped his hand across his face. 'If anything, it's getting hotter in here.'

Still staring at her, he pulled his heavy jacket off, taking the tweed cap with it, and letting everything fall in a wet heap behind him. He looked younger without the 'Farmer Giles' outfit; not much older than her, in fact. He wore a faded blue T-shirt, so old and loose that she could see the ropes of muscle in his deeply tanned neck and shoulders, and a pulse beating beneath the sinews. She wouldn't mind sitting here, looking at his neck all day.

'You see? You're sweating,' he said. 'That makes two of us. I can't think why it's suddenly so hot in here. Not running a fever, I hope?'

He laid a hand across Janie's forehead like a nurse. Her skin prickled up her neck as his face drew closer again. There was a ticking sensation just inside the opening of her pussy, a tiny muscle contracted the moment he touched her. What had Sally said about being in the taxi with Mastov? That all it took was one flick of his fingernail after months of dreary celibacy. This prickling all over her certainly wasn't fear. She didn't want to escape. She never wanted to move again.

The man's damp hair stood up in dark tufts where the cap had ruffled it and she could see one black wisp slowly reshaping itself into a tight curl behind his ear as it dried.

'I'm not ill, no,' she said. 'I just put too many clothes on when I came out. I forgot that it's supposed to be July.'

'Don't normally need logs in July.'

'It's not normally so damned freezing in July. At least, it is in our cottage.'

He pulled his sleeves down his arms and Janie watched the material wrinkle on his skin. Before she could stop it her mind had burrowed under the shirt, wondering whether there were curls on his chest or down on his stomach, like there were on his head.

'Stay here and get warm, then,' he said. 'Your cottage must be even more derelict than this place.'

'I should go,' she said, without making any attempt to move. But while she kept her eyes on his brown neck, her mind remained further down his body. Nothing could stop it, nothing could stop the insistent private twitching and aching inside her. She was mentally unbuttoning his jeans, seeing the wiry curls springing in a nest of hair round his resting, waiting prick.

They were level with each other, he still kneeling in front of her, she sitting on the hay bale, chests heaving under their damp summer clothes, and now Janie was wrestling with a ferocious urge to touch him. Her head felt fine now, apart from a slight throbbing where he'd said there was a cut. But she still wondered if she was seeing things. One moment she had been trudging through a field in the middle of a storm, head teeming with images of other people cavorting and having sex, starved of any experience to call her own, her own body fidgeting with that new, unwelcome hunger. The next minute she was being hustled into a dilapidated barn by a stranger who looked as if he might as easily ravish her as kill her. It was as though her restless state of mind had summoned him out of thin air, like an apparition.

The rain drummed, the wind whistled, and the heat

radiated out of the stranger as he took a long strand of her hair, wound it round his fingers and rubbed it under his nose to sniff it. She could see her reflection: two miniature Janies in each lens of his glasses, with huge bug-eyes and tiny chins. Something in her memory stirred. She had stared into someone's glasses like that before, years ago; seen that alarmed, wide-eyed reflection, and in that remembered scenario she had been sitting bolt upright in a barn full of straw, just like this.

'I used to know someone with hair just like yours,' said the man, as if he could read her mind. 'Same colour, same smell. Do you mind that I'm touching it?'

He separated his fingers and let the strand of hair unwind and fall back against Janie's breast. Instead of returning his hand to rest on the hay bale, or using it to lever himself upright so that they could both leave, his fingers tangled themselves under her hair. He started to slide his rough hands down her neck, lifting her wet hair away from the clammy skin, and stroking his fingertips where her pulse was hammering. Sparks of electricity seemed to crackle off her. He shifted very slightly back on his haunches, and held her away from him. He stared at her neck, her throat, down at her dark-red shirt. Janie followed his gaze. The shirt, like most of her clothes, was loose, but her march through the rain had made the fine linen cling to her, emphasising the twin curves of her breasts. The man slowly formed a smile as he took in the bulges of soft flesh, and Janie pushed her shoulders back so that the breasts were clearly outlined – two inviting mounds waiting to smother him. It was just as Sally had suggested – some lucky guy was going to press his face in there. And Janie's tits, her whole body, had been tight with longing ever since the remark had been made.

'All in one piece, doctor?'

The man's fingers pressed harder into the dip at the base of Janie's throat, causing her to catch her breath.

'All very much in one piece. I was just checking you hadn't hurt your neck as well from that bump. You'll live.'

'Not if you keep strangling me. I should go,' Janie said again, tilting her head away from him. He had just appeared in the farmyard; crept up on her she thought. Perhaps he had been watching her. Perhaps he had been watching the cottage. He had big hands that were squeezing her neck, for God's sake. They were in a deserted barn in the middle of a rainstorm and, even if she screamed, no one would hear her.

'Of course you should,' he answered. He took his hands away and rested them on his legs. Now her neck felt cold. 'Although I'd rather you stayed. It's damn lonely, this place. I'd quite forgotten. But I don't normally wrap my hands round the necks of intruders. Then again, you don't fit the usual description of an intruder.'

'Which is?'

'You know, balaclava, hairy, carrying a sawn-off shotgun ... Male.' She waited. 'They're not usually swathed in someone else's anorak, smooth-skinned, carrying a couple of logs ... Female. But still I have this weird feeling I've met you before.'

'That must be the oldest line in the book.'

'I know it sounds crass, OK. Then I guess you remind me of someone I used to know. And I think I remind *you* of someone. That's the reason that you're not afraid of me, as most people would be. You should be trying to run away. I'm pretty menacing, don't you think? Especially when I catch people breaking the rules. I mean, you've seen my shovel.'

One of his front teeth overlapped the other very slightly, though the others were dead straight. His smile broadened, and the uneven teeth simply made the smile more attractive. His lips were red, and wet where his tongue ran across them while he waited for her to speak. She struggled to keep a straight face.

'No, I'm not afraid of you. I'm just waiting for my chance. I'm not leaving without my logs.' She didn't want to say 'I'm not running away because I'm horny as hell.'

'You're putting it on. You're not a natural-born felon. So why so brazen?'

'It's concussion, probably, or too much wine. My friend and I have been carousing all afternoon.' Janie raised her chin. 'You probably recognise me because you spotted us arriving at the cottage over the field. Difficult to miss us, with all our bags and stuff.'

'That's not it. I only arrived here myself this afternoon, and I've been up here all that time. Too wet to go out spying on the neighbours. Didn't even know I *had* neighbours.'

'Well, you're wrong about one thing. I haven't a clue who you are. All I know is that you're not the cross-eyed Maddock, which is a relief. We both know what I was doing here, but what were you doing, prowling about in the rain as if you own the place?'

She gripped the hay bale, but it scratched her hands. Too much conversation. Her horny mood was ebbing. Sally would be ashamed of her. Ensconced in a lovely warm barn, inches away from a red-blooded male, and talking about head injuries and cross-eyed farmers instead of getting down to some serious seduction? Sally would have had his trousers down by now. But then again, Sally wasn't here, was she?

Her other voice told her that talking was a good

thing. This was a man-free holiday, she remembered. Anyway, Janie wouldn't know how to set about getting his trousers off. On the other hand, if she didn't keep talking she might just grab him and start shouting, 'My friend says I'm frustrated. So fuck me!'

Shards of excitement jabbed at her again, daring her, urging her on. Different parts of her were desperate for him to carry on touching her, even if it was only on her neck. She was starving, she was frigid, and her cunt had closed up. Having felt him touch her once, her whole body was clamouring to feel one flick of his fingertips.

He was so close she could count every bristle pushing through the dark skin on his chin. She focused on his mouth.

'I'm the four-eyed farmer, if you must know.' He pushed his specs up his nose, putting on a sheepish expression. 'And I do own the place.'

Janie tore her eyes away from his mouth. 'And I'm Old Macdonald.'

'Seriously, Miss Marigold. I've bought this farm. I should have told you at the beginning. So, you see, I'm allowed to be in this barn, because this is my barn, and those are my logs. Whereas you are a trespasser.' He jabbed a finger towards her nose. 'So it's me who should be asking the questions.'

'I thought it was all going to be pulled down.'

'Once you'd nicked the logs?'

'Look, I never dreamed anyone would actually want to *live* here.'

'And I never dreamed it would have so much potential,' he grinned, rubbing a hand through his hair. 'Particularly with such a luscious new neighbour.'

'Two – there's two of us,' she corrected him, mentally kicking herself as soon as she'd said it.

'Two luscious neighbours, eh? I'll be round for a cup of sugar, you can count on that. Two of you. What a bonus.'

'Well, now that we're neighbours, perhaps I should tell you my name,' Janie offered.

'If you did that, I'd have to punish you for trespassing, wouldn't I?' he said. 'But then again, I don't want you suing me for personal injury. Lord knows the entire farmyard is a health hazard.'

'Best if we just remain anonymous, then,' said Janie, ever the practical one.

'Let me just check you over, then, once more just to be safe, before I escort you from the premises,' said the farmer, sounding suspiciously like he had an ulterior motive.

'I think you'd better,' she agreed, suddenly realising this was an open invitation for this rough-looking stranger to continue touching her.

His hands came back to her shoulders, and he started to massage the bones so that she was forced to relax.

'So you don't mind?' he asked.

Her neck went limp. She ought to stand up; she ought to leave. But she was glad his hands had come back. She wanted them to move down her body. He was promising, not threatening, and he was only inches away. She gave a shiver of impatience. Maybe whatever he was promising, punishment perhaps, was the one thing that would knock this confusion out of her. Sally would say that all Janie needed was a damn good rogering. That was her remedy for everything. But that was hardly a punishment, was it? More of a reward.

One of the farmer's fingers hooked under her collar and started to stroke the white skin beneath. There was something exquisite in the way that solitary finger finding its way under her shirt made Janie feel totally naked. The tiny spot that he caressed sent sexual messages throughout her entire body. Already the backs of her knees were buzzing, and a tiny pulse had started up in the one corner of her groin which hadn't already been twitching. Her sensitive breasts tightened and started to swell, rising up like dough, as if offering themselves on a plate. Her nipples now screeched to be seen as they hardened and poked against the cloth of her damp shirt.

Something rustled over by the door. Janie heard the shovel scrape slightly and the door rattle as if the handle was being tried. She stiffened and turned her head to listen.

'It's the wind,' said the farmer, turning Janie's head back to face him. 'We're quite alone.'

He held her chin in one hand, and took his glasses off with the other, folding them and tossing them on top of his jacket. His eyes looked even darker without their disguise, his face younger but even more determined.

'Some horrible animal, more like, about to attack us,' said Janie. 'One of those big cats one reads about.'

'Not on my farm.'

Janie felt she was chickening out again. He had referred to her as 'luscious', for goodness sake. Surely it was worth being a little bolder, just this once. 'Before I go ...' she hesitated, 'perhaps you could ... check that cut once more? I'm starting to feel a little dizzy again.'

'Look,' he said, touching her forehead again. 'The blood has dried.'

She tried to put her hand up to the cut, but he took hold of her wrist.

'Does it still hurt?' he asked.

She hesitated, but only for a second. Her game of seduction had begun.

'Yes. Here,' she said, bending her neck so that more of her shoulder was exposed. He flicked her hair away and touched her neck. She bit her lip, undid a button and pulled at the shirt again. Her head was spinning with this new daring. There could be no mistaking the signals she was giving out.

'And here.'

He pushed her shirt further down her shoulder and traced the ridge of her collarbone, treading his fingertips across the exposed skin and under the shirt again, threatening, no, promising, to creep down towards her breasts. Janie's breath was coming in uneven gasps of longing.

His features became blurred and fused in front of her. She closed her eyes, letting her head droop backwards as the soft caresses lulled her. There was some scuffling in the straw as she started to slide forwards off the hay bale, while at the same time he came closer, and their legs collided. He bent towards her shoulder and she could feel his breath hot on her skin. She moved her head round to meet him until their mouths met. They both waited, mouths barely touching. Her breath stopped totally then. She couldn't move away. Her lips softened and parted, but he didn't respond. She started to breathe into his mouth. She slid her hands round and up his back, and felt a quiver run down between his shoulderblades. Her hands pressed harder against him. She was as desperate to touch as to be touched. She flicked the tip of her tongue against his teeth, and then around the inside of his lips; he tasted of tobacco and coffee, masculine, salty, sweet, wet, warm. She pushed her tongue further in, waiting for him to rebuff her, but now his lips closed around it, trapping it, sucking it in between his teeth, so that her face was moulded into his and her breasts and body were pressed against the length of him.

This was why she had come out in the rain, fizzing and burning with unresolved longing. She had needed to walk out into the fresh air, in search of some kind of relief, and here it was, in the big warm shape of a strange farmer, and they were kissing in this barn like teenagers. Janie willed the stranger to carry on kissing her, sucking her tongue. It was like setting a taper to a candle; she was smouldering from her feet upwards.

'What am I doing?' he groaned, his mouth sliding sideways. 'I only meant to bring you out of the rain, I only meant to look at you, then send you on your way. Tell me to stop, and I'll –'

'Don't stop. Don't dare stop,' she hissed, nuzzling against his mouth. 'It's been too long, and it's only a kiss. We're adults, and we're enjoying it. Pretend it's your *droit de seigneur* if it makes you feel better.'

He rubbed his lips across hers. 'It does. Though I'm not exactly the Lord of the Manor, and you're not exactly Little Bo-Peep. I mean, look at you.'

'I'm not Bo-Peep, I'm a brazen hussy, caught stealing by the master.' Janie grinned. 'You have to touch me, and see.'

They were enclosed in the darkness. Everything suddenly felt wicked and dangerous. She wasn't sure she'd be able to find her way out of the rickety barn even if she wanted to. His face was a pale oval in front of her. Hers must look the same to him, thought Janie, especially as he had taken off his glasses. There was no point wasting time staring at each other in the dark. When he didn't reply, or move, she wriggled backwards onto the hay bale and lay down. He remained kneeling, so she reached up and pulled him down on top of her.

He hesitated, then let himself sink down. He took her arms, and held them above her head. The hay tickled and dug through her shirt, so she raised her spine off the bale to escape the prickles. Her breasts arched towards him in an open invitation.

He gazed down at her, silently biting his lips. His nostrils were flared with the effort of trying to breathe calmly. He was straddling her now, heavy on her legs. One hand held her arms down while the other started to massage her shoulder where it had left off before, then, at last, it moved down her chest in a slow circle to reach and take hold of one of her breasts. He rubbed his hand under her arm and down the side of the soft mound, pushing it into the centre and letting it fall back again, feeling its weight against the palm of his hand. Janie's breath came in shallow gasps as she lay there, taut with anticipation. She feared that if she breathed out he would vanish in a puff of smoke. She tried to spread her legs a little to ease the excruciating delight building up inside her. He shifted his buttocks and pressed down on her, still pinning her down. Through the thin material of her trousers she could feel the thick outline of his cock contained within his blue jeans. It jutted right up inside her thigh, nudging against the cleft of her pussy, but for now she wanted to concentrate on the circling motions of his hand, fingers digging into the malleable flesh of her breast, increasing in strength and tempo as their joint breathing grew heavier.

'I couldn't stop even if I wanted to,' he murmured. 'Your breasts. They're so juicy, so welcoming. A real woman's shape. I always wondered how they would feel.'

She strained upwards to catch what he was saying,

but again she heard the door rattling in the wind. It was warm and quiet in the barn, and she had forgotten the storm. The air rushed through the crack in the door like hushed voices.

'Go on, feel me, feel how big they are,' whispered Janie, feeling suddenly bold. She pulled his other hand over her neglected breast and arched her back so that everything was thrust towards him. He rubbed the palms of his hands in widening circles, over the top of her shirt, letting the fabric join with his fingers in massaging her flesh then, pushing the tits together roughly, he gathered them up in his hands, so that they billowed over the edges. His strong farmer's grip crushed them in his fists so that the pain radiated into pleasure. He kneaded them roughly, then drew his thumbs back and forth, flicking across the distinct points of her nipples so that they stood up more stiffly beneath the loose shirt. Pangs of desire shot through her. The memories of pleasures past were dim, but slowly they were returning.

She moaned out loud before she could stop herself. It was like being woken from a deep sleep. Sally would probably say it was just like getting back on a bicycle. Janie tossed her head from side to side to get Sally out of her head and to get back to the pleasure starting to overwhelm her. She wanted to lift her shirt up, show him her bare white tits with their raspberry-red nipples, ripe for sucking, but he had hold of her arms and, anyway, he was intent on balancing and feeling her tits as they were, hidden under her shirt. The greed and excitement in his face was infecting her. She became frantic, wriggling and twisting underneath him. She wrenched her hands free from his and took hold of his hips, pulling him up a little so that she could unbuckle his belt. He was still wearing his T-shirt and her shirt was still buttoned up, but there was no need to undress, and no time.

His mouth was open now, too far away for her to kiss it again. He was breathing harshly and she panted wildly as she stretched herself under his hands and tore at his jeans. However out of practice she may be, and however much Sally may have mocked, here she was, spread out beneath a gorgeous stranger practically in the open air. This was what Janie had been missing. She wasn't interested in the luxury of waiting, she wanted to find the length of this man's stiffened cock, hold it in her hand, discover what the feel of her body was doing to him, how hard it was making him. She needed to feel him inside her. It was time. Now.

A draught whipped across her face, cold on the patch of stomach exposed by the rucking up of her shirt. Janie heard a cough, or a snort, somewhere nearby. There was no mistaking it. She couldn't decipher what or where it was. The old barn seemed to have inhabitants of its own. The wind whistled across the rafters in short gusts that sounded like laughter. The stormy weather was hurrying her, and across the field Sally was waiting in the cottage.

Sod Sally for intruding, and sod the creeping sensation she suddenly had, of being watched. The farmer's jeans were undone now, and Janie reached down to find his cock, but he grabbed her wrists and forced them back over her head, pinning her down with one hand while he drew his cock out of his jeans himself. It seemed he liked being in control. He let it nudge in between her legs then yanked her trousers and knickers down. The hay scratched into the crack of her bare bum as she wound her legs round his hips, straining her groin up against his, unable to wrestle her hands out of his grip. She wouldn't stop writhing until she felt his stiffness sliding its way inside her.

Now something really was shifting about in the corner of her eye. She flung her head towards the door. One, maybe two heads, two pairs of eyes, were framed, totally still, just inside the doorway. She couldn't make out if they were young or old, male or female, as the fading light was behind them and it was almost pitch-dark in the barn. The only line of light was the one that travelled from the door, placing the writhing pair on the hay bale right in the spotlight.

She struggled beneath him for a moment, squealing to get his attention and dropping her legs down. They had to stop. Someone was going to march right in and catch them. There was nowhere to hide.

'Look there, someone's there, someone coming,' she croaked at him. She was torn, distracted, but exhilarated by the fear of discovery. It was like doing it behind the bike sheds, or in the park. The farm had always spooked her whenever she went exploring there, but that was part of the fun, and never had the scariness of it actually turned her on before. Then again, never before had she laid down in the barn to be fucked by the farmer. Not even Sally could muster a fantasy involving cross-eyed Maddock.

Her farmer glanced in the direction of the doorway as well, but he didn't flinch. His eyes were glazed with desire. 'Nothing there,' he said. 'You don't want to stop, do you? 'Cause I don't, and I'm not going to.' He shook his head at her, grinned slowly, and stretched himself over her again, one hand still kneading her breasts, pushing them roughly together, feeling them give under the palm of his hand.

An explosive rush of excitement spurted through her, crazy and hot. She was past caring if there was really someone there. She was probably imagining it in the craziness of the moment. In any case, the thought of someone watching them, riveted to the spot, breathing hard and clutching themselves as they watched the two indistinct figures screwing, was suddenly intoxicating. She was going mad. She kept her head turned towards the doorway, challenging her invisible spectators.

'Watch me, then,' she hissed at the invisible audience, flinging her head back. 'Go on, watch us, fucking here in the barn like animals.'

'Stop rabbiting, wench,' he breathed hoarsely. Her thighs came up again to grip his and she pulled him towards her. Her words were stopped by her own moan of pleasure as he started to run his cock up the soft skin of her inner thighs, its blunt head nudging towards her cunt like a heat-seeking missile. He guided it through her swollen wet lips and burrowed in between them, parting them to make way. She wriggled his cock deeper and deeper inside her, clinging with her inner muscles to take in its delicious length. No niceties, no teasing, just on and on and up and faster. As its length slid past her clit she felt her desire grow to bursting point, ready to shatter and melt her, stoked up by the afternoon's frustration.

He pulled back for a tantalising moment, running the head of his cock round Janie's tender groove. Her moans subsided, then, with a monumental jerk of his groin, he forced the whole stiff length of his cock into her until his balls banged against her splayed buttocks. He pulled his hips back until the length of his cock was nearly out, groaned with the effort of pausing, then thrust the meaty shaft in deep again and again so that Janie heard herself shriek with pleasure. He shuddered out towards his rapid climax, ready to shoot his load into her, and she wondered if he, too, was releasing months or years of frustration into her willing body.

The eyes gleamed in the doorway as the voyeurs watched, and Janie knew what they could see: a man's body flexed over a woman's, humping on the hay bales, both semi-clothed, blue T-shirt, red linen shirt with arms outstretched, only the pale curve of the man's buttocks visible where he had yanked his jeans down enough to get his cock out. In the gloom they would not be able to see the muscles tighten in his arse, but they would make out the thrust of his groin as he drew his hips back and pounded forwards between the woman's parted legs. They would be able to see her scraping with each thrust up the hay bale beneath him, hair tangling in the straw. They would be able to see the man and the woman rutting. They would be able to hear the whispering and the moaning.

His body was welded to hers now. One of his hands still clutched her breast as if it was a buoy, but the other released her wrists and spread out to support the small of her back, lifting her body right off the hay as her thighs clamped round his waist. Cold air tickled her spine where her shirt fell away. Her pleasure peaked with the sudden reminder of the outside world, and darts of desire chased her on towards another, higher point of climax. Sharp animal groans escaped from between her gritted teeth. In response he thrust into her with his own gathering shout of triumph. He crushed her as he slammed into her one last time, the bale slithering across the floor, scraping her back across the sharp sticks of hay until the insistent pricks of pain jabbing into her skin finally pierced the bubble of lust and burst it open, drowning all her senses in a warm flood.

Finally Janie's body shuddered to a halt. She let her

arms and legs flop sideways and took his weight as he rested on top of her for a moment. He raised himself up on his elbows and heaved himself off the hay bale. Her limbs were heavy as she slowly drew her knees up to her chest. The warmth of her satisfaction was ebbing away, she was getting cold, and her skin itched from the bed of hay.

'How could I have done without it all this time?' she murmured to herself, watching the sinews ripple in his back as he scrabbled in the straw for his glasses.

He glanced back at her, and Janie realised he hadn't been able to see a thing without his spectacles. Now his eyes were direct and focused again, and he had obviously heard her remark.

'What a way to put a seal on this place,' he said quietly. 'I've wanted to do that for years.'

'What do you mean?' She hadn't the energy yet to sit up. 'You've wanted to do that for years?'

'I mean I've wanted to catch a beautiful thief stealing logs on my property, just so that I could take her prisoner in my barn, and punish her by shagging her across one of my hay bales.'

'So you do fancy yourself as the Lord of the Manor after all.'

The farmer started to speak, but then they both jumped as the door banged against the shovel he had propped there, knocking it over with a clatter. Unmistakable footsteps splashed away through the puddles outside. They heard a burst of coarse male laughter, and then a moped started up, bumped over the sodden ground, and buzzed away up the track.

'I was right. I tried to tell you! Those eyes at the door. They *were* watching us!'

There was a knot of horror mixed with surprised laughter lurking in Janie's chest and she hugged her knees closer, trying to hold fast the intensity of the past few moments. Then reluctantly she shuffled back into her damp knickers and trousers.

'Does that bother you?' he asked, helping her to her feet and walking her towards the door. They both peered round the murky yard. There was nobody else there. 'Didn't ruin what happened just then, did it?'

She blushed like a teenager as she pulled on her jacket, feeling awkward now that they were upright and outside. Even talking about 'what happened' might make it disappear.

'They couldn't have seen much.' Janie shrugged. 'But it was pretty wild, wasn't it? Doing it, and being watched. Doing it on the hay. All of it was wild.' She looked at the ground and scuffed her boots, her face growing redder.

'I'd like to do it again some time,' said the farmer.

He twined a strand of her hair round his finger as he had when they'd first sat down together on the hay, and pulled her head towards his for a moment.

'Claret hair,' he went on thoughtfully, then stepped abruptly out of the barn into the darkness. 'I'm the lucky one, discovering such sexy neighbours. But I'll have to do something about my employees.'

'Employees?'

'Yes, our admiring audience. Those lads with the moped are my workforce for the summer, helping me restore this place. Old cross-eyed Maddock's son is helping me, as well, and he hired them. He went on ahead of me just now, and I thought they'd gone with him. Good thing *he* didn't see us at it. He would probably have thrown a bucket of cold water over us!'

Janie shuddered, crossing her arms over her breasts, and he laughed.

'At least you don't have to face them. I'm supposed

to be buying them pints in the village pub down there in five minutes.'

The image scanned across Janie's brain once again of her body beneath his, the two figures rocking like clockwork inside the gloomy barn, illuminated by the weak twilight, his buttocks, barely visible beneath his tee shirt, flexing between her grasping thighs. Then she imagined the faces of the watching boys, eyes watering, mouths open, desperate with lust, young cocks hardening in their mucky jeans at the sight, and something came alive inside her.

'Next time we should really give them something to gawp at,' she said. He glanced at her. He wasn't smiling. He was a stranger again. She pulled her hood up. 'Whoops, time to go.'

'You forgot something,' he said, pointing at the log-pile. She bent to pick up a few logs, clutched them in her arms and faced him again, unwilling to leave. They stared at each other for a long moment. He took her jacket and held it open, letting his eyes stray down her red shirt again. Her nipples gave a last, lingering tingle.

'Next time I'll have to exact further payment,' he said.

'Thanks. For the logs.'

Janie watched as her mystery-man turned and walked back towards the farmhouse. He kicked open the door and disappeared. Silly to expect him to walk her home, she thought. This was Devon, after all, not Dalston. She squelched through the patch of mud and climbed over the fence, then flung her head back and breathed in deeply. She felt invigorated, like she'd been an old suit of clothes hanging in a cupboard, and now he had shaken her out, moths and dust flying everywhere.

Her feet moved faster through the wet grass at the

edge of the field. She was keeping this encounter to herself for the moment, challenge or no challenge. Sally was more than capable of muscling in and taking Farmer Giles over for herself, and Janie wasn't prepared to let that happen. Not until she'd been back for seconds.

She hitched the logs up in her arms, and started to race back across the sodden field towards the glowing light of the little cottage.

3

Sally lay on the sofa, stroking her stomach. The rain hissing on the window was making her dozy. Her hand was warm inside her jeans, and she lay there happily absorbing the peace after the chaos of the recent weeks. She couldn't remember when she had last been alone. Janie was great, soothing and admiring company, and staying with her was like stepping into a warm bath. But still, Sally wasn't good at being on her own for long. Not even twenty minutes. And she couldn't bear the silence.

She jumped up off the sofa, feeling slightly dizzy, and went to get the wine out of the fridge. She didn't want to wait for Janie. She poured herself a big glass, then paced round the sitting room, peering out of the windows. There was nothing out there; just a grey sky streaked with a kind of livid white as the day began to die. And branches: branches round the window, branches in the distance, branches punching the air as the wind tossed them.

Couldn't live down here for long, she thought. No cars, no shops, no men. She'd never leave the curtains open once it was dark in London – too many weirdos prowling about – but she didn't feel the same fear here. There was no-one for miles and nothing to see if they *did* peer in. Sally drank some more wine. It swirled comfortably round her skull and the delicious, familiar sense of abandon kicked in. She picked up one of Janie's paintbrushes, which were standing in glass pots, ready for action. Janie may have looked like she was on another planet half the time, but she always had a project going on. Where was she, anyway? Sally wondered. Had she stumbled upon a gypsy woman selling trinkets? Fallen into a cow pat? Got run over by a tractor? How hard was it to pick up a couple of logs? Sally would have gone out and sawn a couple of those stupid branches off a tree, just to be quick. Janie must have been gone half an hour. The grandfather clock in the hall wheezed, started to chime, then thought better of it.

Sally changed the music, selecting some mournful Mahler. Mustn't go to sleep, she thought. Just try to think. She sat down on the sofa and stroked the paintbrush against her cheek. A project. If Janie had a project, even if it was painting this little hovel, then Sally should have a project as well, otherwise she'd go out of her mind with boredom. She needed to think about something more exciting than playing Babes in the Wood down here. She needed to think about the future.

Her waistband felt tight as she lay back on the sofa, and she unzipped her jeans. She'd been out of work a mere couple of weeks, but it showed. She always ate more when she was idle. She glanced towards the window, and pulled the jeans right off. That was better. Her stomach and legs felt free now, and the heaters had warmed the room so it was perfectly cosy to lie there half-dressed. Besides, she still had on Ben's lovely jumper. Sally tickled the brush over her face again, as if she was applying blusher, then she flicked it up and down her neck. Wonder what Janie would use this brush for, she thought. It was quite thick, with a sturdy handle, but the bristles were soft as kitten fur, still brand new. She'd like to help with the decorating, even if it was just choosing colours. Janie might not be adventurous enough. They could make this cottage over completely; perhaps get *Cute Cottages* magazine down to do a 'before and after' feature.

She felt a familiar singing in her ears as a possible new business idea germinated. She scrabbled for her mobile phone, then realised there was no signal down here. That summed it up, really: total backwater. She took another slurp of wine. She'd definitely call the magazine later, from outside, where she could get a signal. She flung herself back into the soft cushions and picked up the brush again, twiddling it like a cheerleader's baton through her fingers before taking the handle delicately between finger and thumb. She touched the tips of the bristles to her leg and flinched as they tickled. She did it again, squirming as her skin became accustomed to the hairy touch, then she flattened the brush over her thighs, sweeping it down to her knees and back again, before flicking the stiff hairs up and down the insides of her bare legs. She started to wriggle about on the sofa as she let her hands guide the brush absent-mindedly. Her jumper rode up her stomach as her hands moved about, and the brush flicked over her knickers. She did it again, feeling the ruffle of her pubic curls. On impulse she ripped the knickers off as well and gasped as the cool air kissed the blonde triangle of curls between her legs. She locked her thighs over her muff for a second, giggling to herself, then parted her legs wider to let the brush explore.

The branches scratched at the window and Sally jumped, but she kept her eyes firmly closed. She wasn't about to be scared by a tree. The front door creaked in the wind and so did the floorboards in the hall, but she knew Janie wasn't back yet.

She started rocking her buttocks on the soft cushions, dancing about on her bottom as the music murmured around her and the paintbrush stroked faster and faster up her legs, over her stomach in circles, and down again, but determined to avoid the crucial spot. For the moment the friction of her butt against the embroidered cushion covers was enough. She would hold the paintbrush away from herself for as long as she could bear it.

Her head started to sway and she stuck the tip of her tongue out to glide across her lips like a cat. She rotated her hips on the cushions, her thighs moving further apart as the paintbrush played between them, still only flicking and stroking. With each stroke of the brush her hips rocked more wildly. The sofa was too soft now. She wanted a hard surface, some discomfort. She supported her weight on her elbows and slid off the sofa onto the floor with a thump. Then she slid both hands between her pale thighs and parted her legs wider, reliving her dancing days. She held the backs of her knees and pointed her toes like a ballerina until she was doing the splits, aware that the shocking pink crevice running between her legs was open now. She could feel the damp slick of her pussy-lips as she eased them apart. Damn this godforsaken place! She wished she had a solid length of male muscle to shove in there. She wriggled herself open and closed a couple of times, relishing the sticky sensations. There was no way she could go for two weeks down here with only a paintbrush for company.

Suddenly, Sally heard another scraping sound. She glanced at the window, the breath caught in her throat. Somebody had decided to answer her prayers – or maybe realise her worst fears. Either way, she wasn't alone after all. Someone was out there, watching her.

It couldn't be Janie, because she wouldn't hang around like that in the garden, she would march round to the front door. The music was too loud to hear footsteps. Although the window was steamed up, it looked like a man, standing in the rose-bed, calmly looking in.

It was her imagination gone wild, she told herself, but despite her alarm she was turned on by the idea. She wasn't afraid. There couldn't be anyone really scary down here. It was just some local, coming past on his way back from sheep shearing, or a tourist getting lost. Give them all something to talk about while they get in the harvest, and give myself a treat into the bargain, she thought. She tossed her head, making herself feel dizzy, then glanced up again. The face was still there. It was definitely male. It wore a peaked cap and had a large unshaven chin. Its mouth was moving, as if saying something, and then there was a tap on the window. Sally crooked her finger at the figure, beckoning it in. The man glanced from right to left, jabbed his thumb sideways, but still didn't move.

Have it your way, she thought. You could be the cottage ghost, for all I care. I'm not stopping now. If anything, this feels even better.

She bent her knees so that her toes were resting on the ground, then relaxed her shoulders into the cushions, and closed her eyes. The paintbrush travelled to the top of her legs, up over her smooth, flat stomach, then hovered over the rise of her pubic mound. The very tips of the bristles picked up the tight curls, and she sighed out loud. Sally wondered what he was thinking. She tried to think of him as Mastov, but that didn't work. Mastov belonged in London, and anyway he was already history. This was someone fresh, and new. She dropped the paintbrush. Her fingers waggled over the soft patch of hair. She tried to keep them back, tried to tease herself for a moment longer, but the foreplay with the brush and the idea of the man watching were too delicious. She burrowed into the curling nest, crowded her fingers in for a moment, then pulled back, her nails tangling in the blonde hair that sprang over her sex-lips. Keeping her thighs open in the splits meant that all Sally's parts felt exquisitely sensitive and exposed. Every tiny millimetre was visible to the man, and anyone else for that matter, but her legs were aching now. She relaxed her thighs a little.

She snatched up the paintbrush and held it like a spear over the inviting target, made herself wait. Made him wait. Let him look for a little longer. Would he be getting stiff, watching the paintbrush which threatened to stimulate her? Her pussy was aching, twitching and contracting like a sponge being squeezed, the tiny muscles puckering to take something in. Anything.

Sally's knees jerked as her hand tired of holding the paintbrush over herself. She gave in. Gently she started to swipe the bristled head up and down the dark-pink slit while her other hand held her lips open. The bristles bent softly into her contours and made small circles round the bud of her clitoris. Her fingers started to follow the movements of the paintbrush, round and in and out, probing until either the brush or her finger – she couldn't tell which – scraped across the hidden kernel of her clit, making it burst into life and start to throb.

Sally wriggled again, throwing herself backwards as her fingers kept guiding the paintbrush, or rather the paintbrush guided them. The conflicting urges were unbearable, to hold back and to plunge in, and her clitoris and everything around it ached with suspense as the brush dipped delicately between her legs. They felt puffy now with excitement. She snatched the brush away, touched it around her clit for a second longer, then gradually increased the tempo until, like a bolt of lightning, the paintbrush hit its mark. She imagined the man crashing in through the window, grabbing the paintbrush from her, rubbing it hard against her, making it work her into a froth, then taking out his stiff cock, tossing aside the brush, and plunging his rigid cock into her instead.

She couldn't stop herself. She started to work the brush furiously up and down the raw slit, rubbing and circling her burning clit until she could do nothing except raise her buttocks right off the cushions and thump back down again, her knees flopping wide open and her moans coming loudly in her private frenzy.

Sally's hair tumbled across her face, blocking out the room and the wind and the rain and even the man outside as she flung her head from side to side, still holding herself open with one set of fingers while the head of the brush rotated mercilessly. Its bristles stroked every available part of her, as if it had a mind of its own.

She turned the brush round in her fingers, grabbed the thick wooden handle, and started to slide it in and out, her small arm working like a piston as she thrashed about. Heat building through her, crashing and burning, her arm with the paintbrush flexing to push the blunt handle inside her one more time then relaxing as the flood broke and the juice started to ooze out of her.

The CD clicked to an abrupt end and the branches rapped on the window again. The warmth of the brush and its friction subsided, and Sally opened her eyes blearily as she came out of her trance. The grandfather clock cleared its throat again. She glanced across the sofa towards the hall, and back towards the window.

It had been her imagination; there was no one there. Time to come to her senses, she thought. She cupped her moist sex, nestling between her loose thighs. Her face flooded with heat, and she drew her legs slowly together. Then she sprang across to the window. She banged her forehead on the glass, trying to see out, but there was no sign of anyone. She didn't know whether to laugh or cry. She reached behind her, and groped about for her jeans. Her heart was juddering. Where the hell was Janie?

'Evening.'

It was the face at the window, except he was inside the house now, standing in the kitchen doorway. His arms were folded across his chest as he surveyed the sofa, the cushions, the paintbrush and, finally, Sally, hopping about with one leg still stuck in her jeans. He had a dark-green shooting jacket slung over his shoulder, shiny with rain and specks of mud. His trousers were also dark green, looked soaking wet, and were tucked into chunky mud-caked boots. As far as Sally could tell he didn't have a gun, although he looked the type who would take a shot at a person just as easily as a pigeon. He had the ruddy cheeks and unkempt hair of someone who lived and worked permanently outdoors and cared little about his appearance. His stubby fingers looked as if they would be happiest wringing the necks of rabbits. His eyes were pale-blue, slightly too small, but piercing and now fixed on the spot where Sally had been writhing on the floor with the paintbrush.

'Who are you?' she said, trying to sound brave. It came out like a lamb's bleat. She was shaking so much that she couldn't get the jeans up her leg.

'Name's Maddock. From up the farm. I was just passing.'

Sally stared back at him. The words took a while to sink in. Up the farm. Not a totally random nutter, then. She vaguely remembered Janie talking about a nearby farm.

'Did you see my friend?'

'Not seen anyone on the road. And once I got here I'm afraid I was a little distracted. Cottage been empty for months, and what do I find the day I decide to come by? A bit of stuff, wriggling about on the floor and giving out a peepshow for free.'

'She's out there looking for logs, and she'll be back any minute,' said Sally, ignoring the stranger's comment.

'Who's that, then? Your friend's another she? No boyfriend down here to keep you company, then? That must be why you're wearing Mr Ben's clothes. I daresay he'd give his latest Porsche to see you half dressed in that.'

Sally followed his eyes as they skirted down her body. The jumper was rucked up untidily round her hips and the damp curls of her pubes were clearly visible. She dropped the jeans and kicked them away, pulling feebly at the hem of the sweater. She was too hot. She longed to take it off.

'I didn't know it was going to be so cold,' she said.

'I'm sure he won't mind. So you've found a whole new way of warming yourself up, and very generous you are to share it with me.'

Sally made a feeble attempt to feign modesty. 'I wasn't sharing it with you,' she protested.

'You saw me looking through the window, and you carried on poking yourself, bold as brass,' said Maddock, a big grin on his ruddy face. 'What man could walk away from that? You even beckoned me in, if I recall.'

Sally was beginning to regret her bold display now she was faced with her audience in the house. 'I thought I was seeing things when I saw you out there. I've had too much wine.'

A smoker's chuckle rattled from somewhere inside his chest, but his face didn't alter. 'Must be good stuff. Mind if I have a snifter of that, then?'

'Help yourself,' she said coolly, handing him the bottle. 'I didn't know they had Peeping Toms in the country.' She curled herself on the sofa, and pulled the sweater down over her knees, then looked up at Maddock. He was built like a shit-house.

'We have all sorts down here.' He chuckled again. 'I'd be glad to show you.'

'One thing at a time, Mr Maddock. Tell me, first. How did you get in?'

'Not that I needed one, but I have a key.'

'You could have knocked. Or used the doorbell.'

'You knew I was coming in,' he said. 'I was trying to tell you when I was outside. You invited me, remember?'

He hadn't blinked once. She kept her eyes on him. She wasn't going to let him win this staring match.

'How come you have a key, Mr Maddock?'

'Maddock. Just Maddock.'

He flung his heavy coat across a chair and stepped in from the kitchen. He had a lumberjack shirt on under the jacket, unbuttoned enough to show a grubby vest, and a wide chest smothered in thick black hair. Sally was determined not to be intimidated by this rustic oaf. The best plan, she decided, was to brazen it out.

'You can try making yourself at home,' she said, 'but, as I said, my friend will be back in a moment.'

Maddock looked immovable and faintly amused. 'Mr Ben give me the key. I come and go as I please when he's away.'

'Well, he's not away,' she spluttered. 'I mean, we're here, not him.'

'I'm to keep an eye on the place: maintenance, and the like.'

As if to prove the point he produced a hammer from behind his back and banged it down on the mantelpiece. Sally jumped, but the surprise was followed by a series of thrills up and down her legs.

'I see you've already got the paintbrushes in.' He gave a dirty laugh.

Sally gripped the brush tighter, and Maddock looked at her, his mouth stretching into a sly grin.

'Janie's doing some decorating. That's what Ben asked her to do. She hasn't said anything about any maintenance man. Hasn't said anything about any man, come to think of it.'

'Good thing I dropped by then, isn't it?'

'You think there's maintenance needs doing here at the moment?' she asked, her voice going higher with each sentence. 'Broken shutters, cracked window frames, that sort of thing?' She unrolled the jumper off her knees and straightened her legs out so they were splayed in front of her on the sofa. The room was baking.

'I'm to come in every day while he's away, Ben says. There's a lot of storm damage to fix, especially up on the roof, and he wants some trees pruning as well.'

Sally felt slightly relieved; at least he sounded like the genuine article. 'I'm sure there's lots you could do for us, but it's too late to do anything about it tonight,' she said, realising that his presence was making her feel deliciously vulnerable and quite turned on. There was no point being antisocial. 'Would you like some more wine before you leave?' she asked. 'It's kind of dull here on my own.'

'Don't mind if I do,' Maddock answered. 'And I wouldn't say it was dull here, not at all. Just think yourself lucky my lads weren't peeping with me. I'd have had to cover their eyes. You town strumpets ... no shame!'

'Come on!' Sally snorted. 'I bet you have country strumpets as well. You'll probably be needing a roll in the hay to cool off after what I showed you.' She absent-mindedly wound the paintbrush through her messy hair.

'In this weather?' he scoffed, approaching Sally and standing over her. 'You must be joking. We're not that basic. A roll on Mr Ben's nice dry hearth-rug would be far more welcome.'

Sally took a swig from her own glass. 'In that case, I wonder how town and country would compare?'

He thumped down on his knees beside Sally and took the paintbrush, shaking it out of her hair. She curled her legs back up again. Her stomach was clenched with excitement. He held the paintbrush up to his face and sniffed it. She could feel the heat beating off him. She would boil if she didn't rip that jumper off soon.

'Perhaps we should suck it and see?' he said.

'Not sure my friend would like it,' Sally murmured, glancing out of the window.

Maddock watched Sally from close quarters for a moment or two, and then his mouth began to split into a grin, slowly, as if it was out of practice. One lower front tooth was missing, which made him look to Sally like a pantomime villain. Slowly he leaned across Sally's body and started to run the paintbrush in circles round her stomach. She lay totally still, but her legs grew slack, and her feet flopped lazily between Maddock's dirty boots.

'Maybe your friend's not getting it,' he teased.

A wicked laugh bubbled up inside Sally's throat. 'But she'll see us. She'll be back.'

'So what. If she's anything like you, she'll enjoy the show. I can tell you're up for it.'

'I'm always up for it,' she said, bold as brass.

'So take the paint brush, and do it.'

'I've had enough of playing with myself,' Sally whined. Maddock was no oil painting; he was brutish, and looked like a bull about to mount. He was a world away from the pale, besuited men she usually bedded. He looked like he'd grown straight out of the mud. He smelled like it, too. But his blue eyes and his thick fingers wielding that paintbrush, and the slow grin, reduced her to jelly.

'Tarts like you have never had enough,' he whispered, too close for comfort. He had the paintbrush in his big fist as if it was a sledgehammer. He leaned closer, and blew into Sally's hair. She clamped her thighs together and tried to struggle up on her elbows.

'Now, you look good enough to eat lying there,' said Maddock. 'You're sick of doing it alone, is that it?'

He grinned a bit more, and at last he looked more like a man and less like an oak tree. Sally grinned back, and nodded. She could see that he was used to quelling difficult animals, or felling whole forests. Let him quell her. She was tired of being bold and brazen. She decided to lie back like a lamb to the slaughter. He pushed his sleeves up gigantic forearms and continued to circle the paintbrush over her skin, moving it down towards her pussy, out along her thighs, then back again. Sally's fingers automatically flew to her golden bush, half covering it, half wanting to reveal it. Maddock peeled her fingers away and pinned her arms out to the sides.

'I'm not into games,' he said. 'Just let me get on with it, woman.'

Sally laughed coarsely, and all at once she seemed to come back to life. 'OK, Mr Maddock,' she taunted, trying to free her hands in order to get the paintbrush off him. 'Show us what you yokels are made of, then.'

Maddock's grin faded just a tad. 'If rough's how you like it, rough's how you'll get it.'

Keeping his eyes fixed on Sally, he poked the paintbrush handle towards her cunt and, without further niceties, eased it inside, angling it so that it could reach higher than she had been able to get it. Then he rotated it firmly from side to side, and with every inch that he pushed it Sally gave a breathless gasp.

He continued to work the brush with one hand, and with the other he unzipped his fly. He pulled out his cock, which was almost erect, and circled his fingers round the base of the muscled shaft and ran them up to the knob, then down again. His foreskin wrinkled away from the rounded bulb, and smoothed out over the surface as the blood pumped through. Sally chuckled again. Maddock obviously had no truck with time-wasting.

The farmhand bit his lip as he rapidly handled himself, his sharp face intent on what he was doing, his eyes fixed on the paintbrush. Sally started to frown, afraid that he intended to jerk off right there in front of her. But then she realised it was not wanking that he had in mind; he was getting himself ready for something a whole lot better.

He walked his knees up between Sally's pale thighs and spread his own legs so that she was virtually doing the splits again on either side of him. Then he slowly withdrew the glistening paintbrush from where its handle had disappeared again into her shadowed hole, and replaced it with the blunt tip of his penis.

The weight of him on her legs filled Sally with renewed energy. She slid her hands under his checked shirt-tails to get at his arse as his muscular buttocks drew back, then inched the stiff length of his dick a little way into her. Her legs came up and wrapped around his hips, trying to pull his groin into hers, but he was stronger, resisting her, always pulling back, totally controlled, tilting his hips slowly back and forth until he was good and ready. At last they were in harmony, like two parts of the same beast, his grizzled head steady above hers. Sally let her head fall back and, as it came to rest on the back of the sofa, she saw the tall shape of Janie standing in the weak light from the hallway.

'Janie!' Sally gurgled, her hair bouncing across the sofa as she tried to lift her head.

'Quiet, woman,' Maddock growled, though Sally knew he had seen Janie. 'I won't be put off my stroke.'

There was a thump and clatter out in the hall. Janie was dropping something heavy onto the floor.

Maddock allowed his hips to increase their speed. Sally tried to twist aside to see Janie, but she couldn't alter his rhythm and her friend became obscured by the back of the sofa. Now her legs had no choice but to grip tighter and tighter round his thick torso as his meaty cock filled her. She blocked out Janie and anything else that threatened to distract her from what he was doing.

Maddock was evidently as strong as one of his own

oxen. Muscles she never knew existed rippled and flexed constantly in his arms, his neck, his thighs. Then suddenly he shifted his position, and sat back on his buttocks. He spread his hands around Sally's hips and flipped her up towards him so that her back was towards the hallway. They sat upright now on the floor, face to face, Sally straddling his knees with her legs still wrapped around his waist. This way his cock was angled right into the small of her back, filling every nook and cranny, as Janie had put it. They paused for a moment, panting into each other's faces, taunting each other to see who would move first, testing themselves to see who would crack and give in to the mounting excitement. Sally was acutely aware of Janie's eyes boring into her back; she hadn't heard her turn and go. She wondered if Maddock would stop.

But then he pulled his haunches back and, like a double act, Sally copied him. He gave a rising yell and she squealed in answer, and then they slammed their hips into each other, pulling back, arching, slamming back so that they shuddered with the impact of bone on bone. They ground against each other one last time, her body filled with his solid maleness. He started to give an unearthly low groan and Sally screeched triumphantly, feeling his body tense up. She bounced her butt across his legs, tightening her muscles round his cock and her legs round his waist until his face grew dark with the effort of holding on. He was obviously coming, his cock pumping into her, his eyes still blazing, never closing, watching Sally as she bounced and arched herself away from him. She took in every last inch of him before she swore she could feel his spunk shooting inside her, and she allowed her own climax to shatter. Finally she let herself fall back onto the floor

as a stifled roar escaped Maddock's lips and he released
her with a crash. They tumbled apart from each other,
both falling onto their backs, chests heaving as they
submitted to their joint climax. She leaned up to look
at his penis; it was still huge and thick across his leg.
She watched until it stopped flexing and spurting, and
until her own inner quivering had ceased.

'I'm sorry for intruding.' Janie's voice cut into the
silence.

They both turned their heads to look at her, too
breathless to speak. Janie started to back out of the
room, kicking over the logs that she had dropped in
the hallway.

Maddock rolled over and sprang straight up from a
crouch like an acrobat. 'Here, give me those.'

He stepped over Sally, his manhood still half-erect.
He squatted down beside Janie, picked the logs off the
floor, and came back to throw them into the fireplace.
Janie just stood there, staring at his bare muscled
buttocks, shockingly white above the tanned legs. He
stacked the spare logs in the basket beside the grate.
Then he grabbed the newspaper Sally had been reading
and started ripping the pages and scrumpling them up
to make kindling.

Janie and Sally continued to stare at him for a
moment, then glared at each other. He was not a man
of modesty. Sally shook her hair out of her eyes and
shrugged. Janie looked livid. To be fair, even someone
less uptight would have been pretty shocked to come
home and see the pair of them rutting on the floor like
that, thought Sally. She sat up and crossed her legs
beneath her. She didn't know what to say.

Janie spoke first. 'I saw everything.'

Maddock struck a match and held it to the newspaper, which started to smoke into life. He turned

round then and looked Janie up and down, kicking off his filthy boots and removing his shirt as he did so.

'At last, a real fire,' murmured Sally, unwilling to address Janie directly and unable to take her eyes off the stocky Maddock, especially now he had demonstrated some other useful caveman skills. 'That's what he's come here for, you see,' Sally ventured. 'Maintenance. He's here to keep an eye on the cottage.'

'And everyone in it, by the look of things,' Janie replied.

'So, did you enjoy watching us, miss?' Maddock asked, for all the world as if he was referring to a display of country dancing.

He squatted down behind Sally and ran his huge hand round to her stomach. Sally's knees twitched together.

Janie said nothing, but her cheeks were flushed. She took Ben's over-sized raincoat off and shook the drops off it before hanging it up.

Sally was tense. It was like waiting for a telling off by the headmistress. Janie came back into the room, twisting her wet hair into a knot at the back of her head, then gripped the sofa.

'What are you doing here, Maddock?' she asked, sounding uncharacteristically fierce.

'Evening to you, miss. It's like your friend just said, Mr Ben has asked me to keep an eye on the place. I'm surprised he didn't tell you. There's a lot of work to be done, inside as well as out.'

'Mostly inside,' spluttered Sally, still hugging herself on the floor.

'I know that. That's why I'm here,' said Janie. 'But we don't need you working on the house at the moment. We're supposed to be having a quiet break here.'

'But there's work that needs doing constantly,' said Maddock in defence.

'You can say that again.' Sally chortled, and leaned against his chest. 'Especially after hours. But seriously, Janie, he could help you. You said you thought the decorating was more than you could do on your own.'

'Not while we're staying here, thank you, Maddock. It can wait.'

'You're beginning to sound like Margot in *The Good Life*, Janie!' spluttered Sally, irritation taking over from awkwardness. 'Honestly! Can't you see he's only here to ... to help?'

Sally flipped her chin at Janie to mock, then smiled back towards Maddock. But he was still looking at Janie, and Janie was looking at Sally as if she would like to slap her. To Sally's annoyance, Maddock got up suddenly so that she nearly toppled backwards. He took a couple of muddy steps towards the sofa and glared at Janie. Sally thought Janie looked suddenly beautiful, standing there flushed with anger, her eyes glittering, and her lips parted as if to spit.

'No need to treat *me* like an intruder,' said Maddock, sounding hurt. 'You and your cousin were the ones who trod all over my dad's corn year after year. We should have taken the shotguns to you back then.'

'I'm not treating you like an intruder. At least, I don't mean to. I just meant that we don't want any maintenance doing while we're staying here. We want to be left alone. My friend here, she's –'

'A nymphomaniac? I know.' He gave one of his dirty laughs.

'– stressed. And right now, so am I. Anyway, haven't you got enough work to do up at the farm? For the new owner?'

'How do you know about him? He's only just got here.'

'I met him just now.' Janie's face went bright red, and she picked at some loose threads in the sofa cover. Sally started to kneel up, anxious to get the conversation back to her and Maddock.

'So you'll know he hasn't a clue about any of it. The farm is none of your concern, miss. Not really his concern, either. Bloody weekenders.'

'Well, isn't our Ben a weekender as well? But you get along fine with him.'

'Mr Ben could charm the pants off a duchess,' said Maddock. 'Frequently does, so I'm told.'

'Oh, when am I going to meet this guy?' wondered Sally. But they ignored her.

'And his family have owned this cottage for decades,' said Janie. 'Since before you were a ... a tadpole, Maddock.'

Maddock and Sally laughed at her, and Janie flushed again.

'That's why His Lordship up at the farm can wait for his renovation work to be done,' Maddock said, turning one of the logs on the fire.

'Whatever. I don't want to argue.'

'I asked you a question earlier,' Maddock continued. He was right beside Janie now, and Sally folded her arms crossly around her knees. They both seemed to have forgotten her.

'And I would like to ask you a question,' said Janie. 'When would you like to leave? Right now or in one minute's time.'

'My question was, did you enjoy watching us?'

'A bit difficult to avoid watching, seeing as how you just strolled in here and started shagging my friend

87

right here on the floor.' Janie still had one foot in the hall, as if she was contemplating her escape. 'Now, I really don't want to hold you up any longer. Don't you have to be somewhere?'

'His Lordship and the lads can get the pints in,' said Maddock. 'I still want to know ... did you enjoy it? Looks like something's flicked your switch.'

'Yeah, don't pretend to be so uptight, Janie,' goaded Sally, crawling on her knees towards the sofa and climbing up. 'Admit it, you were turned on just then, weren't you? Sex in the sitting room on a rainy night with a bit of rough. What could be a better way to pass the time?'

Maddock kept his eyes on Janie, unflinching at Sally's description of him. 'And that was just the warm up,' he said. Then he suddenly yanked the big jumper off Sally, tugging her T-shirt with it. She giggled. Her slim torso was the same milky white as her legs, and her breasts tipped out of her tiny T-shirt as Maddock removed it. She knew her tits were pert and sweet, very different from Janie's large round ones. Sally glanced down at her own body then smirked proudly round at Maddock. He didn't return her look, but still stared past her at Janie. Sally followed his line of vision, and saw that Janie's shirt was damp, and the sharp points of her nipples poked through the material.

'Come over here by the fire, Janie,' urged Sally, stretching out her hand. 'It's lovely and warm now.'

Janie edged round the corner of the sofa. She grabbed Sally's abandoned glass of wine and took a deep slug.

'Maddock, who is he? The man who's bought the farm?' Janie asked suddenly, sounding civil for a moment. 'The man you're working for?'

'Some bloke. A doctor or something. I call him His

Lordship because he's taken over my dad's farm and it's going to take some getting used to.'

'Oh boring, boring,' whined Sally, hopping off the sofa. She skipped into the kitchen, letting her tits bounce up and down, and found some candles and matches. She lit them, and turned the sitting room lights off.

'What are you doing, Sally?' Janie sounded nervous.

'Making us more comfortable.' Sally pulled a pile of cushions onto the floor in front of the fire. 'We don't want to talk about business! I think it's time we concentrated a little on you, Janie, since you're feeling left out of the action.'

Sally pounced on her friend, pulling her away from the sofa and onto the cushions. Maddock moved up from the fireside to join them, and twisted Janie's chin towards him.

'I agree. I think you should try a little bit of what's good for you,' he said to her. He nudged at Sally, who frowned for a moment then rolled away across the cushions and put on another CD, this time of a woman singing low, mournful songs.

'Wimpy music, this is,' said Maddock. 'Oh, well, bit of atmosphere, I suppose.'

His face remained very close to Janie's and Sally saw her friend recoil slightly, as she had done herself when she'd first clocked the surly face and the tiny red veins in his skin. She realised that some of the marks were scratches and scars. She didn't like him staring at Janie like that. Maddock's hard blue eyes were like glass, as they flicked over her features. He raised his other hand and Janie flinched sideways. He sniggered, and held her chin tight so that she had no choice but to return his hard glare.

'Do you posh bitches really think all we farm hands

do is fuck and clobber each other?' he hissed, lowering his hand so that his fingertips travelled over Janie's reddening cheeks and down her throat. He nodded slowly, winking over her head at Sally.

'Don't be ridiculous,' Janie replied, raising her eyebrows in an attempt to appear relaxed, even though the action actually made her look more snooty.

'Right then,' he nodded. 'I think your little friend here wants to have some more fun. I'm sure Mr Ben wouldn't object if we got up to no good in his house.'

'He'd probably approve!' chimed in Sally.

'I don't want him to know,' Janie protested.

'By the way, we farm hands do like to fuck,' interrupted Maddock. 'And we're not always fussy who it's with so long as it goes like a truck.'

'You pig!' spat Sally.

'In fact, the lads will be green when I tell them what I found in Master Ben's cottage. Certainly helps if the birds have got good bodies too,' he continued softly. 'Especially plump, ripe ones like yours, Janie. You look like you don't screw nearly enough. Now's your chance.'

Sally sniggered loudly, to remind them that she was still there. Janie raised her hands to try to push Maddock off, but he chuckled and held her face again. Sally saw Janie's tits squashed up against his chest. He drew back and peered down at them, then he glanced across at Sally, who was still topless.

'Tell your friend to relax,' he told her.

'Come on, Janie. Relax, we know him. He's nice. He'll make you feel good.'

Maddock nodded at Janie, then released his grip on her face and had the linen shirt off and over her head before she could take a breath.

Now her breasts were nearly bare, her flimsy bra

only just covering them, as they threatened to escape out of the top. The material stretched taut over the swollen mounds. Maddock slid his hand over the smooth curve of her breast. Janie bit her lip, and Sally's own nipples contracted at the sight of Maddock barely touching Janie yet making her stand quietly in front of him while he undressed her.

'You could join in, if you like. Don't want you sulking over there.' Maddock was reading Sally's mind. 'I'm sure you'd fancy a threesome.'

'I love threesomes. Just not with my friend,' Sally snapped, and Janie glanced across at her as well, as if seeing her for the first time. There was something strange about Janie. Her hair and clothes were messed up, for one thing, but then she had been running through the rain. It was something else, though. She looked feverish, almost, and had done when she stood at the door watching them. Either the sight of them humping had really turned her on, or shocked her, or she was ill, or something else had excited her or frightened her while she was out.

'What took you so long, Janie?' Sally asked loudly.

Janie opened her mouth to speak, but Maddock put his hand over it. 'Quiet, woman. You've had your turn.'

Sally rocked back on her knees. She didn't mind being bossed around if he was planning to give her one. In fact, she found it a novel kind of foreplay. But she was sure Janie wouldn't welcome all this macho stuff.

'Janie?'

But Janie didn't answer. There were hectic circles of pink in each cheek, and she avoided looking at her friend. Sally didn't know whether to jump up and kick Maddock out, or stay where she was and watch what he was going to do. But it wasn't up to her, because he was already doing it. He had Janie pressed hard up against his ribs and then he lifted a hand and planted it squarely over one breast. Then his fingers dived into the hot, damp crevice between her tits and Janie let out a squeal and grabbed onto his shoulders, not to push him away but to keep him there. She was already hooked.

Maddock ogled her breasts greedily. He frowned with concentration as his fingers slowly explored the soft mounds of flesh, cupping them like scoops of ice cream and lifting them out of the bra cups. Sally saw Janie's nipples begin to burn, berry-red.

'You like that, don't you? Stunning boobs,' Maddock murmured, then ran his tongue across his thin upper lip. 'Full, just as they should be. Bigger than your little tits, tartlet,' he said, without much more than a half-nod in Sally's direction. 'Look at that. And growing bigger all the time.'

Instead of putting her off, his rasping quiet voice seemed to put Janie into even more of a trance. He was acting differently from the way he had taken control of Sally, but then she'd been ready for him. Janie would take a lot of coaxing, or so Sally reckoned.

Maddock weighed both heavy breasts on the palms of his outstretched hands, just as if he was about to milk them. He bounced them up and down and squeezed them at the sides so that the nipples jutted forward. On impulse, Sally suddenly scrambled up behind Janie and scrabbled at her thin bra-straps, then flung the flimsy underwear to one side. Janie instinctively went to cover her tits, but Maddock grabbed her wrists and held her arms open. Sally hovered for a moment, wondering if Janie was afraid, but to her amazement she saw a smile tilt the corners of her friend's mouth.

'Better naked, isn't it?' Maddock crooned. 'We can all see you properly now. Don't want to stop, do you?'

'I should, but you know I can't,' Janie whispered.

'In all your glory. Just look at them.'

Maddock pushed Janie's breasts together hard, flicking one thumb across both nipples as if striking a lighter until they stuck out like bullets. Another stubby finger ran up and down the deep cleavage until it filled with sweat, and Sally saw answering beads of perspiration break out along her friend's upper lip. Janie pushed against Maddock harder, and dug her nails through his vest as she knelt up. Now her bare breasts were level with his nose and he gave a low whistle.

Sally bobbed up behind Janie again and tugged at her loose trousers. She would assist Maddock in his little game, but she wasn't prepared to be a spectator for long. She would soon want the limelight back for herself. Janie didn't resist, but let Sally take off her trousers so that all she wore were her knickers.

Maddock blew across the breasts pressing in front of his nose, still squeezing them together. Sally's own tits began to set up a low throbbing at the sight. Then his teeth closed round one burning nipple and he sucked hard, drawing the teat outwards with his teeth while he pinched the other hard between finger and thumb. Janie groaned in instant pleasure, and jammed his face between her tits, shifting her knees wider as she did so.

Sally could tell Janie was already fighting the desire that was starting to pulsate inside her and, although she was jealous of the attention Janie was getting, she was fascinated to see her friend in this aroused state.

On impulse she picked up the paintbrush and playfully flicked it under Janie's bottom, then jumped back as her friend started wildly jerking back and forth, pressing her hard nipples further into Maddock's mouth. She opened her legs as she knelt there, and as Maddock continued biting her nipples, first one and then the other, Janie started to touch herself with her fingers, rubbing them hard against her newly awakened pussy, tilting her bottom so that her own fingers could give her some relief.

Sally was overcome with curiosity, and flicked the paintbrush in between Janie's fingers. Janie groaned out loud, and Sally jumped back again, as if she'd been caught stealing. It looked like Janie would soon bring herself off, leaving Maddock's stiffening rod free for Sally to enjoy a second time.

As if he'd heard Sally's thoughts, Maddock yanked away from suckling at Janie, leaving her nipples jutting into thin air. Then he lowered Janie down in front of him so that she was on all fours, her butt pressed back into the sofa, and her face now staring into Maddock's crotch. Sally saw her bite her lip with frustration at the way he had dropped her breasts just when she was starting to lose herself.

Both girls waited for him to speak, but he was silent, just running a finger thoughtfully down his scarred cheek as he reached one hand down to grasp his bollocks. Janie groaned again, completely lost, and lowered her torso to the floor so that her swollen breasts could rub against the rough surface of the cushions.

Maddock stopped moving, as if waiting for something. Janie raised her head from the cushion and his thick penis, erect again, sprang forwards and banged into her face. Sally had an even better look at it this time. It was dark-red with blue veins raised along its short, thick surface, but it was stiff as a fist and standing out at right angles from his toned body. Janie scrambled forwards, grabbing at herself again, but

Maddock held her down on all fours. He settled himself on his knees, running his fingers through her sleek copper hair to release it from the knot. Sally saw a couple of stalks of hay drop from it. Maddock prodded the blunt end of his cock into Janie's cheekbone, then dragged the rounded knob across her face towards her mouth.

Janie's lips opened as she drew in another breath. Sally wondered if her friend had ever sucked cock before. The first time was always something of an eye-opener, to say the least, and what a dick *this* was to practice on.

Sally reckoned Janie didn't know what to do, because she tried once more to get up on her knees, and rise up to the level of his face. Sally saw Maddock frown, and she leaped forward from her ringside seat and pinned Janie's hips down to keep her in place.

Maddock edged the bulb end of his hard shaft towards Janie's mouth and the plum-coloured tip slipped smoothly between her parted lips. She tried to swallow, but in doing so she touched the moist tip of Maddock's cock with her tongue and it jumped between her teeth, and probed deeper towards her throat.

Janie mirrored the action of his cock in her mouth with her own fingers, probing and pushing as many as she could into her gaping pussy. I'd never do it in front of anyone else, she'd said. Sally's skin felt hot and cold.

'Aren't you going to help her?' Maddock murmured suddenly, looking across Janie's head at where Sally was sitting close behind her. 'Look at that lovely pussy just aching to be licked out. I can't be in two places at once.'

Sally couldn't do it. For all her experience she had never gone down on a mate before, and she wasn't going to start now. She reckoned she owed it to Janie to leave her to it. She shook her head and crawled back towards the fireplace, but Maddock was no longer looking at her.

Janie opened her jaw wider over Maddock's still-stiffening penis, then closed her lips tight around it and started to suck. His penis seemed to be filling her whole mouth, punching out her cheeks. Maddock held her head and guided it back and forth slowly along the length of his shaft. Janie had got the hang of it. She nipped the taut, engorged muscle again with her teeth and he let out a groan. He spread his legs, tensing his meaty buttocks to aim at an even better angle.

With every move of Janie's mouth along his shaft, her fingers travelled deeper inside her. Sally wondered whether to go to work on her friend with the paint-brush; it wouldn't be the same as finger fucking her, but she couldn't move, enthralled and appalled by the experience of watching, and in any case they were both managing perfectly well without her.

Janie lifted one hand and cupped Maddock's swinging balls, and increased the tempo of her lips and tongue. She tickled the balls as they banged softly against her chin, then squeezed them hard, and suddenly Sally saw them retract into his groin as he plunged his cock further down Janie's throat, pushing through her teeth so that she made her jaws go slack again to accommodate his size.

He held her face between his hands, covering her ears and, as their movements became more and more frantic, Sally was aware of new, strong spasms clenching and unclenching deep inside her as she watched.

Maddock jerked back and forth, grunting lewdly, and nearly knocking Janie backwards with his two final thrusts. His fingers twined through her hair as he pumped his juices into her mouth and Sally knew she was tasting for the first time the sweet salt of his thick spunk. She mentally applauded Janie for swallowing so carefully – always a point-scorer. Before he had finished, Maddock tugged Janie's head away, his still-rigid cock emerging from her mouth like it had from Sally's own cunt, wet with saliva and spunk and jerking with the aftershocks of his climax.

Sally's mouth fell open. She grabbed her own pussy, which was convulsing frantically as she started to come. She watched Janie's fingers being gripped and swallowed as she ground them up inside her and at last Sally's own excitement collided with the astonishment of where she was and what she was doing. She gave a low, jagged moan as her own long-awaited climax rippled through her.

Meanwhile Janie arched her back, stiffening like a cat on all fours to seize the moment, shivering as her own moans were forced out of her. Then she fell slowly forwards onto the cushions.

Maddock started to clap his hands, breaking the mood, and Sally joined in. Janie remained lying on her front.

'Janie? Are you alright?' Sally hissed, reaching over to tap her friend on the shoulder.

Janie rolled over reluctantly and made a grab for her shirt. 'Of course I am.'

'Thank you for your hospitality. Mr Ben would be proud,' Maddock said, yawning and picking up his clothes. Janie and Sally watched him in silence.

'I told you, I don't want Mr Ben knowing anything about this. Any of it,' Janie said. She had gone back into headmistress mode, sitting up slowly and sliding her arms into her shirt sleeves.

Maddock wiped a hand across his mouth and

coughed. 'He likes me to report all goings on at the cottage. You never know what riff raff might try to break in.'

Sally laughed at that. 'He'll be wishing he was here, not in boring old Amsterdam,' she said.

Janie said nothing, but looked out of the window at the darkness. It had finally stopped raining. In the sitting room there was no sound apart from the crackle of the logs in the grate. Maddock picked up his jacket and stood up. He tugged at his forelock.

'So, ladies, I hope you were pleased with the service. And now I must be off.'

'Hey, not so fast, matey,' said Sally. 'We might not be finished with you!' She scrambled to her feet and followed Maddock through the kitchen. He pulled on his smelly jacket and stuffed the peaked cap back on to his head. Suddenly he was just a passing farmhand again, not a raging sex machine. His blue eyes flickered over Sally as if he'd never seen her before.

'Got to make my report, haven't I? About town versus country, remember?'

'Town wins hands down,' Sally started to argue, but he was gone, slamming the back door behind him. The wind managed to deposit a quick blast of cold air in her face, and Sally scampered back into the sitting room to huddle by the fire.

'What the bloody hell were you playing at?' Janie exploded, buttoning up her red shirt. 'The pair of you, making free in Ben's house. This'll be all round the village by morning!'

'He came snooping round the garden, and saw me here on my own. I was horny, and bored. And what about you? I didn't see you fighting him off!'

Janie was silent, curling herself into the corner of the sofa and staring into the fire.

'You don't fight off people like Maddock.'

'Why? Has that happened before?'

'No.' The anger went out of Janie, and she looked up at Sally. 'Not with Maddock. Not with anyone. I've never done that before.'

'What? Sucked cock?'

Janie blushed and wriggled in her seat. 'None of it. I've never done that, and I've never done it in front of someone else. At least, not until today.'

Sally came to sit beside Janie, and tugged roughly at her arm. 'You should have warned me about the wild-life around here. I wonder if there's more where that Maddock came from?'

'Very likely. All lurking in the hedgerows, peering in through the windows, right now, laughing their heads off.'

'So much the better. You can forget your man-free zone, doll. I think we're going to find there are more macho bumpkins with more sex drive and more swinging dicks round here than we can shake a stick at!'

Janie got up to pull the curtains, and just caught sight of the tail lights of Maddock's Land Rover bump-ing up to the road.

'There he goes, on his way to the pub to meet with Farmer Giles.'

'Who?' called Sally, pulling on her jeans at last.

'They'll be exchanging notes about the London bints who are staying at the cottage.'

'Good. Let them. Because they ain't seen nothing yet. By the way,' yawned Sally, kicking the cushions to one side and walking into the kitchen to peer into the fridge for some food, 'why *have* you got straw in your hair?'

* * *

'Pub's heaving tonight, isn't it? Summer rush, I suppose.'

The city gent shoved his way through the crowd of drinkers and addressed his comment to the man already waiting at the bar of the Honey Pot Inn, who didn't reply.

'Everything alright, Jack? You're not your usual debonair self.' The city type extracted a piece of straw from his friend's spectacles, and another from his collar. 'You look like you've been through a hedge backwards. Talk about the rustic look!'

Jack roused himself and smiled.

'Pint, Jonathan? I'm getting them in for the lads, and for Maddock when he gets here.'

The city gent squinted through the haze of smoke towards the corner table.

'Not interrupting anything, am I? Only –'

'Not at all. I've had enough of ordering them about for one day. It's a relief to see you, to be honest,' Jack assured him. 'Only what?'

'Only you looked miles away just then. If I had a penny for every thought I've dug out of people, I'd be –'

'Even richer, I'm sure.' Jack laughed, then the faraway look came back into his eyes. 'But actually all I was thinking about was marigolds.'

'Marigolds?'

Jonathan spluttered into his pint. The dark barmaid glided up. She pointedly started to wipe the bar with her cloth, moving her arm slowly back and forth, and Jonathan stopped drinking to watch her.

'It's this girl, you see.' Jack's voice was virtually impossible to hear above the hubbub. 'She was nicking logs, up at the farm. I'm sure it's Janie. Her hair smells of marigolds. It always used to smell of marigolds –'

'Well, *hello*.' Jonathan gave up listening to Jack. 'New barmaid?'

The woman glared down her fine nose for a moment, then rewarded him with a dazzling, scarlet smile.

'New to you, perhaps. That's six pounds fifty please, Jack.'

'You belong here already, Mimi,' Jack said, handing over the money. 'Can't imagine the Honey Pot Inn without you.'

'And you're here for the whole summer, I trust?' queried Jonathan, eyes now glued to the barmaid's generous bosom, which was encased in a low-cut black sweater.

'If anything takes my fancy enough to stay,' she said, swinging her hips as she scooped up a handful of glasses.

'Or if any *body* takes your fancy?' Jonathan called as she swayed up to the other end of the bar.

'You want to watch it with her, Jonathan,' Jack warned. The pub door swung open, and Maddock banged his way through. 'Someone's beaten you to it.'

'Nonsense,' replied Jonathan, keeping his eyes on Mimi's neck until she turned round again. 'No-one ever beats me to anything.'

Jack started to reply to Jonathan's fighting talk, but was in time to catch the wink passing between Mimi and Jonathan.

'I have to hand it to you, Dart,' he laughed, lifting the tin tray loaded with glasses. 'You have them eating out of your hand, don't you?'

Jonathan laughed too, taking out a business card scribbled across with his mobile number. He flipped it expertly across the bar so that it landed on the drawer of the till just as she opened it. Mimi took it, and slipped it into her cleavage. Then she swung round the corner of the bar and was gone.

'How rude of me, ogling the local talent,' Jonathan said, following through the crowd. 'You were saying, about the marigolds?'

'Oi, you two!' shouted Maddock, and the two men winced. 'You should check out the crumpet staying at Mr Ben's cottage! Delicious redhead, cute blonde.'

'Tell us more, Maddock.' Jonathan nudged Jack, who shrugged his shoulders and sat down at the table. 'Do tell us more.'

4

Janie woke up with her heart pounding, as if someone had startled her or she had something urgent to do. She had barely slept all night, despite being exhausted. Her mind raced and her body tossed and turned. The rain had eased off in the night, and for a short while the silence had started to relax her. She thought about serious sunbathing and swimming, of the summer really beginning, but here was the rain again, cats and dogs, casting a dull light over the growing day.

She was in Ben's huge bedroom with its white-washed brickwork and dark beams crisscrossing the ceiling and walls. Lying like a starfish under the snowy duvet, she could briefly pretend that she was waking up to a normal seaside visit, just like every other time she had been down here: quiet, uneventful, usually solitary. If she tilted her head she could see the willow tree through the low window, and beyond it the hedge bordering the farm. Was Farmer Giles asleep in the ramshackle farmhouse, or was he staying in the grand Art Deco hotel up the coast, towelling himself after a shower and stuffing those spectacles onto his nose to brood over a sheaf of building plans? Had he and Maddock had a good laugh about her last night in the pub? Very probably. She curled her legs up, prickling with humiliation. The starkest picture she had from yesterday was of Maddock's penis leaping and spunking down her throat, his hands warm and gnarled on her hair. She remembered her own fierce rush of triumph at successfully sucking him off. Then there was the weird knowledge that Sally had been sitting in the room with them, unusually quiet, watching it all. But she didn't want to dwell on any of that. It had all come too fast after her encounter in the barn. Or maybe it was that very first bout of sexual contact for ages that had made it all happen with Maddock; made her permanently insatiable. *That* was what she wanted to revel in as her toes stretched to the end of the bed. Her sexual re-awakening at the hands of the handsome farmer.

There was a slight bump from the attic above her. She waited for more: the sound of footsteps, Sally getting out of bed. Janie tensed. She didn't want to talk to Sally; she didn't want to talk to anyone just now. But thankfully there were no more bumps. Sally would have turned over and gone back to sleep, hopefully. God knows what she would be dreaming of, but one thing was for sure: Sally would be seeing her mate Janie in a whole new light after yesterday.

She flung the duvet aside and got up. It was still only eight. She pulled on a tight T-shirt and her bleach-spattered dungarees and creaked down the wooden stairs. She was sure they were listing more violently than last year. Ben always said that subsidence in a remote place like this didn't bother him. If the cottage collapsed one day, he would simply bulldoze it all and build another one.

Janie wanted to be busy. She picked up the cushions which had been left scattered on the floor the previous night and dropped them at random onto the sofa and chairs. There was a faint smell of wood-smoke in the room, and Janie found that her eyes were pinned to the spot on the floor where Maddock had jammed her face into his crotch and she had sucked on his cock like it was going out of fashion.

'I should go back to bed,' she muttered to herself, yanking the chairs and sofa round into some semblance of sociable positioning. But then she thought of Sally, still asleep, who had sat back and watched her sucking Maddock off. Worse, she had seen her frisking herself with her own fingers. She had seen Janie with her tits out and shoved in a strange man's face. And Janie had let herself into the cottage and seen Sally right in front of her, coiled round Maddock as if he was a tree trunk, and rutting with him all over the hearth-rug. What kind of holiday was this turning out to be?

Janie picked up the cushions all over again to plump them up, and saw one of her paintbrushes dropped there. As she dropped it into her pocket she started to flush, thinking again of Maddock and his big boots and his swinging bull's balls and his muddy fingernails and sharp teeth. She knew his rough edges were right up Sally's street, but she couldn't deny that Maddock had pulled her into some pretty explosive action as well, made her do things she had never tried before, nor even had time to contemplate with her Farmer Giles. Her breasts ached this morning, and she had bruises on her hips and knees. There would also be scratches on her back from the straw. The farmer had been gorgeous and warm, and almost gentlemanly, considering what they were doing. She wanted to think about him, but his face and body kept merging with Maddock's in her tired brain.

This morning there were no men, no Land Rovers, no barn doors and shovels scraping. Just the dripping of the rain off the thatch, and the grandfather clock ticking loudly in the hall. She punched a button on the radio to let the idle chatter of the DJ distract her, then went into the kitchen, set the coffee pot on the go and began preparing to sand down the cupboards.

'Dressing like Andy Pandy isn't going to disguise what you did last night,' remarked Sally suddenly from behind her.

'I thought you were asleep,' mumbled Janie, scraping furiously. 'Coffee's on. I've got work to do.'

Sally pushed past her, yawning. Her matted blonde hair stuck up at the back like a baby's, and she was wearing one of Ben's striped office shirts.

'That's Ben's shirt. Didn't you bring your own?' said Janie.

'Found it in my bathroom. He won't know. I was cold in the night. What's it to you, anyway, misery guts?'

'Nothing. Just that we're staying here partly as guests. Doesn't mean we can just make free with all his things.'

'Bit late to start worrying about all that,' said Sally, hitching herself up on the bar-stool beside the fridge, and reaching for the cups. All was silent and a little awkward until the coffeepot began to sputter and hiss. Sally slid lazily off her stool and poured herself and Janie some coffee and added three sugars for herself. She stirred and kept stirring until Janie stopped sanding her cupboard and looked round.

'That's better,' said Sally, who had been watching her. She crossed her ankles, pulling the shirt as far down her thighs as it would go. She had white fluffy socks on. 'Now, are you going to tell me what's eating you? As if I couldn't guess?'

Janie started ripping at the edges of her bit of sandpaper, but shrugged.

'If I've done something wrong, just tell me,' said

Sally. 'This is the first morning of our glorious holiday. We don't have to fall out, do we?'

Janie shook her head, still concentrating on the sandpaper she held. She wished her mate would put some jeans on, or knickers at least.

'Two things are wrong here, I reckon,' said Sally, slurping her coffee and shifting back onto the stool. Her bare buttocks squeaked on the seat. 'One, we both went over the top last night, exposing ourselves to each other like that, not to mention giving our all to that Maggot, or whatever his name is.'

'Maddock.'

Janie blushed scarlet again, and even Sally clapped her free hand over her mouth at the name. Then she snorted coffee down her nose as she started to laugh, and that started Janie off as well. She plonked down her sandpaper, picked up her coffee, and leaned against the sink.

'And we weren't even particularly pissed!' she said, relaxing some more.

'Er, speak for yourself. I was bladdered. In fact, that makes *your* behaviour far worse than mine, if you were supposedly sober! That's the funny thing.' Sally wiped her nose.

'So I'm the pot and you're the kettle.'

They laughed again, and then just as abruptly stopped. Both stared at the floor, obviously remembering some of the really intimate details.

'Sort of a case of, you show me yours, I'll show you mine!'

'Alright, Sal. I'm sorry. I think that's it. If I'm completely honest, fantasising about hot sex with a guy is one thing, especially after my years in the wilderness –'

'Certainly the wilderness down here.'

'But seeing your mate at it, all her bits –'

'Then her seeing yours!'

'Well, much as I love you, I wasn't ready for that,' said Janie. 'And I wasn't ready for you pushing me into it with that Maddock.'

'We led the horse to the water, and it drank! You came into the room with that Wild Woman of Borneo look. I could tell you were up for it, even if you didn't know it yourself. And Maddock could smell it a mile off, even though he doesn't know you.'

'But I can't believe I did it – did something – with Maddock of all people! His dad used to scare us shitless when we were kids.'

'Well, it wasn't his dad, was it? This Maddock was like a bull in a brothel. He'd have gone on all night if we'd persuaded him.'

'Do bulls go on all night?'

They creased with laughter again.

'So am I forgiven for leading you astray?' asked Sally, sliding off the stool and pouring some more coffee. 'Though you've got just as much of the dirty slapper in you.'

'I'll forgive you if you go and get dressed. I don't think I can take any more naked bottoms. I just want to get back to normal.'

'But what the devil shall I wear? Versace, or Westwood? We're not going anywhere, are we? Look at the pissing rain.'

They both peered out of the kitchen windows and sighed.

'You can wear something suitable for cooking,' said Janie. 'That's what you can do today, while I'm stripping these cupboards.'

'And I've got just the dish.' Sally picked up her coffee cup and started to stump towards the stairs.

'What's that?' Janie called out.

'Shepherd's pie, of course!'

'Great. And I like it with plenty of shepherds in, please.'

Janie opened the back door to let some air in while she got out the white spirit. A brisk breeze and a handful of rain nipped in and slapped her round her hot face, and she closed her eyes. Today was going to be good, after all. Despite propping the door open while she cleaned the cupboards with the white spirit, it still made her feel light-headed. She left the cupboards to dry, and went into the little room.

'Today's a work day, madam,' chided Sally from behind her. 'No slacking.'

Janie turned round. Sally was wearing nothing but some expensive French knickers and a camisole, all topped off with a ruffled floor-length cook's pinafore which she had tied in a huge bow at the small of her back.

'Get the fire going, and then you're going to dress up as well,' she said, and Sally dropped Mastov's negligee over her friend's head. Janie let the silk slide lasciviously over her hair and cheeks. It barely made a sound as it merged with her own skin.

'I'm supposed to paint the kitchen cupboards wearing this?'

'Well, I'm supposed to fill your freezer wearing this.' Sally sketched a little curtsey, nearly tripping over the pinny. 'Now, show us yer onions.'

'In the little pantry thing. Now, first the undercoat, then the petticoat.'

They changed the radio station to one playing constant music, and got to work. After fuelling themselves with toast and marmite, Sally began preparing the lunch. The aroma of onions soon filled the kitchen as Sally chopped and peeled the vegetables and got under

Janie's feet. Both the girls started sniffing and wiping their eyes at the combined effect of paint and onions, and Janie had to fling the back door open again.

'Get the mince sizzling, and then come out of there,' she instructed Sally, feeling quite peculiar and walking through to the sitting room. 'My head is spinning with all the fumes.'

She twiddled the poker in the grate and picked up Sally's negligee. Quickly she stepped out of her dungarees and T-shirt and dropped the garment over her head. It slithered down her body, making her shiver with its cool touch. She looked at herself in the mirror above the fireplace. The light from the flames leaped over her features. The creamy silk looked good, bringing out a slight flush in her own pale skin, but her bra looked too hefty under the delicate spaghetti straps. It totally detracted from the design of the bodice.

She glanced into the kitchen. Sally was dipping her little finger into the mince and sucking it. She frowned, then picked up the jumbo tube of tomato purée and squeezed it bang in the middle, letting a long red snake wriggle out into the steaming mixture. The tip of Sally's tongue was trapped between her teeth as she watched the purée's journey into the mince. Janie reckoned she could guess what was going through her friend's mind as she flicked one last drop of purée from the tube's nozzle and licked it off her finger.

At least she was engrossed, thought Janie, and she unhooked her bra and tossed it aside. The negligee was so well cut that the bodice clung to her ribs and stretched tight across her stomach, forming a natural support for her breasts. At the same time, the constant slippery touch of the silk wandering across her nipples made them stiffen, and her tits firmed up in response so that they rode higher on her ribcage. She stretched her arms above her head, coiling her hair up, then let everything drop and turned to look over her shoulder. The back of the negligee was cut right down to the twin dimples above her bum.

'Get in here and taste this, Janie!' called Sally. 'I reckon we could live on shepherd's pie and Chardonnay all week!'

Janie glided into the kitchen, and Sally whistled.

'I told you it would suit you better than me. You look like a princess. You even hold yourself better when you're wearing that.'

Janie flicked her hair over her shoulder like a Hollywood starlet and blew Sally a kiss. Then the two of them bent over the bubbling, meaty mixture on the Aga.

'This reminds me of Paris,' said Sally, slurping on her wooden spoon. 'Jonathan and I went to this restaurant one evening, and they invited us into the kitchens. He knew the chef, or something.'

'A friend of Mastov, perhaps?'

'Very likely. My God, *very* likely. That Mastov has fingers in all sorts of pies. As I've already discovered.'

They laughed, and Janie watched while Sally mashed the potatoes.

'We ate so much in Paris, but the food and wine was so good it just made me feel full and horny, rather than full and bloated. It's no wonder we had to shag at least three times a night.'

'Don't make out you're suddenly some sort of gourmet,' objected Janie, helping to fork the buttery mash over the meat. 'It was just his incredibly long dick that kept you at it, you said.'

'How do you open these old-fashioned oven doors, then?'

Again they bent over in front of the Aga, Janie

holding the heavy door open while Sally heaved the enormous pie dish inside. Warm air wafted out of the oven at the same time as cold air whistled over their backsides.

'Two Thin Ladies. I like it.'

Sally cursed as she slammed her finger in the door. Janie knocked her head against a cupboard as she straightened, leaving a dash of white undercoat on her hair.

A tall, fair man dressed in impeccable tweeds and cashmere was leaning in the doorway, arms folded and looking them both up and down. Suddenly Janie felt quite girlish and awkward.

'For Christ's sake!' exploded Sally, turning on the kitchen tap full blast to run water over her finger. 'Does no one ever knock around here?'

'Certainly not,' replied the visitor calmly, stepping into the kitchen and shutting the wind and rain out. He walked past her and untied the big bow at her back so that her pinafore fell limply down in front of her. 'Cute butt, as ever. This the new style of television chef? Linguini in lingerie? Knocking it up in knickers?'

It was the first time Janie had ever seen Sally lost for words. Her mouth opened and shut a few times, and then she yanked the pinafore over her head and hurled it to the floor.

'Just what the *fuck* –'

'Language, in front of ladies,' he said, stopping in front of Janie. 'You always did have a mouth like a sewer. Now then, let's remember our manners. Good morning.'

He took Janie's hand, twirled her round once, then kissed her fingers, watching her all the time with navy-blue eyes. Janie couldn't see past his shoulder, but she could hear Sally making rude puking noises. The man just smiled, still holding Janie's eyes, and he waltzed her slowly backwards into the sitting room. The silk floated round her legs and, although she couldn't dance like Sally, her body felt fluid as she moved. He twirled her round again, and her arms flew out as she spun.

'I didn't think you'd leave those mean streets totally of your own accord, Sally. Now I see how you were persuaded to come out to the country, to the back of beyond,' he called out, lowering Janie down on the sofa and walking over to the CD player. 'And now I've seen your delectable friend, it's no wonder you never brought her to meet the lads in the City.'

'She wouldn't want to come to the City to meet odious creeps like you. I wouldn't want her breathing the same air.'

Janie had seen Sally riled, but never like this. She was motionless with fury, her fists clenched by her sides, her small face tight with loathing.

'But your friend – sorry, your name?'

'Er, Jane. Janie.'

'Jane, you look as if you could perfectly well choose which air you breathe, without Sally's protection. She's just a little upset, that's all.'

Sally sprang at him then, unable to contain herself. She literally wrapped her fingers and nails round his neck, her bare legs round his middle, and hung onto him. Janie jumped back. Sally was drawing blood from the man's cheek.

'Sally, what's going on? You two know each other?'

The man laughed, a deep, cold laugh, and unpeeled Sally's frantic limbs from around his ribs. He tossed her easily over to the other armchair, where she landed on all fours like a cat.

'The devil. We were talking of the devil,' spat Sally, brushing her hair off her face. 'And he's appeared. How did you know I was hiding in this cottage?'

'This is Jonathan Dart? The man from Paris? The bastard who shafted you?'

They didn't answer her. They were now too busy circling one another. Or rather, Sally was stepping round him as if he might scorch her.

'Maddock told me where you were. We got talking in the pub last night. He told me all about it, in fact. I knew, from his description of what this floozy was doing with a paintbrush, that it was my Sally. Nothing's secret, or sacred, around here. Although I didn't recognise the description of the "posh bitch" who was here with you. I gather you give great head, Jane.'

'What paintbrush?' asked Janie, glancing round at her decorating stuff.

'You'll have to show her. Cracking stuff, apparently, so Maddock told me.' Jonathan winked at Sally, and she raised her fists again.

'You two must have business to sort out,' Janie muttered, standing up and elbowing her way round Jonathan, who had barely shifted his position in front of her, despite the attack from Sally. He caught hold of one of Janie's wrists.

'Business can wait. It can always wait, can't it, Sally? I've seen something I'd far rather explore.'

'You can keep your hands off Janie for a start!' screamed Sally, launching herself at him again.

'Hello? Anybody there? I was just looking for – whoa, cowboys, what's going on in here?'

As Jonathan lurched sideways, Janie saw her farmer entering the room, pushing his glasses up his nose and tipping his cap back on his head. Her stomach lurched and she kneeled up on the sofa where she'd fallen in the scuffle. She found it was impossible not to move seductively in the negligee, and already Jonathan's dubious attention had flattered her into life.

'It's you!' she breathed, at a loss for anything else to say, and Jonathan and Sally both stopped fighting. Sally dropped off his shoulders like a discarded wrap, and skidded across the room. The two men looked huge, and she looked tiny.

'It's like bloody Piccadilly Circus here today!' she cried, delighted. She pulled on the farmer's sleeve, and he came to stand by the fire. 'Come in, come in. Just in time to interrupt actual bloodshed. Perhaps you could get rid of this reprobate for us. He's not welcome.'

'It didn't look like that to me,' the farmer remarked, taking off his glasses to polish off the steam. 'Looked like you were all getting on famously. What's going on, Jonathan?'

'Nothing, Jack, all under control. Did you know you had wildcats for neighbours?'

Janie and Sally gaped stupidly round. The aroma of shepherd's pie began to permeate the room, and somebody's stomach rumbled. Both the men started to laugh.

'Do you mind if I find my way round your drinks cabinet?' the farmer asked Sally. Janie fumed. It wasn't Sally's drinks cabinet. 'I think we all need to start again.'

'Well, I'd be *very* glad to start again,' Sally said loudly, leading him into the kitchen to find some wine. 'Just not with Mr Dart, here. Can you get rid of him for me? I swore I'd kill him last time I saw him.'

'Not my place to get into your argument. In any case, I couldn't possibly chuck him out of here. For one thing, it's not my house. And for another, it turns out we both own properties close by, which makes us neighbours. Life in the country is known for its hospitality. I'm sure your friend told you all about that when she came back with the logs last night?'

'Do you know, she didn't say a word when she came back with the logs. Why? Did you bump into each other last night? What happened?'

He started to reply, but they must have moved to the other end of the kitchen, because now Janie could barely hear what they were saying, and, anyway, Jonathan was sitting beside her on the sofa and looking at her again with those unwavering eyes. He placed a hand on her thigh.

'Do you mind? I adore the feel of expensive fabric.'

The silk wrinkled up her leg, ruffling over her fine hairs, and she caught her breath.

'You know him?' asked Janie. 'The farmer?'

'In the end everyone gets to know everyone else around here, even us weekenders.'

'That's just what he was saying.'

'That's Jack. He's just bought the farm over the way.'

Janie tried to crane past him to look into the kitchen and hear what they were saying in there, but she could only hear muffled voices and then the familiar sound of Sally's throaty chuckle. She might as well have had a megaphone to tell the world, *I'm on the pull here*.

'Let her get on with it. He'll have trouble resisting if she's got the throttle out, believe me. But she'll be crawling back in a minute. Did you hear what I just said?'

'Yes, you said Jack. Ben's friend, Jack? Ugly Jack? Jack from my childhood?'

'Could be. He was saying he used to play around here as a kid. Said he'd bumped into an old friend just yesterday. Was that you?'

For some reason Janie's eyes welled up. The pictures jerked across her mind's eye like an old cine film. Not the wigwam fantasies, although she could 'Jack' those up easily enough, but the real pictures: the grubby boys and the irritating little girl always trying to join in.

'Pushed you around, did they, as kids?'

She turned her eyes on Jonathan. He was too smooth and sophisticated for Janie's taste, and had seriously damaged Sally's prospects, but he had a way about him that was hypnotising. She understood how he had got through Sally's defences. He seemed to be looking right into Janie's mind; perhaps it wasn't so difficult, particularly if Jack had already told him all about their escapades as kids, and their adventure in the hay barn, but to have five minutes of this man's total attention was mesmerising.

She heard a scuffle and a cough in the kitchen and, as her eyes darted sideways to see what was going on, Jonathan caught her chin in his hand and kept her face in front of him.

'Little boys are all the same. That's how I know. They can be smelly and horrible, especially to little girls.'

'He said he knew me, when I met him yesterday. But I didn't recognise him. I thought it was just a line.'

'If I'd spent my childhood climbing up trees and scampering across cornfields with someone like you, I wouldn't forget, either. So he's not such an idiot.'

Jonathan's fingers were gentle on her face, and Janie couldn't turn away. She shifted on her legs, and it brought her closer to him. The silk of the negligee moved across her skin, echoing his fingers, and rustled. He heard it, too, because the hand that was on her thigh tightened, and moved slowly upwards, taking the material with it, up towards her hip and baring more and more of her leg.

There was silence from the kitchen now. Despite the warmth that was stealing through her under this man's fingers, Janie wanted to know what they were doing. She didn't want Sally getting her paws on Jack. She heard the kitchen table leg scrape on the flagstones, and the sound of a wine bottle being put down on the counter.

'She's playing a game to annoy us both,' Jonathan hissed, again reading Janie's mind. 'Both of them want both of us but, you see, their plan is about to backfire.'

Janie relaxed a little, and turned back to him. While he had been speaking the silk had rustled all the way up and over her hip, leaving it pale and gleaming in the dull wet light. He left the material draped there, and let his hand wander further on, underneath it, over her warm stomach, across to the other hip, then back to her stomach, where it paused. Janie tensed, staring at his face but seeing, from the corner of her eye, his hand spread across her hidden skin. She arched away from him slightly and, as one breast brushed against his cashmere sleeve, her nipples sparked into life.

'That's more like it,' he said. 'You may look like some uptight princess, but you're hot, aren't you? A little like Sally, but you keep it well hidden.'

As if in answer the kitchen door swung shut, either kicked that way or blown by the draught from the back door. Now they were completely separated from the other two.

Janie didn't want to think of Sally's little tits pressing against her farmer; pressing against Jack. He was Janie's Jack. She'd seen him first. She wanted him to fuck her again. She didn't want him entering that soft golden bush and groaning over Sally's triumphant little body.

'She doesn't want me to have you, either, you know, but we're going to teach her a lesson. It's not why I came here this morning, but it'll work just as well to bring her to heel.'

'What do you mean?' Janie had one ear cocked towards the kitchen while his words purred into the other ear.

'I mean they'll be more interested in us once they see how well we're getting on without them.'

'We should just use each other, you mean?'

His even features opened into a smile and, although Janie could see it was the smile of a man used to getting his own way, her own mouth started to curve up in comprehension. She liked the sound of her own voice, saying something so calculating, cynical, almost. She was learning to play this game. Learning either to pretend to be someone else, or learning to let loose the cooler Janie lurking just beneath the surface.

'Honey –' he chuckled '– tell me, is this really such a chore?'

All the while his fingers had never stopped swiping and stroking across her hips and stomach, never going higher or lower. That entire area of her skin was alive and singing with his touch, and warm, as if it was accustomed to this attention. Her body relaxed, folding into itself, but her mind still kept darting through that kitchen door.

'Don't look so anxious,' urged Jonathan. 'Can't have that kind of tension when I'm around.'

No wonder he'd gotten inside Sally's knickers quicker than you could say 'elastic'. He was like one of those horse whisperers. A woman whisperer. He got them where he wanted them. But she wouldn't wait around for the nasty side of him. She just needed him for this moment, to transport her away from the image of Sally wriggling up to Jack, teasing or even mocking him into submission, seducing him so that he had no choice but to ram up inside her.

'What are they doing in there?' asked Janie.

There was definitely something, a groan or a sigh, and they both heard Sally's high giggle – the one that signalled she was in for the kill.

'Not making apple pie, that's for sure,' remarked Jonathan.

Janie frowned, turning her face this way and that, but Jonathan just kept on watching her, and surreptitiously pulled the silk garment up her body so that more and more of her became visible.

'She'll have her tongue down his throat by now,' Jonathan crooned. 'She's not always known for her subtlety.'

Janie's lips parted in dismay, but he prevented her from speaking by brushing his dry lips across her mouth; not exactly kissing her, but leaving his taste on her lips to silence her, and it worked. He had an expensive, sharp smell about him that spiked the air around them both. Janie closed her eyes, and tried to persuade herself that it was just the two of them on the sofa, just the two of them in the cottage.

'He'll be making a feeble attempt to push her away, get back in here, but he'll be getting hard, despite his desire for you. She's very skilled at that.'

Jonathan dropped his hand from Janie's face and brought it to her hip, so that now he had both her hips cradled in his hands. Despite her jealousy Janie's own body couldn't help responding to the constant sweeping of his fingertips. That fidgety warmth that she had felt yesterday, listening to Sally's story, was back in earnest, the little muscles around her fanny tightening involuntarily and a definite moisture slicking from inside her.

'And she'll be unable to wait for long, once she's turned on. She'll be creaming herself by now, I expect, especially knowing that we're next door, that we could barge in at any moment. She'll be rubbing herself up against him. He may be resisting still, but it won't work. She'll see that he's a bit of a gentleman, a bit shy, not like me, and she'll make him touch her, feel her wetness through those French knickers, which, incidentally, I bought for her in Paris.'

'What a naughty thought!' gasped Janie, biting her lip and shifting on the sofa without realising what she was doing. 'Wearing a gift from you while she's making out with him.'

'Honey, you're getting the idea. A quick learner.'

'And this negligee is not mine. It's something she was given –' Janie couldn't resist adding her own little piece of spite '– by another man, last weekend.'

'Really?' It was Jonathan's turn to be put out, but only briefly. He smiled again. 'Better and better, though I can't imagine her wearing it. While you look as if you were born to drift about wearing white gossamer.'

Just then one of the kitchen chairs fell over with a crash. There was an exclamation from one of them, followed by the heavy double thump of bodies falling onto a wooden surface.

'Didn't take them long, did it? She'll have just removed that lovely underwear. Perhaps she'll be fingering herself; men like to see that. She won't be able to wait, though, and nor will he, not once that cute bush of hers is on display. Any man with red blood in his veins would be unable to resist her powers of persuasion, and she's on a mission this morning.'

'Don't tell me any more,' pleaded Janie. 'Let's just show them, like you said.'

He lifted her body across his tweed lap, shifting himself so that she was straddling him with her back to the kitchen. He continued to run his hands up and down her sides, underneath the silk, and she held her breath, waiting for the moment when they would make contact with her tits. She could feel the acorn-hard nipples making points through the thin fabric, riding high and hard on her round, eager breasts, and now everything was level with his face. It was only a matter of time before he touched them. The sharp sensations already slicing through her were too strong to ignore. It was as though she was constantly on the boil, or at the very least simmering, like Sally had said. It was as if, just under the surface, the basic urges that had been awakened in her yesterday were waiting to be jump-started each time someone came near her who even looked at her in a certain way. Not just that, but she realised, after five minutes with this guy, that just by the way she dressed or moved, just allowing a tiny shift in her attitude, her body was bursting with more promise than she had ever dreamed of. She couldn't stop now, no matter who or how many friends or enemies might be rutting away in the kitchen.

She arched herself away from him, revelling in this new, constant sexiness that crawled all over her skin. She was learning to tease herself into the bargain. As his hands were busy under her legs, undoing his trousers, she brought her own hands up and started kneading her breasts through the slippery silk. She loved the feeling of fabric on skin, pushing her big mounds together so that their nipples stood out, then releasing them so that they bounced apart, and fondling them again. Jonathan's eyes were still on her face, and that only excited her more. Her own hands on her breasts, touching them through the silk, was utterly delicious, and she wanted to make him touch her. Her breath came more quickly, and her hands worked faster and rougher on her breasts until she found her buttocks starting to gyrate on his knee. But although she was enjoying it, she forced herself to release them. She grabbed the back of the sofa, resting her forearms on either side of his shoulders, and pulled herself up so that she was raised a couple of inches above his groin. By kneeling up like this her tits were in front of his nose. Her pussy could wait. They were frozen in that position for a moment, challenging each other to move first, then, supporting herself on her knees so that her thighs started to shake with the effort, Janie hooked her fingers under the spindly straps of the negligee and flung her arms free so that the white silk spilled down her torso and settled around her waist.

'He'll have his trousers round his ankles by now and she'll be totally naked and spread out on the table like a ploughman's lunch. He won't be able to help himself, he'll be pushing his fingers into her cunt while she wriggles about and traps him between those dancer's thighs of hers. She'll be glancing at the door, mark my words. She's just as anxious as you.'

'I said, no more.'

At last Jonathan's eyes snapped obediently down to the glorious cleavage in front of him. His hands roved up and grabbed her bare flesh, and he pulled her body towards him so that slowly he could slide his face inside the warm cleavage. Janie held herself very still, once again holding the back of the sofa. She arched her bottom right away from his crotch so that she couldn't even feel what was there, although her pussy felt as if it was being dragged towards a magnet, the tiny muscles around her cunt grasping at the anticipated pleasure like mini tentacles.

Then the foot of one of the kitchen table legs started squeaking. There was a pause, then the table leg started to shift, rhythmically, across its square patch of tiled floor.

'She's pulling him into her, that greedy little pussy of hers, the golden curls parting to drag him in.'

Janie was split in two, one half of her poised over the promise of her own ecstasy in the shape of Sally's ex-lover, the other half desperate at the thought of Jack being goaded and pleasured out there in the kitchen. Sally didn't even know who he was. She didn't know that only a few hours earlier he had been inside Janie, shoving her across the hay bale with the force of his screwing just like he was shoving Sally across the kitchen table.

'She's getting her evil way,' remarked Jonathan softly. 'She'll be on her back on the kitchen table, she's always liked hard surfaces, and she'll have her legs wrapped round him like a limpet.'

Before the picture could lodge itself in Janie's brain, Jonathan licked at the heated flesh of her breasts. She threw her head back, and pushed herself harder against his face. His tongue flicked over one stiff nipple, then across to the other, darting like a snake's. Stabs of desire shot directly from her nipples to the opening of her pussy, tightening the furrow there as her knees weakened.

She pushed the back of his head towards her, forcing his mouth harder onto one aching nipple. His lips and teeth closed slowly round it, the pressure to bite increasing little by little. She fell against him and his teeth got a grip and pulled the nipple into his mouth.

At last, he was sucking, his tongue flicking and circling. Then he was moving to the other nipple, and Janie was sinking her weight slowly down, unable to support herself on her weakening legs. She could have let him go on like that, but other parts of her were burning for release now as well. She was still seething at the thought of Sally and Jack humping on the kitchen table, but was also burning with a kind of reckless greed. The urge to lower herself onto Jonathan was overpowering her.

There was a muffled male groan from the kitchen and the thumping and squeaking of the table legs accelerated.

'She won't find in his trousers what you're about to find,' murmured Jonathan, emerging from between her tits and leaving them singing for more. His smooth blond hair fell over his forehead and messed up his groomed appearance. It made him look far more attractive, and made Janie feel far more powerful. She didn't want to speak, though she didn't mind listening to his insidious commentary. She just smiled, and finally lowered herself down onto him. She rested there, feeling the long, thick shape of his cock running straight across his lap, dividing her pussy-lips. She felt a manic grin spread across her face, and bit her lips so as not to squeal with alarm. It was like sitting on one of her logs.

'Sally told me you were well hung,' gasped Janie, drawing her hips back to find the end of his cock, and sliding back along it to land against his groin. 'But I just thought she was bragging. I've never *seen* –'

'And you never will, honey, believe me. Take it, feel it, feel what she's missing right now.'

Janie reached down between her legs and took hold of his dick. It was worthy of legend. The smooth, taut surface was already damp from where she had been sitting on it, and that sent stronger thrills of excitement through her. She took it in both hands, hitched herself back on his thighs for a moment to lift it and stare at its incredible, swollen length. Though engorged with blood, it looked unusually colourless. As she held it and looked at it, and ran her hands along the shaft, it leaped up at her, the bulbous end already winking with a droplet of pre-come. It was as if someone was already sluicing her through with hot juices.

'No need to be so gentle with it,' goaded Jonathan. 'Take it, princess, it's all yours.'

Janie raised herself up on quivering thighs and placed his rounded tip against her pussy. Instantly it made contact with the burning nub of her clitoris and it was Janie's turn to groan out loud. The very sound of her own uncontrolled voice sounded filthy in her ears, and she realised that Sally and Jack could probably hear it through the ajar kitchen door, but there was nothing she could do to stop it, and no way that she wanted to.

'Listen to this, guys,' she hissed, edging Jonathan's cock inside her and letting her pussy-lips nibble their way down its length. She paused every so often to adjust her knees and to luxuriate in the huge, animal mass that filled her. She lowered herself still further, wondered how much room there was, and felt herself expanding to accommodate him; felt herself impaled on a great rod. It felt almost as if she could lift her legs away and balance herself, cunt on cock, spin round on it even. It was quite out of this world and accentuated by her sitting above him. He lay there, hands loosely on her hips again, her tits bouncing and brushing against his face as he watched her.

'So easy,' he murmured, tightening his grip on her

hips as she finally reached the base of his cock and they both waited for the inexorable movement to begin. 'You've made this so easy for me.'

Just then Sally called out in a stream of gibberish, and the two bodies in the kitchen crashed down once, twice, three times on the surface of the table before she cried out in a long, low howl, which gradually whimpered into silence.

Janie waited, put off her stroke for a moment, but Jonathan's cock seemed to continue swelling inside her and she had no choice but to move, to start easing herself up and down the long shaft. Once she had started she couldn't stop because, as she raised herself off it, every inch of it rubbed against every screaming inch of her, so she could only go so far before slamming back down on him, groin on groin. When she did that she could feel the end of his knob stretching her deep inside, testing her to the limits, teaching her, for heaven's sake, what she was capable of taking.

'No rush, honey. I'd like them to see us. But let's catch up a little, shall we? Let's have the last, long laugh.'

His hips echoed the rhythm of hers. He backed himself against the sofa as she moved off him, then slammed up inside her as she came back down, and she could hear her voice rising in a crescendo, saying nothing but trying to articulate the extraordinary, ter-rifyingly powerful sensation of being impaled on this vast pole. It gave her more and more pleasure, as rivulets of fire seemed to streak up the sides of her cunt, like his cock was some kind of torch. Her inner cavity becoming a mass of vibrating mad ecstasy. She kept her eyes open, and watched the shaft moving in and out, as his eyes focused on her bouncing breasts. He pushed back against the sofa and tensed himself, then looked her straight in the eyes and pumped his spunk into her so that she was thrown upwards with the force of his thrusts. She cried out each time he lifted her, her own screams and his thrusting and her finger rubbing over her clit finally giving way to a wild, shattering climax that had her arching her body and then collapsing onto him, her legs spread out on either side of him, and her bare torso smothering him.

The kitchen door opened with a crash and the other two shuffled in. Jonathan could see them across Janie's shoulder, but she wanted to keep her face hidden while she regained her breath. Jonathan patted her back a couple of times, and then unceremoniously heaved her off him, then packed away his subsiding erection and did up his corduroy trousers with a brisk *zip*. Janie huddled away from him, pulling up the straps of her negligee, but still hiding her face.

'Why so coy, Janie?' Sally asked from behind her. She had the pinafore haphazardly wrapped round her, but the French underwear was missing. 'That was a splendid show! But, then again, how could you fail to look superb, bucking about on that?'

'Why shouldn't I?' Janie flashed back. She was not having Sally hurling insults, particularly not in front of Jack. 'I'm allowed to try out your ex for size if I want to. It's what you would do!'

Sally whistled and fanned her face as if insulted.

'So it *is* Janie. Little red-haired cousin Janie. With the marigold hair.'

Jack was staring at Janie as if Sally and Jonathan weren't there. He had a different sweater on today, even scruffier than yesterday's, and his jeans hung loosely off his hips where he hadn't finished buttoning them up. Now that he had come out from behind the kitchen door and she could see him clearly, she wanted him even more. She started to draw her knees up in front of her, but thought better of it, and curled herself sideways instead, draping one arm along the back of the sofa. Jonathan crossed one leg over the other, for all the world as if they had just been sharing cucumber sandwiches.

'I came to check if I was right,' said Jack. 'That it *was* you, that's all.'

'Yes, Jack, it's me.'

'Ugly Jack? From the wigwam?' Sally butted in, hands on hips like a fishwife. Jonathan chuckled and swung one polished brogue up and down. Jack buttoned up his jeans, still staring at Janie, and her stomach melted at the glimpse of furry stomach under his sweater. He stepped past Sally to go back through the kitchen.

'Hey, don't go, Jack,' Janie cried. 'We need to catch up.'

'Can't you see what kind of gorgeous, horny woman she's grown into?' taunted Sally, staying close beside him and pointing at Janie. 'You had your chance when you were kids. She was nuts about you. But now? Well, now she's anybody's!'

'You were always so shy,' Jack said, ignoring Sally, but not coming back into the room. 'We always wondered how you would turn out, Ben and me.'

'I'm not just anybody's!' Janie protested. Beside her, Jonathan cleared his throat.

'I have to go,' said Jack. 'Things to do, sorry.'

'Stay and have some shepherd's pie,' Sally chimed in, wrapping her arm round Jack's waist. 'You weren't in such a hurry to leave ten minutes ago, when I had your trousers round your ankles and your cock right up the tradesman's entrance!'

'Get out while you can, Jack,' drawled Jonathan.

'These two are randy little polecats. I never dreamed that Sally here would have a friend who was as horny as she is, but the pair of them obviously need sorting out on a regular basis. Let's face it, I'm not sure you're the man to do it.'

'We'll see about that,' replied Jack. His mouth hardened. He unwound Sally's arm from round his middle and looked again at Janie. She started to get up off the sofa, but he was already halfway out the door.

'I'm here all summer, Jack,' she murmured. 'It's not like he says, despite what you saw here today. It was the paint, and the onions. They went to our heads. We're just here to relax, me and Sally. Just minding our own business. There's plenty of time for you to find out what I'm really like.'

To her relief a slight smile dimpled his cheek. Then he raised a hand towards Jonathan, and was gone. They all looked at one another, and then Sally could contain herself no longer.

'How the hell did you find me?' she demanded, marching across to Jonathan. 'I came here to get away from the whole damn lot of you.'

'Your agent, sweetie,' drawled Jonathan, brushing a speck of dust off his sleeve. 'She's very indiscreet.'

'I'll kill that Erica when I get back!'

'I'll leave you to it,' sighed Janie, unfolding her limbs from the sofa. Jonathan's hand came down on her leg and squeezed it.

'No need, my dear. I'm going, too, but I'll be back. This little cottage is like a honey pot. I doubt any of the local males will be able to stay away. I'll sniff Miss Sally out when she's in a better mood, and when she's prepared to listen to what I came here to say.'

'Hell will freeze over first!' shouted Sally, and Jonathan roared with laughter.

'I take it there's no invitation for *me* to partake of the famous shepherd's pie, then?'

'No one will be eating it if I don't rescue it from the oven,' Janie remarked, and she slithered out from under Jonathan's hand and darted into the kitchen. She was knocked backwards by the heat from the Aga, but the pie looked just perfect, and her stomach rumbled as she put it on the table and retrieved the abandoned bottle of wine. Jack hadn't shut the back door properly and she went to close it, flaking off some old red paint from its surface and smiling as she did so. Her anger at Sally making a beeline for him like that had subsided into something more constructive. She was climbing up on to Sally's level – or descending, whichever way you looked at it. Either way, she was only more determined, not less, to get the man she wanted back to the honey pot, as Jonathan had called it. She hadn't planned to, but she could stay all summer if that's how long it took.

'Paint and onions.' Jonathan was roaring with sardonic laughter in the sitting room. 'Now I've heard all the excuses.'

Janie heard Sally swearing and shouting at him, and then there was silence. She wondered if they were making up, and couldn't resist peeking through the door to see if it was Sally's turn to swing on Jonathan's big dick, but her friend was standing on her own by the window, staring out at the rain, and Jonathan had gone.

'He really gets to you, doesn't he?' Janie said quietly, fiddling with the corkscrew.

Sally spun round, still pink with fury.

'Got to *you*, more like. What were you thinking of, squirming all over him like that?'

'Oh, no you don't!' Janie tilted her chin, quite ready

to fight, but Sally's shoulders suddenly drooped and she came slowly across the room.

'He's the only one who ever has,' she admitted, taking the corkscrew out of Janie's hand. 'Got to me, I mean. You've seen what he can be like, but I'll be damned if I'll ever let him see it.'

'Come on, let's forget those blokes and eat this delicious pie. Never knew we could be so domesticated.' Janie changed the subject, pulled Sally back into the kitchen and picked up the chair for her to sit in.

'You're cheerful,' Sally grumbled, as she picked up her fork. 'He certainly pumped you full of life, didn't he? Just wait till I get my hands on him.'

'You weren't slow to jump on Jack, either. Come on, that's what you always do, but for me, all this is like – it's like ice melting, or something. Something's happened to me and I feel like I'm waking up from a coma.'

'Meanwhile, I feel absolutely knackered,' said Sally.

Janie swung her arm round, scattering the mince and potato she was serving onto two plates. 'Look, we're going to eat this pie, and we're going to do a whole lot more cooking this afternoon. We need our strength.'

'Hark at you! I'm the one who should be in trouble, after snatching Ugly Jack from under your nose, and you're suddenly Miss Domestic Goddess.'

Janie sat down and took a forkful of the lunch. She let the meaty goodness roll round her mouth while she thought about what Sally was saying.

'Let's just say I've had my eyes opened,' she said, finally.

'Your legs, more like,' chided Sally.

Janie chuckled – a new, sexy, pleased chuckle. She helped herself to some more pie. She had never felt so hungry.

5

The next morning was also spent cooking and painting, with both Sally and Janie trying not to look as if they were straining for the doorbell. To cheer themselves up in the absence of any visitors, they decided to dress as they had yesterday. That is, in precious little.

Just as they were finishing their lunch there was a rapping on the front door. Both girls dropped their forks in surprise. Janie was on her feet first, smoothing the silk negligee down her sides and flicking her long hair back over her shoulder. She felt a flush of anticipation spread across her cheeks and swirl down to her stomach. It was as if she was always going to be permanently ready now, for whatever male-shaped promise arrived at their door.

'Oh, no you don't,' Sally squeaked. 'Let me, I'm the polecat around here.'

She was the quicker of the two, and dashed in front of Janie through the sitting room, the pinafore still flapping around her legs.

'Sally Seaman? Good morning. You called us, yesterday ... about the feature? We're from *Cute Cottages*. I'm Shona Shaw, but we seem to have come at a very bad time. Perhaps it would be better if we came back another day?'

A tense-looking peroxide-blonde woman in a tight pink suit stood on the doorstep, accompanied by a spindly young man wearing a striped jumper and clutching a camera. They were both staring at the half-naked Sally and the see-through Janie, who were shivering as the wind swept past their visitors to get inside the house.

'Sally?' Janie looked at her friend. Sally looked completely blank, and then clapped her hands to both her cheeks in a coy, Bo-Beep kind of way.

'Oh, hush my mouth, I forgot to tell you. I had the idea yesterday morning, just as the lady says, and I called *Cute Cottages*. Before all the excitement, you know, with our gentlemen callers –'

Janie kept the look of righteous indignation on her face, but inside her the giggles were threatening to bubble over.

'Go on,' she said sternly.

'I should have told you,' Sally stammered. 'I spoke to this, well, to this lady here.'

This lady here wasn't going to help. She was too busy eyeing the bizarre costumes Janie and Sally were sporting. The photographer was trying to hide behind her shoulder pads. Everyone was shivering.

'Still not clear, Sally,' Janie insisted, twisting her mouth to speak into Sally's ear and folding her arms in what she hoped was schoolmistress fashion.

'And I thought they could do a feature on the interior design work you're going to do on the cottage. You know, a "before and after" scenario.' Sally dug her elbow into Janie's side. 'It's just crying out for it, don't you think? And it would be superb copy for your professional profile, too.'

A smile slowly stretched across Janie's face.

'Can't leave that business head of yours alone, can you?' she crooned, chucking Sally under the chin. The tense peroxide and the spindly photographer cleared their throats. Another blast of wind shot straight off the sea and licked between Janie's bare legs. She allowed another beat of suspense, then beamed graciously at their visitors.

'Forgive me for being so suspicious,' she apologised, stepping aside while Sally reached forwards to take their arms. 'It's just that we have so many callers here, all hours of day and night, and I have to make absolutely sure – I never can tell who my friend Sally has propositioned – I mean, *invited* – to descend on us!'

Sally closed the old front door deliberately slowly so that it creaked in a horror-movie manner, and ushered the uneasy pair into the sitting room.

'There's so much to show you. Such a lot of work to be done, and we haven't had a moment to get started. So many interruptions.' Janie flung her hair back and smoothed the negligee down over her hips, then started gesticulating round the room like a ballet teacher. 'Honestly, whoever said the countryside was for pansies? Now, this is the main sitting room, which of course we will be stripping to its bare essentials.'

Like a conjuror's assistant, Sally sprang about the room, following the line of Janie's pointing finger to indicate the imperfections. At the word 'stripping' she tore off a long, jagged swathe of wallpaper from beside the fire, and rubbed her fingers on the marbled patch beneath.

'Damp,' she muttered, wrinkling her nose.

Janie kerbed her anxiety at the sight of all the reddish powder cascading round Sally's head. If that really was as serious a damp problem as it looked, then it would take more than just her, more perhaps than just Maddock and his merry men, to sort it out – but that was just tough. They'd started, so they'd finish. She pushed her guests down onto the sofa, and noticed how it seemed to be sagging even more from the recent action it had endured. Shona Shaw's prim buttocks were perched exactly where Jonathan had sat yesterday; where Janie had been pole-dancing, using his cock as a prop.

'Coffee?' she trilled. She needed five minutes to gather her skittering thoughts or else she would fall prey to the laughter that threatened to engulf her. She snapped her fingers at Sally, who shuffled up to her meekly, tripping over the long cotton pinafore, and bobbed a curtsey. That did it.

'We'll just sort that out for you,' Janie choked, fiddling with the bow of Sally's pinafore. 'The coffee, that is. How rude of me not to think of it sooner. Perhaps you'd see to that, Sally, and then I think that we ought to get dressed. You know, properly. You must excuse our appearance. We were expecting –'

'More gentleman callers,' Sally piped up, twirling away from Janie's bossy hands, and displaying a totally bare bottom as she bustled into the kitchen. The pair on the sofa were still open-mouthed with disbelief.

'Don't go away, will you?' Janie beamed. 'I'll be with you in two minutes.'

She rushed up the stairs and pulled on her faithful dungarees along with a long-sleeved T-shirt. Suddenly she felt faintly ridiculous. There was no point pretending it was warm enough to be prancing about in a negligee. In any case, if Jack came round later, she could always boot Sally and any other hangers-on out of the room, peel off the dungarees slowly, deliberately, in front of the fire, make them somehow just as alluring as the negligee. She had learned a lot in the last couple of days, in particular that it was her body, not her clothes, that the men wanted.

When she came back down the stairs Sally had produced the coffee and was sitting cross-legged by the fire. The pinafore was stretched like a tent across the tops of her legs so that the slightest dip of a curious neck would afford a perfect view of her pussy. Shona Shaw was glancing anywhere in the room but at Sally, while the photographer was slurping at his coffee as if it was the last drink on earth, squinting furiously into its grainy depths.

'Thank you, Sally. I think you should cover up, now. The housemaid's outfit will do, or perhaps, as it's a day of leisure, some sensible gardening gear.' Janie turned to Shona Shaw. 'We're a good pair, actually. I'm the creative designer, she's the dogsbody.'

Sally coughed loudly and flapped the pinafore. Janie went and stood over her, draping her arm across the mantelpiece. Shona slowly crossed one leg over the other with a swish of stocking and flipped her note-book to a blank page. The photographer hadn't yet taken off his lens cap, but was huddled next to her on the sofa, clutching his bony knees.

'Light the fire, would you Sally, before you get dressed?' Janie asked, smiling over Sally's head at the visitors. 'Lovely real fire, even in summer. It makes you want to just lie down on this rug here, wriggle about in front of the flames, you know? Especially when the weather is so shitty. But we never close the curtains. Not like you would in London. No need for that kind of privacy out here in the country. We're open house, you see.'

'For all gentleman callers,' added Sally, bending over the hearth.

Shona cleared her throat. 'Let's get down to business, shall we? Tell me, if you love the cottage so much, why do you want to change it?'

'Well, we've worn it out, you see.' Janie ran her finger thoughtfully along the mantelpiece.

'People come to visit, and we rarely let them get

away within twenty-four hours. It's like a love shack, really, and we want it to stay that way. But the décor is, well, more Goldilocks than Goldfinger, don't you think?' Sally piped up, bending right over to light the fire so that the crack between her butt-cheeks widened and the photographer gulped his hot coffee down too fast.

'Yes, and when our visitors are not fixing things with their hoary hands, everyone out here seems to be hung like donkeys,' Janie added thoughtfully, tapping her chin and cocking her head as if the idea had just occurred to her. She looked hard at the young photographer, as if seeing him for the first time. He had beautiful green eyes, spaced far apart, she noticed, and jutting cheekbones like Rudolf Nureyev. 'Not like our boys from the smoke.'

'Who are all hung like chipmunks,' chimed in Sally.

'They'll never seem so manly. Not after the men we've come across, as it were,' Janie was still examining the boy. 'What's your name?'

'Derek,' he croaked, and licked his lips.

'Time to get out your Hasselblad, don't you think, Derek?'

Sally sat back on her haunches and reached lazily under the pinny, flipping it aside to scratch at herself and giving a little titter of pleasure as she did so. Janie kept her face straight and perched on the arm of the sofa next to Shona. The lady editor nibbled her biro and uncrossed her legs again, keeping her eyes nervously on Janie.

'Perhaps a guided tour?' she suggested, tottering to her feet. She turned her back to Sally, holding the notebook in front of her like a shield.

'Absolutely, Miss Shaw. And I think we should start

with the bedrooms, don't you? Always the cosiest part of a cottage like this, and actually the least run-down. Not that we've spent much time asleep, have we, Sal?'

'No, Janie,' agreed Sally, rearranging her pinafore demurely.

'Clothes, Sally, please. We don't want our guests thinking we're on heat. Coming, Derek?' enquired Janie.

Derek was still drooling across at the fireplace, and didn't hear her. Sally rose smoothly from her cross-legged position and gave the pinafore one last sideways tweak. Young Derek sat up straight as if he'd been shot.

'One or two of the bedrooms have already been decorated by my cousin, the owner,' explained Janie, as she took Shona's Chanel-pink elbow and steered her briskly out into the hall, 'but there are other parts of the cottage and garden that need attention.'

She noticed that Derek's hair was very neatly combed into a side parting, and she ruffled it with her fingernails as she passed him. He swiped one hand absently across his locks, then stood to attention, and allowed Sally to lead the way.

'Come and see the attic room,' she said to him as she skipped up the staircase. 'There are spectacular views, you know. You can take pictures, while I get changed.'

'Hasselblad, Derek,' barked Shona. 'In here. *Now*.'

After showing them round, Janie and Sally left the journalists alone to tramp over the cottage and take their shots. Sally, dressed in Ben's old jumper again and the infamous denim miniskirt, stoked up the fire.

'There's no excuse not to do the work now, is there?' she remarked.

'Just as well you're here to help, then, isn't it?' replied Janie, suddenly sombre. She glanced out at the dripping leaves around the window. 'Anyway, it was always my intention to make good use of our time here.'

'And so you have, doll, though not perhaps as you planned.' Sally paused, then went on casually, 'You could always get that Maddock along to do the job. He might be along later on, anyway, you know. Checking things out, sniffing about.'

'You hope. Why did you make that call, Sally?' Janie demanded, nailing down what was bugging her. 'I mean, it's turned out to be a great idea, but why behind my back like that?'

'Honest answer?'

Janie nodded.

'I thought it would liven things up a little. Keep my toes in the water, keep my pecker up, so to speak, while I'm stuck – while I'm staying here. And get you some publicity into the bargain.'

'I see,' Janie mumbled doubtfully. 'So you're bored already?'

Sally wasn't an ex-performer for nothing. She snuggled up to her friend on the sofa, and tickled her under the armpit till Janie laughed hysterically.

'Janie,' Sally said. 'Do I *look* bored?'

'Excuse us.'

Shona and her assistant were in the doorway.

'It's a wrap then, is it, Derek?' giggled Sally, leaping away from Janie, who resumed her stern expression.

'We'll have to run this past the editor.' Shona's face was very flushed. She glanced at Derek, and her face softened a little. 'It'll make a marvellous feature, after all. I wasn't too sure, at first, but it's perfect for our magazine. Come along, Derek.'

Derek trooped obediently after her, throwing a sorrowful look over his woolly shoulder.

'Best little whorehouse in Devon,' he muttered behind his hand.

'And you be sure to visit again soon, now, honey,' crooned Sally, in a perfect Dolly Parton response.

'More to that boy than meets the eye,' remarked Janie, as the front door rattled shut.

'He's a "before and after" feature waiting to happen,' chuckled Sally, as she watched the car jerk unevenly through the potholes a few minutes later. 'Pure as the driven snow when he left London this morning, and now look at him! Corrupted the moment he sets foot inside the witches' cottage!'

From Sally's vantage point, she could see the journalists clearly through the rear windscreen. Shona's head was up very close to Derek's in the front of the car, and he, aware that the girls were watching, was attempting to accelerate manfully away from the cottage.

'Look! She was as turned on by us as he was. I bet she'll have him in a lay-by before they reach the M5.'

6

The silence was almost high-pitched. It sang in Janie's ears, accompanied by the thump of blood that supplied oxygen to her body. The only other sound was the occasional squawk of a sea bird. She reached her chosen spot and stood still for a moment while she got her breath from the climb through the uneven sand dunes. Her eyes watered as she looked out to sea. Apart from some sailing boats leaning into the wind on the horizon, the beach was deserted.

The temperature had soared, in more ways than one. After three more days of enforced seclusion in the storm-battered cottage, the rain had finally retreated overnight and a rectangle of bright-blue sky had woken Janie early that morning. It was a belated answer to her prayers.

There had been no more visitors in the rain. Janie and Sally had spent another couple of days holed up together, stripping paint and washing curtains but, despite the diversion of the photoshoot, Sally's cold had got worse, she'd retreated to her corner of the sofa, and tempers had begun to fray.

'Come on, the holiday has begun!' Janie had chirruped that morning, tearing up the spiral staircase to Sally's attic. She'd flung the door open into the dark-red room. Sally was awake, and muttering into her mobile phone.

'Only place I can get a signal,' she'd grumbled,

putting her hand over it. 'That's how I got hold of those magazine people.'

'Get off the phone! No more work! We're going to the beach. Holiday time!'

'Too grotty. I think I've got sinusitis. I'm just speaking to Erica –'

'Whose Erica?'

'My agent; my head-hunter.'

'What for?'

'I might go back to London. I'm sick of doing your decorating, and all the talent seems to have melted away as rapidly as it appeared.'

'Well, we can go and find some! Look, the sun's out.'

'Yes, I'm still here, Erica.'

Sally had rolled over under the rumpled quilt, clamping the mobile to her ear, and a hard lump of anger expanded in Janie's chest. Sally was like a spoilt child. The minute things didn't go her way, or there wasn't enough entertainment of the male variety, she flew into a sulk.

'And there was I, thinking we were having a lovely girlie time of it these last few days. Stuff you! Go back to London then.'

Janie bent her head now and spread her towel out on the sand. She regretted saying that. She didn't want Sally to go, especially in a poisonous mood, and especially when there were no clouds tainting the bright blue sky. But Janie had driven a couple of miles to get to the beach. She wasn't about to go back to grovel.

A movement caught her eye just as she was stripping her clothes off. Two people at the far end of the beach were running towards the water in wet suits, dragging their surfboards. She couldn't tell with the sun in her eyes whether they were male or female.

From where she stood they were simply silhouettes; very agile silhouettes. Within minutes their surfboards were on the water and skimming off in front of the wind. Janie watched the silver splash of the waves and couldn't resist the invitation. She tore everything else off and half slid on her backside, half scrambled down the dune and across the beach, her heavy breasts bouncing against her ribcage and her loose hair slapping against her shoulders. She screamed out loud as her toes hit the freezing shallows, but she waded in confidently, bending to scoop and splash the water over her limbs, feeling the skin cower into goose bumps. Then, with a gasping breath, she plunged forwards into the waves, following the distant surfers. Her mind emptied: there was just her, the sea and the sky.

Janie swam until her limbs were numb from the Atlantic cold, and then she turned back to shore, her legs wobbling like a new-born colt's as she staggered through the waves. Water ran down her legs from her dripping bush to tickle her thighs. She jogged on the spot for a moment, sure that no one else was around, her nakedness no longer hidden by the ocean, and then she ran towards the shelter of the dunes.

'Must ... get ... fit,' she panted as she flopped down onto her towel and let the sun start to warm her. It gradually seeped through her skin and into her aching muscles. Eventually her heart stopped drumming and her chest stopped heaving for breath, but her body still buzzed with exhilaration. She turned onto her back and stretched her legs out luxuriously, pointing her toes across the big towel. A breath of air tickled the hidden layers inside her slightly parted sex-lips, and she opened her legs a little wider. Her fingers groped about in the sand to find her bag but she couldn't reach it, and instead her hand flopped down onto her stomach. She nearly screeched with electrified pleasure. She snatched her hand away, and brought just the very tips of her fingers down on a different place: the hairless groove that ran along the top of her leg towards her pubic mound. Again her skin shivered beneath her touch. She remembered that the skin was the largest organ of the human body, and today that organ was the most sensitive, too. It was as if a taper had been applied to it, kept it smouldering, and every time it was touched, even by her own fingers, it would burst into flame. She knew one place that would be more sensitive than all the others. She allowed her hand to stray over her breasts, just a gentle brush across the top, firmly avoiding the nipples, and she felt them swell hopefully under her touch. There was a fluttering in her stomach, and she dropped her hands, smiling broadly to herself, letting the sun rest on her closed eyelids. There was so much promise in her body, she thought. Promise she'd never before believed in; promise that had occasionally blossomed at the hands of one or two past boyfriends. But that had only ever been for a few months at a time, and then she had allowed it to wither away again. Now she knew that, as Sally had predicted, her lust might well remain permanently on the boil. But how was she going to keep this new hunger satisfied?

She allowed one hand to return to her flat stomach, and moved her palm over it in small circles, sending messages all over her body that caused her nipples to pucker up and the inner fluttering to quicken. Her thighs fidgeted across the towel, parting still further and, while she moved one hand to her breast, the other hand sidled downwards until it met her warm nest of dark hair. She entwined her fingers in the wet curls, pulling one or two strands upwards out of the tangle, straightening the hair, feeling the roots tug on the excruciatingly tender skin underneath. Her middle finger extended down to her crack and she gave a half gasp, half giggle, as she felt the blood-heat warmth spread inside the moistening lips. That wasn't just the damp from the sea, she thought, although she wondered, as she lay there caressing herself, what she would taste like now. She wiggled her finger, felt the soft sliver of sensitive flesh, and shocked it into tingling response. Janie moaned softly, sure that the sound was only in her ears.

A shadow crossed her closed eyelids, and she shifted, thinking it was a cloud obscuring the sun, but it seemed too solid for that. She opened her eyes and saw a tall shape standing a couple of feet away. Sally? she wondered stupidly, raising herself onto one elbow. Her tit swung against her arm and, as she raised one knee to get herself upright, a droplet of juice ran out of her crack and across her thigh.

It wasn't Sally. It was one of the surfers. He had his short wetsuit rolled down his torso, and his back to the sea. He could see Janie clearly, but she was half blinded by the glare. She raised one hand to shield her eyes and examined him more closely. He was lithe and tanned, and his face was young, so young. Tiny gold prickles of barely-shaved stubble speckled his brown cheeks. Hectic flushes of blood were just visible under the skin. She tried to remember her own youth. It wasn't that long ago, for heaven's sake. He was seventeen, maybe. Definitely a boy rather than a man, and yet his body was worked on, hard, no ounce of puppy fat, and his arms were big with muscle.

Janie let her eyes flutter slowly back to his face. She

opened her mouth to speak, but he wasn't about to make polite small talk. His bright-blue eyes were fixed on her tits, as they hung there boldly in the sunshine. Of course, raising her arm to shield her eyes had only lifted them higher. The realisation of her pose, like some sort of nude sculpture there on the towel, triggered her nipples into an intense reaction and, despite the heat of the sun, they shrank into tight arrowheads, which pointed directly at him.

The young man swallowed, registering their message, and shifted his bare feet in the sand. She thought he might be trying to get away. But he stayed where he was. Through his tight wetsuit she could see his groin bulging against the black neoprene. She itched to know if he wore anything underneath.

'Surf up today?' Janie heard herself asking into the tingling silence. She could imagine Sally cackling at such a clumsy attempt at surf-speak. 'I thought there were two of you out there.'

The boy nodded and tossed his head back towards the waves. His hair was beginning to dry into bleached strands.

'My brother's still out there. I got a cramp.'

'I can see that.'

The flutter she had felt earlier in her stomach was back with a vengeance, and felt more like hysterical determination. The old Janie would have lifted the towel by now to cover her nakedness. She might have made some shy, dismissive remark to send him on his way, but his frank stare at her naked body and his unmistakable hard-on were too tempting for her to let this scenario pass.

'Want some lemonade?'

'My dad says you should never accept drinks from

strangers,' he croaked with a lopsided grin, and Janie laughed. She took the bottle from the cool bag and waved it at him.

'You're big enough to look after yourself, I should say,' she remarked, patting the towel beside her. He stepped closer, leaned across her, and took the bottle for a swig. 'So, what brings you here? Do you know this part of Devon?'

'No. It's my first time.'

More colour flooded his cheeks as he said it, and Janie knew to keep back her dirty chuckle. Instead she quietly took the lemonade from him, keeping her green eyes calmly on his burning blue ones, and without wiping the neck of the bottle she flicked her tongue round the wet rim before tilting her head back to take a deep swallow. His eyes were fixed on her long throat as the cold liquid swished down.

'I mean, it's the first time we've been down to this coast,' he stammered. 'Dad's rented a place for the summer. He insisted we come here this year. Normally we go to Constantine Bay, in Cornwall. The surf's miles better over there. So's the surfing crowd. I mean, it's just dead round here, isn't it?'

'That depends what you're after,' Janie replied lazily. The bottle was still poised above her open mouth as if she was about to give it head. She licked it again, then wrapped her lips round it, swallowing a little more lemonade, then she screwed the lid back on. On an impulse she put the bottle down, not back in the cool bag, which would have been the sensible option, but between her legs, resting it up against her pussy, and stifled a gasp as cold plastic met sensitive, warm flesh. She leaned back on her elbows, forcing herself not to grab the bottle and start rubbing it up and down her thirsty slit. The urge to do that wouldn't go away, but then, nor would the boy. 'There's plenty to entertain you if you know where to look,' she said.

'I'm beginning to realise that.'

Without the lemonade bottle the boy didn't know what to do with his hands, and he started rolling the wetsuit back to cover his stomach.

'It's too nice out here today to cover yourself up. It may not be the Med, but this lovely weather has got to be a record for Devon. Sit down for a moment. Like you said, there's nothing to do round here, so there's no rush, is there?'

'No rush,' he echoed, and his young voice dipped violently into a deep manly timbre, at odds with his adolescent face. Janie's pussy gave a couple of uncontrollably cheeky twitches that practically nudged the bottle away. She watched the young surfer wrestle with the twin urges to come and sit near her or to stand there and remain cool. Time to be a little less obvious, thought Janie. She relented and drew her legs up so that her bush was temporarily hidden from his confused, hungry gaze, but of course that only brought the bottle harder against her, its long shape pushing between her pussy lips and nudging against the tiny bud of her clit. As she gripped it between her thighs, she could feel the droplets of condensation mingle with her own moisture. Her breath was beginning to rush again, as if she was still swimming. She wanted to show the boy what she could do with the bottle, but it was too soon for that, and might be too shocking. She hitched herself up the towel, pulling her shoulders back in an effort to look more sophisticated, but all that did was thrust her breasts out so that his baby-blue eyes, which had struggled to keep politely to her face, swivelled back down to watch the instant tightening of her red nipples.

'It may be a bit quiet in this neck of the woods,' said Janie, 'but where else can you get quite so close to nature, after the city smoke? I expect that's what your dad was after.' She virtually whispered, trying not to giggle out loud with delight. Something in her warned her to act very calm and very still so as not to alarm him. 'That's why I'm stretched out here, starkers. Never do that in London, do you? Hope you don't mind me being topless like this?'

He shook his head violently, like a little boy trying not to tell a lie and, at last, like an animal tempted in from the wild, he squatted down just by her feet. He rubbed the salty strands of yellow hair off his hot face, and kept rubbing.

'So. You here on holiday, or what?' he asked.

He couldn't take his eyes off her tits, even though he was attempting to make conversation. She didn't dare look down at herself in case she distracted him, but she could feel her nipples hardening and darkening more and more every time his curious eyes returned. His pale-pink tongue slid across his white teeth and he gulped. Janie kept her smile faint but encouraging.

'It's a mixture,' she answered. 'Work and play.'

'So which is this bit? Work or play?'

A soft wind came off the sea and ruffled his hair. He swiped it impatiently out of his eyes. Janie felt her own hair tickle her face, and the wind caressed her bare skin like delicate fingers.

'Oh, that's easy. Play,' she whispered, not knowing if the wind had snatched the word away. 'This bit is definitely play.'

She tilted forwards onto her knees. Now she was right by him. She paused for a moment as he blinked hard, focusing in closer on Janie's tits. Then she picked up one of his hands from where it was digging frantically about in the sand, lifted it like a warm animal and placed it on one swollen breast. Her nipple spiked up even more, and poked against his palm. His mouth dropped open, and Janie's head fell limply back on her neck as his fingers closed round the mound of smooth flesh. She spread her knees a little to balance herself more comfortably in front of him, then leaned her hands behind her on the towel so that her spine was arched and her breasts were pushing at him, jumping up with each heartbeat.

The dry grass rustled in the slight breeze, and far away the waves curled with a collective sigh onto the beach. Both the surfer and Janie were breathing fast, their breath mingling with the wind. At last he brought his other hand up, and both her breasts were enfolded in his hesitant fingers. He glanced up at her, his blue eyes blazing with a crazy request for permission, and her insides melted. Again her head felt limp and heavy on her neck. Already she wanted to subside beneath him, open her arms and her legs to him, let him grab and take and thrust and pummel. She wanted to make him into a man. But she also had a glorious, blue-eyed opportunity here. Privacy, sunshine, open air, and a young man with the body of a god waiting for her to show him the way. And she had all the time in the world.

The fluttering in her stomach tightened into a clump of fierce desire. She watched his fingers digging into her breasts, moulding them, making them rise, letting them fall. Then she knelt up and placed her hands on his shoulders and pushed her tits into his eager face. There was an electrifying pause. She felt his breath whistle against her flesh. What had Sally said? 'Some lucky bloke is going to nuzzle in between those breasts and love them.' Yes, she wanted her cleavage to be his

first real woman's cleavage. Forget any teenage groping he might have enjoyed. She wanted this to be
something he would remember forever; she wanted
this to be his first time, with her playing the older
woman. She wanted to smother him, keep him there.
He nuzzled his face in between her breasts, pressing
them into his cheeks with his hands, and then he drew
back. Janie cupped one breast and offered it. She
rubbed its taut dark nipple across his mouth as if
urging an orphaned lamb to suckle. The tip of his
tongue flicked out tentatively. Her knees wobbled, and
she clutched more firmly to his shoulders, to keep her
balance and to keep him in place right there, her tit
angled right into his mouth.

His tongue flicked across the nipple again, and his
hands, that a few minutes ago had been wrestling with
a surfboard, squeezed Janie's breasts together until
they sang with delicious pain. Then his soft lips nibbled
her nipple, his tongue lapping round it, and he drew
the burning bud into his mouth, pulled hard on it, and
began to suck. Janie looked down at his bleached-blond
head, the salt water dried in granules and flecked white
across his cheekbones. She wanted to stay like this
forever. She looked away over his head, across the
dunes and over the ocean, experimenting with the idea
of distancing herself from what was happening, but
his mouth, his teeth, kept tugging at her aching nipple
and pulling her attention back. Charges of sheer electricity started to streak directly from that spot down
through her body to her empty, waiting cunt.

He had got the hang of it now. He had the other
breast up by his face, and turned his head this way
and that, lapping and sucking, snuffling through his
nose to breathe, groaning, biting and kneading harder
as if he owned her breasts now. It wasn't enough for

one breast to be suckled, they both had to be stimulated, and then she began to experience the promise of real, selfish satisfaction. In an echo of the increasing ferocity of his mouth and hands, Janie pushed herself more roughly against him, seeking, searching for more pain at her nipples to communicate more pleasure through the rest of her. She parted her legs and lifted her knees to plant them on either side of his still-kneeling thighs so that she was straddling him, and still had his head crushed between her tits. Slowly she pushed at him so that, still sucking on her nipples, he lowered his back onto the sand. He kicked his legs out straight underneath her, and then she was on top of him, her tits dangling over him, their size and weight accentuated by their new position, the round globes pale in his tanned fingers. She tilted her pussy desperately towards his groin and rubbed it briefly against his wetsuit. Even through the tough material she could feel the length of his dick. Keeping her tits over his face, she grabbed at the wetsuit and started to roll it off him like a second skin. He raised his hips obligingly, unquestioningly, eagerly. Janie wondered if he knew how big his hard-on was. She yanked the wetsuit down and his erect penis thumped free, juddering out from the rough tangle of blond curls, golden-brown like the rest of him. Its surface was smooth like velvet, and the mauve plum emerged eagerly from beneath his soft foreskin. She held her hand out, and the gorgeous dick sprang into it. Now it was her turn to fold her fingers round something, and as she did so its owner bit her nipple hard and she yelped with delight, leaning over him to settle herself above her new toy.

'Just take a little break. Try something new,' she whispered, both to herself and to him. She started to wriggle back down his body so that his head followed for a moment, still nibbling at her nipples, but then he fell back as she slithered down towards his groin and he could only grab at her wet hair. Her face reached his cock, which stood up like a beacon. The tip was already beading in anticipation, and she thought how much sweeter it would be to go down on this fresh young stick of rock than Maddock's rough, rustic old pole. Nevertheless, she was glad Maddock had shown her how to do it, because now she could exercise it as her own skill. So, with no further ado she opened her mouth and drew it all in until the boy's round knob knocked at the back of her throat.

He made a sound, exquisitely shocked. She held his buttocks and felt them clench as she sucked on him, nibbling down to the base of his shaft and licking and sucking the sweet length of it. He started bucking gently, crying out in amazement. Janie wondered if his pert little girlfriends gave head like this, and doubted it. After all, she hadn't a clue at that age! She hoped he would think he'd died and gone to heaven. Any minute now she would be going to heaven, too. She was just preparing the way. As she sucked, she rubbed her tits and her pussy up and down his stretched out legs. She felt him pull at her hair, and she had to slow herself down. She didn't want to waste this golden moment by coming all over his leg. Her pussy was contracting frantically now, and she knew she was leaving a slick of juice on his legs.

Janie gave his cock one last, long suck, pulling it towards her throat and nipping it with her teeth, then she let it slide out along her tongue and into her waiting hand. Quickly she clambered back on top of him as he started to rise up on his elbows, seeking her tits again. She pressed him gently down on his back, and tilted herself over him. They had moved some way from the towel now.

'See how beautiful it is,' she crooned at him, showing him the length of his shaft encircled by her fingers. 'See how well it's going to fit.'

She smiled as he watched her raise herself up on her knees and aim the tip of his cock towards the warm hole hidden in her own soft bush. Slowly she let it rest there, at the entrance, nudging past the wet sex-lips and into the coppice of curls. She waited, and his eyes snapped towards hers. Janie smiled again, and lowered herself a little more, gasping as each inch was filled, then she reached under him and cupped his balls in one hand and he bit his lip with another loud groan of surprise. The tension was ecstasy, but she couldn't hold onto it for much longer, and slowly, luxuriously, Janie let the boy's penis slide up inside her, all the way to the hilt. It was tempting to ram it, let their hips start jerking, but once it was right in she forced herself to pull out again. He frowned, perhaps thinking she was rejecting him, but she eased herself down again, moaning and tossing her head back, so that the next time she did it he was with her, pulling his own hips back, waiting when she waited.

His eyes were on hers again, but as she sighed out with the delight of being filled, and bent over to let her tits swing across his mouth, his eyes flipped sideways and his face froze. His hands came up to her hips and held her still. She didn't move. She didn't want to, and she couldn't, but then she saw a shadow fall across his face.

'Hey, guys, don't let me interrupt. This looks like fun.'

Another voice, very similar to his, spoke from somewhere above and behind them. Janie kept her eyes on the boy's face, reckoning that she would know what was going on from his expression. Then she heard the unzipping sound of another wet suit, and the boy's eyes widened. First he shook his head furiously, and then a filthy grin spread across his face. Not a grin she had taught him, thought Janie. He looked back at her with a new, domineering expression. My God, she thought, thrown off-balance. Already he's learning. After another glance at the newcomer her boy reached up firmly to take hold of her breasts.

'My older brother,' he croaked. 'Back from the surf.'

He pulled her forwards so that her tits dangled into his mouth again, and her butt was raised in the air. Janie tried to protest but she couldn't move, so gorgeous was the feel of his now confident and almost aggressive mouth sucking on her sore nipples, firing them up once again. As first one nipple then the other settled into his mouth, so she automatically started up her rhythm again, sliding up and down his cock to try and ease her increasingly frantic urge to come. She could feel her inner muscles tightening each time to grab hold and keep him inside her, and his cock hardening even more with each thrust. She was just poised to ram herself down onto him harder than ever when she felt her buttocks being pulled apart and the warmth of another male body pressing up against her back.

'Can't let you have all the fun, bruv,' said the voice. 'Got some catching up to do, mate. If she doesn't mind, of course.'

The first boy pulled Janie down harder on top of him so that her tits were squashed against his face and his dick was rammed right up inside her.

'You don't mind, do you?' his brother murmured in

her ear. 'Just say. You don't mind, do you? Want to hear you say it.'

'No,' she puffed, barely able to speak. 'Don't mind . . . want it . . . want you to do it.'

Amazing how quickly he had learned when it was time to take control, she thought vaguely, watching the younger boy's mouth smile round her nipple as he heard her speak. There was something else going on now, though. She reckoned she could recognise sibling rivalry when she saw, or rather, sensed it. It was not that different from the 'friendly' rivalry between Janie and Sally. But too many different sensations were swirling around her head to allow much rational thought, and she let herself fall, or rather be pulled, first forwards, her tits licked and sucked to burning point by her accomplished pupil, and then tugged backwards by his invisible brother, who now had his own erection wedged up between her arse-cheeks. He was sliding his hand up and down the warm crack, sliding right under her to reach the tender spot where the first boy's dick had spliced her. He parted her thighs still further so that as well as having a big dick inside her, another dick was tickling her exposed clit. Janie's head started to swim. She gyrated as if dancing on the boy's pole, flinging herself wildly about as the urge for satisfaction and the loss of her previous control started to overtake her.

Both the brothers took hold of her then and made her stop, and she found the pause to be as arousing as the wild movement, because all her tiny internal muscles kept on working. The boy beneath her took her arms and kept her suspended above him, so that he could continue suckling her nipples. He stopped the thrusting inside her for a moment and she let the hovering orgasm recede a little while they relished the wait. Then she felt the invisible brother bring his stiff cock once again to her butt and, instead of sweeping it down through the crack, he started to push it towards the puckered hole of her anus. She held herself rigid. She could feel he had lubricated it, most likely with the suntan oil that she had lying on the towel, so his cock was all slippery yet rock-hard. At first, her hole tightened like a fist against the intrusion, but at the same time a throb ignited like a pilot light somewhere inside her, just the other side, she supposed, of that thin wall separating the two orifices. She opened her eyes and found that, although she was lying over the boy, her neck was arched as if to see over the dunes. Just one glance at his blond head engrossed between her tits increased the deep throbbing inside her. It felt as though the other little hole loosened to let the invisible brother in, because she could feel his thick knob pushing inside a fraction. Her own shy muscles tried to push it out at first, and then slackened to accommodate him. Then it was grabbing, gobbling, welcoming the new length of male hardness. Inch by inch it eased into her anus and she felt light-headed with the knowledge that she had two thick cocks wedged inside her, and she was welcoming them both. Every muscle both inside and out strained and yearned to keep them there and to milk them of all the hot pleasure they had to offer.

The invisible brother was deep inside her now, and she felt his thighs propping up her own. Then he started to rock back and forth, his breath hot on her neck. One big hand fanned out over her stomach to support them both in that position, and she let the rocking move her body, carefully at first – she was still unsure of how the complicated design of her body could manage two cocks at once. Would it hurt or damage her? she wondered. She'd read articles about taking 'double penetration', and knew that it was perfectly fine. And anyway, how could anything that felt as good as this be wrong! She relaxed, and then it was like she had two entirely new bodies, front and back, both with conflicting zones of exquisite pleasure heightened by the novelty of this undiscovered ability, and by not being able to see the invisible brother but guessing that he was as gorgeous as the other one. She fell, first forwards onto the rigid cock inside her cunt, then back onto the one inside her anus, and it was as if they were both spurting jets of fire up her. As she moved off one the other penetrated her, and she felt the storm of orgasm gathering at both entrances; she was sluiced-up and ready, and, as she heard the gathering shouts of the boys combined with her own moans being snatched away into the sea air, it was suddenly happening. They were all three rocking frantically, both boys ramming their cocks up her in unison so that she was spiralling down onto them at the same time. She welcomed the burning heat, her first boy smacking and pummelling her tits back and forth over his face until he couldn't hold his spunk back any longer and the tide came spurting out of him. This was met by her own gripping, convulsive orgasm and then the hot jizz of the invisible brother literally bringing up the rear, as his come rocketed up her. He laughed and yelled out loud and, at last, she toppled sideways, still gripping both boys inside her, and they lay in a muddled heap on the sand while the tide came on up the beach and the seagulls wondered what the tourists were coming to these days.

7

'Yeah, yeah, lovely cottage and everything. I mean, I'm lying here on a patchwork quilt, looking up at exposed rafters, nothing but blue sky out the window – and what do you know?'

The voice at the other end of the mobile squeaked and Sally shook her head impatiently.

'No, nothing else exposing itself around here. It looked promising at first. One or two extremely gorgeous locals, but then it was ruined when an unwelcome visitor pitched up. And Janie's had my nose to the grindstone – mind you, we've had work to do for that magazine feature I told you about – and I've not been able to shake this bloody cold off, and now it's sunny, and I'm bored, and all I want is to –'

The voice squeaked again, and Sally sat up in her bed, the better to gesticulate. She thought she heard a door banging downstairs, and she jumped up and secured the latch on her own door. She didn't want to face Janie just yet.

'I've had enough R and R to last me a lifetime, Erica. I was just going to say, all I want is to come back to London. Get my life going again . . . yes, put your feelers out. I'll let you know when I'm on my way.'

Sally chucked the mobile on the quilt and glared at it. It was her lifeline to civilization. She walked over to the telescope and fiddled again with the knobs, trying to switch it on, or whatever you did with telescopes, but there was nothing but a black circle to be seen. She looked along its long white shaft, pointing towards the horizon – she didn't even know if it was north or south from here – and wondered where Janie had got to.

She should have gone with her to the beach or wherever she'd gone. Janie was only trying to help. But this didn't suit Sally. None of it: not the paint-stripping, the sanding, the scrubbing, the painting, the hammering, nor the nailing. The house was taking shape already, admittedly, and Janie had tried to cheer her up with the promise of a trip to Exeter or Bristol to order some new furniture, but Sally wouldn't co-operate. Janie was the expert now, and Sally wasn't used to following instructions. Worse, Sally wasn't used to seeing Janie blossoming like this, dancing, for heaven's sake, to CDs, jumping every time the front door rattled, and trying to talk about what happened that morning Jonathan and the dishy Jack rolled up. Sally didn't want to think of Janie in her silk negligee, straddling Jonathan (*her* Jonathan), her glossy red hair flowing down her back as she slid slowly up and down his cock while his familiar hands gripped her hips to help her take the strain. She didn't want to think about Jonathan's face being hidden by Janie's energetic body, and neither of them knowing that in the kitchen Sally and Jack had been pretty swift on the table, both anxious to get instant gratification and then see what was happening on the sofa next door. Even though Sally had started the whole shebang, she had discovered, once she had Jack on top of her with his glasses steaming up and his fine cock up her, that she was only cutting off her own nose to spite Jonathan's face – and she was in the wrong place with the wrong guy. But she had misjudged her friend, for, rather than fighting a battle, Janie had simply joined in the game in her own quiet way, and Jack and Sally had come back into the room and had stood there watching. It was the first time watching someone else having sex had been more horribly riveting than tasting her own enjoyment, and Sally had been seized by a mixture of envy and pure, unadulterated rage.

She spun the telescope violently round so that it rocked on its tripod, and went to the little en-suite to turn on the shower. It was boiling up there under the rafters, and she had to admit that the garden looked enticing, all dark shadows and bright green grass, still wet from the rain, the drops glittering in the new, strong sun.

The water pressure was dismal up there. She let the water run for a moment in the shower and went back to the telescope, hoping she hadn't damaged it. Cousin Ben would be furious if she'd been messing with his equipment, although the chance would be a fine thing.

'You like your instruments the longer the better, eh, Sal?' said a familiar voice. 'If you're too stubborn to let in the real thing, why not see if that telescope fits?'

Jonathan. What a cheek he had! Sally was too tense, too teeming with all the images and thoughts crowding the peace of the room, to turn round and face him. She gripped the telescope and stayed where she was, following its blind gaze out of the window.

'How did you get in?' shrieked Sally in annoyance.

'Maddock let me in. I –'

'She's not here,' she spat.

'Jane's not here? Damn, I was looking forward to another *tête-à-tête* with her. Such big, beautiful breasts, such eagerness, such starvation, and yet such elegance.'

Jonathan laughed, and tucked in the rumpled patchwork quilt before sitting down on the end of Sally's bed. 'Such a shame you hid that light under a bushel all these months.'

Sally wheeled round, remembering too late that she was stark-naked and glistening with sweat.

'I told you, she wouldn't be seen dead propping up bars and being drooled over by people like you.'

'I wouldn't be so sure. She got quite the taste for *people like me* the other day, don't you think?'

'Screw who you like. I don't care any more.'

Sally wondered for a split second whether to grab a T-shirt or something, and then she found she didn't care about that either. She held onto the telescope as if for support and wiped a hand across her dripping nose.

'Hey, hey, what's happened to you? The spirits in this cottage sapped you of your strength?'

Sally didn't answer, but inside she wondered if he had a point. She looked at Jonathan as if for the first time, and her gut twisted with desire, made all the fiercer by her renewed, vicious loathing. He wore a plain blue polo-shirt and chinos just the right side of casual and, as he crossed one leg over the other to swing his foot idly in his usual manner, she saw that he wore genuinely weather-beaten deck shoes.

'I'm having a shower,' she said at last, and felt her whole body flush, her gut twisting again like the ropes on the boat Jonathan would be sure to have to go with the shoes. 'So you should leave.'

'I've come to talk to you,' he answered, still swinging his foot and smoothing one hand across the old quilt as if to soothe it. 'I meant to speak the other day, but everything was all too amusing, and neither of you she-cats gave me a chance.'

'There's nothing to say. You see what you've done to me. Wrenched the job I loved away from me, as well as most of my friends –'

'Hardly friends, darling –'

'– reduced me to a life of seclusion, flopping about

163

in the middle of nowhere, doing odd-jobs about this dump because I can't get work anywhere else and, to top it all, wrestling with a stinking cold that I haven't been able to shake off since I got here. Godforsaken shit hole.'

Jonathan waited for a moment and, to her surprise, didn't laugh in her face.

'I've come to fix all that,' he said.

Sally snorted and took a couple of steps over to the tissue box beside her bed, aware of her tits tipping jauntily from side to side as she moved. This was not at all the impression she was trying to give, but she was sure her flesh was firm enough to stand up to his unwavering inspection. To hide her rising confusion and lust she jabbed the tissue box at him.

'Come to fix my flu, have you? You can even tell colds to take a running jump, and they'll listen?'

'I want you to come and work in a brand new venture with me and a partner. But only when you decide to return to London.'

Sally's mouth dropped open behind the tissue, and she turned away to blow her nose all the harder. Through the window she suddenly saw Maddock's muddy Land Rover driving slowly along the road from the sea. It slowed down at the turning to the cottage, but then accelerated away before she could wave or attract its attention. Something inside her calmed down as she watched it go. The words 'fish' and 'sea' sprang to mind. There was always someone else, some-one waiting out there who would make her feel better in an instant, if she only got off her arse and went to look for him.

'A bit sudden, I know, and I wouldn't blame you if you told me to –'

'Drop dead, Jonathan. Yes, that's all I have to say to

you!' The fire was in her belly again, and she rose up on her toes as she yelled at him. 'I don't need you or your fancy new colleague to help me out of a hole. Things are just fine the way they are.'

Jonathan spread his hands in surrender and uncrossed his legs, ready to stand.

'If that's how you feel,' he said. 'But I don't think you really mean it. You're not cut out for a life of leisure. Just hear me out, would you? It's a very attractive proposition, and we both agreed that you were just the girl for the job.'

'I wouldn't spit on you, or your new colleague, if you were burning to death,' she half sobbed, half shrieked, hurling herself towards him. Following fast on the heels of her venom was the familiar hysteria, the exhilaration that always fired her when Jonathan was around; that fire that had never been far away when she was cutting through that City jungle. She knew that she should be screaming at him, but instead she found herself laughing maniacally as he stood up and caught her just as she was launching her fingernails at his face. His fingers closed round her wrists, and he held her in mid-air for a moment before lowering her to the floor, making her feel like a feeble schoolgirl.

'It was only a suggestion. I should have known better. I should have known how bitter you'd be after what happened.'

He turned to go. Sally grabbed at his arm and pulled him back.

'That it? You're going to give up that easily?'

'I only wanted to express how sorry I am for what happened, Sally. I was a fool. That's why I tracked you down, rented a house near here, wanted to speak to you, try to make it up to you.'

'I don't believe in this new Saint Jonathan. I won't listen. You'd have to try a helluva lot harder than that.'

She dropped his arm and stalked away across the room, which was filling with steam from the shower and making them both sweat.

'I've had enough of fighting – even with you. So I'll be off. Go and pack up the house and return to London.'

He was ready to abandon her again. He was halfway out of the open door. Sally backed away, on the other side of the room, towards the shower room. She was immobile with anger and disappointment, the same emotions she'd felt when he'd stuck that knife in her back those few months back. But that anger was very close to desire, and it threw her into turmoil now as it had then. They glared at each other through the steam.

'Lily-livered to the end,' she spat. 'Can't even persuade an old flame to try again. I thought better of you, Jonathan Dart.'

She stood for a moment longer, then flicked her fingers dismissively and stepped into the shower room to open the little window and let out some of the steam. She paused, her face poking out into the warm sunny air, but she couldn't hear him, either leaving or staying. She stepped into the shower and grabbed the shampoo.

'What's that song?' she grunted, still not sure whether to laugh or cry. She stuffed her head under the jets of water. 'Gonna Wash That Man Right Out of my Hair.'

Jonathan was right there, cramming himself in behind her, shirt and trousers and shoes rapidly soaking through. His tall frame filled the shower cubicle, but Sally climbed up him like a monkey up a tree, gripping her knees round his hips and tearing at his shirt, pulling it over his head, slithering down again to unbutton his trousers, throwing them over the top of the cubicle, running her hands down his wet sides while he stood perfectly still, amusement playing round his lips. Then she took the soap in her hand and rubbed it frantically between her palms to get the suds going. She dropped the soap and took his half-erect cock in her hands and started to lather it, tucking the still-soft end into one hand and swiping up and down the shaft with the other. She watched it quiver and rise through the bubbles, extending like the telescope, lengthening from his flat stomach, smoothing out the skin, ironing out any wrinkles until it was straight, smooth as plastic and even longer than she remembered. It emerged strong and proud through the pink bubbles of Ben's soap. She pulled it roughly, making it even longer, and lathered the big balls that hung beneath it. Jonathan's height made the end of his prick jab into Sally's stomach even when she was standing on tiptoes.

His head rolled back against the shower wall, but still he waited and smiled and hardly touched her. He knew how to drive her crazy. Making her work like this only drove her wilder, because she knew how sensational the end result would be. They had never done it in the shower before, and at last the cosy cottage bedroom took on a whole new decadent light. The smile stopped playing and Jonathan's lips dropped open as she moved her hands harder and faster up and down his shaft, working the soap into a luxurious lather. Sally felt his dick jump and pump, and she watched her own fingers, tiny as they gripped him. Then she left his cock and slid her hands back towards his balls, cupping them with one hand while the other travelled further back, up between his buttocks. She let her soapy forefinger dart straight into his tight butthole, forcing a reaction from him, and she cackled softly as, at last, his hands stretched out helplessly and grabbed at her hips, then circled her waist and pulled her right into him. His cock was now jammed upright between her tits, and at last they were moving in rhythm, joined together again. Sally pushed her whole torso against him. She reached under him, and felt his balls retract with his mounting excitement while her finger poked higher and higher up into his tight crevice, reaching for the spot where she would tickle and prod and he would jump and gasp.

Her nipples were hard as they pressed against him and her stomach twisted again and again as she felt his penis grow longer, pinned as it was against her. She looked up at Jonathan and remembered how it had been between them – their brief but overpowering affair. That trip to Paris, their earth-shattering fight and his bitter betrayal. But now she was safe. She'd gone through the hoops of fire and was, in a way, on her own turf. She could do and say what she liked. She was doing what she liked right now, and Jonathan Dart was at her mercy, practically on his knees in the shower with her while she probed his most tender parts and kept him where she wanted him. She would always want him, despite his dirty dealings.

He began to shudder, and his hands clenched harder around her narrow hips, and then, just as she was about to scrunch his balls hard and strike up through him to set fire to that tiny spot, he took her hands and forced her to release her hold on him. The bubbles were running away and his cock was gleaming and clean, bouncing under the pounding needles of water. Sally licked her lips greedily, reaching out for it, but he spun her round so roughly that she grabbed onto the chrome shower pipe to avoid slipping over on the soapy floor. He pressed himself up behind her so she could just make out his blurred reflection in the steamed-up shower panel. He lifted her so that her feet rested on the step which ran round the base of the shower tray, and cupped one large hand under her dripping bush. He parted her lips and thrust his fingers inside her, the water and soap mingling with her own juices. Sally's cunt was already contracting wildly to take in his long fingers, but he pulled them out again abruptly and parted her legs wider and wider until she started to rise right off her toes. She had always loved the way he made her feel like a living doll. The difference in their height had always made people comment when they had worked together. You could tell people were imagining what positions worked best, how a man rumoured to have the biggest schlong in London could fit it inside such a tiny woman, but there was no one to come forward and confirm that she had the most accommodating cunt in the UK.

Sally felt her stomach give a kick of desire as his familiar hands manipulated her into position. She was practically swinging off the shower rail now, and she knelt on the tops of his slightly-bent legs as he grappled her from behind. She knew he was strong enough to support her like that, and as he raised his pelvis she lowered her eager crotch to meet it. And then she felt it, the tip of his cock, ready and waiting, hard as iron. She rested her cheek against the panel for a moment, ecstatic to feel his shaft in there, wanting the moment of anticipation to go on forever while the water shot down onto them. And then another thought stole into her head: the thought of Janie, only a couple of days ago, sliding up and down that very same pole, tossing her hair about while she made free with Jonathan's cock. Well, she was going to erase that pretty picture right now.

With a muffled shout of private glee, Sally steadied herself against the panel. She felt him solid and strong behind her, flexed and ready, and then she rammed herself down onto him, inch after glorious inch, filling herself with Jonathan's huge length. She descended slowly and triumphantly until her buttocks were squashed up against his stomach and his magnificent cock was practically holding her up. She let her hands go and heard him laugh, and then he tilted himself forwards so that they both started to fall. Sally let out a shriek as they landed on their hands and knees half in, half out of the shower. She started to crawl forwards, still impaled from behind by the biggest dick in the land. But he yanked her back inside the cubicle so that the water, now running cold, kept showering onto their backs. The cold seemed to make his cock even more rigid as it reared up inside her. Her nipples and the surface of her skin shrank against the cold water, tingling with tension as he started, very slowly, to thrust himself inside her, so that she was pushed and pulled across the slippery plastic floor with whatever movement he chose. Her hands and knees squeaked with the friction, his hands holding her wet bush against him, not needing to do anything more to stimulate her, just letting her tight pussy welcome and engulf him so that they were welded together. They were the beast with two backs, rocking back and forth on the floor, his prick bashing and thrusting so that she was pushed out of the cubicle and pulled back in. The water got colder and colder, and Jonathan pumped faster and faster, and Sally couldn't tell whether she was shivering from cold or from uncontrollable excitement. She felt him accelerate his thrusts, and he started to breathe into her neck, resting his mouth and teeth there while he pumped and then lifted her off the ground with the force of his orgasm. Sally wiggled her hips from side to side to give herself more friction as she rubbed her clit. She felt her own muscles close round him like a vice then yield themselves into an explosive climax as he pulled her right up against him and pumped his juices into her while hers flowed and mingled with the freezing water and the ebbing bubbles.

In an echo of their dwindling fluids, the water from the shower slowed, dripped, and then stopped, and Sally fell back against Jonathan's chest, glad in a way that she couldn't see into his face; glad to feel him inside and behind her, not able yet to admit that he had her by the short and curlies, and always would.

'There. Knew you'd come round,' he growled, squeezing her hard. She smiled to herself, then pushed his arms away, and tilted her arse towards him. She crawled forwards so that she could relish his cock sliding slowly out of her. She heard it flop heavily onto his thighs, then she was up and out of the shower.

'You mean *you* came round,' she retorted over her shoulder, as she wrapped herself in a towel. 'You were practically on your knees. You're on your knees now! Just where I like you.'

Jonathan looked up at her, sleek and wet as a seal, then got up to follow her out of the shower room. She didn't offer him a towel. He walked around her bedroom examining things, still dripping wet, his penis still half-cocked and bouncing in front of him. Then he went up to the telescope.

'You can probably see to Plymouth with this,' he said, tilting it up to his eye. He hooked a foot round the leg of a bar stool that was tucked into the corner of the window, which Sally hadn't noticed, and perched himself on it.

'I've tried fiddling with the knobs,' she said, sidling up to him. She wasn't used to this comfortable silence between them, especially after such stupendous sex. She was still waiting for his act to drop; the peacemaker to disappear and the old, evil Jonathan to reappear.

'Your speciality, my girl,' he laughed softly. At last he was looking at her, and they smiled at each other. 'But you didn't twiddle this particular knob expertly enough. Look, it's working now.'

He hoisted her up onto one of his knees and she stared through the lens. At first it was all blue sky and the odd nodding tree branch, and she felt as if she was tipping downhill as Jonathan aimed it towards the sea, focusing it so that the blurred blue turned first into clear sand and then the individual stalks of sea grass waving in the slight breeze.

'How do you know what I'm looking at?' asked Sally.

'Because I can read your mind,' he chuckled, stroking her buttocks where they were planted on his leg. She felt an answering twitch of renewed desire in the moist crack of her pussy. 'Seriously, there's a little monitor attached here which gives you a miniature of what the lens can see, like a video camera. You should be trained on the beach now, or the dunes just behind it. You won't get the focus as far as the surf, because the dunes are in the way.'

'Oh my God!' cried Sally, clutching with both hands onto the shaft of the telescope. She settled more comfortably onto Jonathan's leg and started to rub herself gently against the bone of his thigh. 'You're right! And there's some people down there, stretched out on a towel, topless, nothing on – it's a couple. Fucking each other's brains out! A man pressed up behind a woman, just like you were taking me just now, doggy style. He's got her by the hips and he's fucking her from behind and she's toppling forwards with his weight but – but she's on top of another guy! They're all humping like rabbits out there on the dunes! Anyone could stroll up and see them. An old dear walking the dog, kids building sandcastles.'

'Let me see!'

'There's two blond guys ... hmmm, wouldn't mind a bit of that myself. There's one – red-headed – oh, my God! It's Janie! She's the sandwich! What is she playing at, the hussy? She's being rogered out there by two hunks in wetsuits!'

'Give me that!' Jonathan grabbed the telescope off Sally so that she tumbled sideways onto the floor. She jumped onto his back while he peered through the lens, swearing loudly.

'I've got to stop them!' he exclaimed, pulling the focus. 'The little bastards!'

'What's your problem?' Sally felt a surge of irritation. Now that he was there, she wanted to get right to the bottom of what was going on. Not only had Jonathan not finished with the begging and pleading, he had not complimented her after getting her in the shower. He seemed to have forgotten all about wanting her to come to London and work for him. Instead he was squinting down a bloody telescope and making a fuss about Princess Janie being taken from above and below by two strangers. Sally shook him. 'Want to have another go at her yourself?'

Jonathan pushed the telescope away and stood up.

'Can you find me some dry stuff to wear? I've got to get down there.'

'No, you can get your own clothes.' She scrambled up on the stool, warm from his bum, and straddled it.

'Whatever.'

'You're supposed to be either fighting with me or wooing me, Jonathan. What's going on?'

'Perhaps it's just the magic of the seaside, makes us all mellow, except I won't be mellow when I get my hands on those two little shits.'

Jonathan marched out of the shower room, muttering and pulling on his soaking trousers as he went, and scuffling his feet into the deck shoes. Sally smirked. He bent down and pinched her face in his hand.

'I have to go, doll.' He kissed her hard.

'Leave them alone. Stay here and pay me some attention. I've got more where that came from.'

'It's a promise, but not now.'

'Janie can look after herself, you know,' said Sally.

'It's not Janie I'm after, you idiot!' he exclaimed, pinching her face again then flinging open the door. 'Honestly, you're obsessed with that girl. No, she can do what she likes, and very nice it is when she does it, if I recall. But I can't stand by and let those boys get away with that behaviour.'

'Why the bloody hell not? If I had the car I'd go down there myself and join in! Give you something to chew on. They look like pretty tasty young dudes to me.'

'You'll go near them over my dead body!'

For once Sally was stunned into silence.

'Don't look so shocked, Sal. I'm allowed to be indignant once in a while, and not just about you, or about business. Because those over-sexed gigolos sticking their bits into your friend are Sam and Tom – my sons!'

He clattered down the stairs and Sally chased after him, her mind whirling. The unattached, enigmatic, cruel Jonathan had sons who looked like a couple of Greek gods! This was something else.

'Wait up, Jono, I'm coming with you!'

He ran down the garden path and she followed him, exulting in the luxurious kiss of the unexpected sun on her bare limbs, her blood still racing after their session in the shower.

'Not this time,' he said, revving up the engine of his 4x4 Merc and blowing her a kiss through the window. 'I'm not having you creaming all over my leather seats!'

'Bastard!'

'We'll talk. I'll be back for more.'

'You've blown it, Jonathan Dart!' she shrieked, hopping up and down on the doorstep. 'I'd rather stick needles in my eye than have you back for more!'

The car jerked as he executed a three-point turn and powered up the drive and onto the road, scattering clods of dried mud.

8

'Such a bollocking! He was like some father from a Victorian novel. It was lucky we'd finished what we were up to, otherwise he'd have ruined an absolutely sensational moment!'

Janie was having trouble suppressing her laughter as they bumped along the narrow lanes towards the village in her battered Saab.

'What was his problem? They're old enough to do what they want, aren't they?'

Janie roared with laughter and slapped the long brown leg that extended from her miniscule polka-dot shorts. She pulled in by a hedge to avoid a dozy tractor. The driver's head swivelled full circle to get a look at the two girls.

'Barely! They're seventeen and nineteen, faces like angels, bodies like –'

'You lucky cow. You're having all the luck,' said Sally.

Janie turned to look at her friend; her face was solemn again. Someone tooted at them from behind to get a move on.

'I'm sorry if it seems like that, Sally. None of this is turning out the way I envisaged. But *you* try resisting that kind of temptation! Golden boy comes and talks to you while you're stretched out naked in the sun, ogles your tits, hard-on fit to bust, young, untried, in dire need of the older woman's touch –'

'Older woman, indeed. You're younger than me.'

'Twenty-nine seems very old to kids of that age, I can tell you,' said Janie.

'Which must make Jonathan forty plus instead of the mid-thirties he told me.'

'Who cares? Who the fuck cares? With him you get three for the price of one!'

Janie stepped on the gas as the road widened, and they bowled along the seafront towards the village. Sally stared at her friend. The red hair was tousled in the wind that blasted through the open window, and freckles were dotted all over her honey-coloured skin. Sally snuffled into her handkerchief, and tipped the mirror down to look at her pink-rimmed eyes and white face. All she'd had time for was a hair-wash this morning, before Janie had forced her out into the sunshine.

'I expect Jonathan will ground those boys for a week now,' Sally remarked spitefully. Janie had had enough fun for one week. She wanted Jonathan to stay away as well until she was able to have him all to herself.

'A bit rich, coming on the heavy father when he has the morals of a donkey, wouldn't you say? Even if he could order them about, which I doubt.'

Sally relented and burst out laughing. She slicked some lipstick quickly across her mouth. 'So it's just you and me today?' she asked.

'That's the idea. To be honest, I feel as if I've gone six rounds with Mike Tyson – I don't think I could take a cock right now if it socked me in the mouth.'

'You dirty mare. Get your mind onto a different track, why don't you. We'll get some food in from the supermarket, yeah, then how about a beer?'

'Whatever you say, dear. Anything to keep that smile on your sulky little face and your bum on that seat. Still want to go back to London?'

Sally glanced out at the little thatched cottages that lined the road, the gardens thick with bushes and flowers, washing lines dancing with towels and bathing suits. Every other car towed a boat or collection of surfboards, and people in shorts strolled towards the sea, all rain and storms forgotten.

'No, I think I'd like to extend my holiday, actually . . . if that's OK with you. I've been a fractious bitch, and I'm sorry. Apart from anything else, look at me, I'm a mess. I'm afflicted with the flu. I must stay here and recuperate. To hell with Jonathan's phony offers of work.'

'What was it exactly he wanted you to do?'

Janie reversed the car into the supermarket car park and got out her shopping list. Sally smiled. Despite all the sexual shenanigans and men coming out of her ears, Janie still couldn't help being little Miss Organised. And thank God for it, the way Sally's head was pounding.

'A drink will make that go away,' soothed Janie a little later as Sally massaged her temples. 'Nothing one of Alf's Bloody Mary's won't cure.'

'Alf?'

'The landlord of the Honey Pot Inn – our next destination.'

They were back on the road, the car bulging with enough food to keep the army in shepherd's pie, apple crumble, every cheese under the sun, strawberries and cream and, of course, all the ingredients for mind-blowing cocktails. The car crawled back between high hedges, every so often a tantalising glimpse of the sea becoming visible through field gateways and breaks in the cliffs. Finally the winding coast-road led them into the village.

'I'll leave you here to get the drinks in. I'd better get

'this lot back to the fridge,' Janie said, as she slowed down outside the pub. The place was heaving. Sally realised it was a Saturday and the entire population of Devon seemed to be spilling out of their cars and onto the unadorned patch of tarmac in front of the pub: everyone from beach bums to crusty old salts fresh from whaling, or whatever they did out there on the ocean.

'I'll come with you. Don't fancy my chances with the hoi polloi,' said Sally.

'Christ, what's the matter with you?' said Janie. She kept the car in gear and revved the engine impatiently. 'You're not afraid to go in on your own to get our drinks, are you? Time was you'd relish the prospect of going into a pub full of men on your own. Time was I'd have cramped your style!'

'Just not feeling brilliant, that's all,' Sally shrugged, but Janie leaned across her and unclicked the seat belt.

'Get a grip, girl. You're becoming a recluse, and that most definitely wasn't the point of this exercise. You haven't stepped outside the cottage in a whole week. Now, I'll be twenty minutes, max. And mine's a pint of Pilsner.'

All eyes followed the choking exhaust of Janie's old car as she roared loudly up the street towards the cottage. Even her driving had changed, Sally thought, feeling in the pocket of her tiny denim skirt for some money. All confident and assertive. Everything about Janie had become more confident. She had a glow coming from inside. Was it really several good doses of sex that had done that for her? And if so, why was Sally still feeling like shit?

She didn't know if anyone was looking at her as she ventured in, but she didn't feel like catching anyone's eye, so made for the dark interior of the pub as coolly as she could in her suede mules. There was a solid bank of male backs between her and the bar and the noise level was deafening, and rising. She felt her own level of irritation rise as she struck out sideways with her shoulder to get between two lads who totally ignored her and started jabbing their fingers into the chests of two blond guys who were leaning over the worn wooden bar. The bar staff were run off their feet and there seemed to be an argument brewing over who was going to be served next.

'Fuck this,' Sally said. She gritted her teeth, and pushed again. The lads may as well have been made of wood themselves, nailed to the floor. Now the blond boys had turned from the bar, and were trying to flick away the lads' jabbing fingers. The taller of them started to argue; Sally couldn't hear the words, but she knew immediately that these two were the hunky surfers Janie had been making sandwiches with on the beach the other day.

She pushed her hair off her hot face, yanked her vest top down (the same one she'd worn that hot day in London) so that her nipples were only just covered, and decided to try her luck with the hunks. They were absolutely gorgeous. Now that really would piss Jonathan off she thought gleefully. She bobbed up between them, staggering slightly on her high heels and grabbed onto the taller boy's arm to get her balance. The men beside and behind her crowded up so they could get a better view down her skimpy top, but the boys she was aiming at didn't even noticed her.

'Hi!' she squeaked above the hubbub, practically jumping up and down to attract their attention. 'You must be Sam and Tom.' But as she jumped something flashed across her head and someone grabbed her round the waist and pulled her out of the way just as she realised that one fist, then several, had started to fly back and forth just above her.

'Out the way, miss,' someone growled in her ear, and she saw that it was Maddock who had pulled her out of the chaos. He still had one arm round her waist, and she felt a luscious softening in her groin at the muscled arm gripping her like that. She wiggled round to get in front of him and started to smile, but he picked her up, his blue eyes staring past her, and practically tossed her towards the pub door, then jerked his thumb at someone to get her out of the way. He waded past her towards the boys, who were now fighting for real. People around them were cheering and shouting, and a woman behind the bar was shrieking. Sally was riveted, although she edged towards the door for safety. Maddock wore a checked shirt and the same old trousers, but no fishing jacket or peaked cap this time; it was too hot for that. His dark hair stood on end, ungroomed, and his strong forearms were smeared with oil, or perhaps something worse. The crowd seemed to part like the Red Sea as he got to the scene of the scrap, and a rhythmic clapping was set up as he grabbed first one lad, then the other, by the scruff of the neck and marched them outside. The two blond boys stayed at the bar, puffed their chests out and gave each other high-fives. They were just turning back to order their drinks when Maddock burst back in and grabbed them as well, and hurled them out through the door before they could blink.

There was a lot of rowdy shouting and applause as the fight seemed to be carrying on outside. Maddock didn't reappear, and a smoky quietness settled inside the pub for a few moments as everyone peered to see what was happening. But in peering through the door they couldn't help but see Sally, and the warmth stole over her like an old friend as she recognised the appraisal in one or two faces when they took in her miniscule skirt and tiny vest. She stepped boldly up to the bar.

'A Bloody Mary and a pint of Pils, please.'

The barmaid didn't answer. She had a tea towel in her hand and was staring over Sally's face at the brawl in the courtyard.

'I said . . .' Sally thumped her elbows on the bar, and the woman blinked huge dark eyes at her.

'Sorry, sorry, what was that?'

Sally repeated her order, realising that it was her turn to stare. Apart from the voice, which sounded pure South London, the barmaid was like something out of a Spanish opera. She had black hair tied loosely up in a knot on her head, arms the colour of cappuccino, and a tight black dress which plunged down her front and her back, and only reached to just below her buttocks. Like everyone else in the pub, the barmaid had trickles of sweat running down her neck and into her cleavage. Sally wiped her own face and smoothed her palms across her bum. She repeated the order.

'Causing havoc as usual, Mimi?'

Maddock was right behind Sally again, pushing up behind her so that her tits were pressed into the bar and she couldn't move. She gave an experimental twitch of her hips. It wasn't accidental. He didn't move, and she felt his groin firmly pinning her to the spot. His arms appeared on either side of her, clutching a grubby tenner.

Mimi, the barmaid, put Sally's drinks down in front of her and curled her lip at Maddock. 'Not my fault if they're fighting over the candies in the shop, is it?'

'It is when you dress like that in front of boys who barely sprout hair,' he answered in his thick Devonshire brogue. 'What d'you expect, my girl?' His breath was hot against the top of Sally's head. She tried to push herself sideways.

'I'll get these,' he said, pushing the glasses towards Sally, and she stopped struggling. She took a gulp of her Bloody Mary. Mimi had put lots of pepper and Worcester sauce in it, and it nearly knocked her off her stiletto mules, but Janie was right. Any lingering traces of flu didn't have a chance once she'd downed this, and she flicked her hair back again and spun round, her back to the barmaid, to face Maddock.

'Thanks, Mr Maddock,' she said, in her best Marilyn Monroe lisp. 'It's me who should be buying you a drink, after breaking up the fight like that.'

'Come and meet the boys,' he said, nodding curtly at Mimi, who stuck her full red bottom lip out in a sulky pout and stalked to the other end of the bar to serve someone.

Sally tottered after Maddock, squinting against the bright sunshine as they returned outside. The crowd had all trooped back inside the pub, and the blond boys had disappeared. There was still no sign of Janie. Maddock led her to the back of the building, where it was quiet, away from the car park. There were beer barrels stacked about and muddy tyre tracks criss-crossing the yard, presumably from the beer lorry, and the ground was still damp after the recent downpours. Apart from a couple of flower baskets at the front of the building, it seemed they didn't go in for tarting up their pubs round here, Sally thought, as she picked her way across the mud. This could equally be Maddock's farmyard. Still, it looked to be more of a local's boozer than one going all-out for the tourists.

The two lads she had seen poking their fingers into Sam and Tom were slumped on a brick wall nursing

their bruised jaws. The pair of them were like miniature versions of Maddock, but scrawny rather than
bulky, and their young faces were still unscarred by
years of combine harvesting and lambing or whatever
had given him all those scratches.

'Now here's someone worth having a scrap over,
boys,' Maddock said, grinning lecherously.

Maddock nudged Sally over to the wall. The lads
looked up, and their pale eyes gleamed. They smoothed
their messy hair back over their narrow heads.

'Get more action from this one than that harlot in
the bar, the way she's been acting up recently,' Maddock said, pinching Sally's cheek. 'Just remember,
Mimi's way out of your league. Your sisters would have
more luck scoring with our dusky barmaid than you
would, if you get my drift.'

'Eh? She's into women now?' one of the boys sniggered. 'Cool. How do you know that?'

'She looks like she'd swing any which way,' the
other lad butted in. 'Like she'd have anyone for
breakfast.'

'I shouldn't have said anything. Just make sure you
steer clear of her,' Maddock snapped, his face flushed.
'She's still spoken for. Those beach boy toffs need to be
told.'

The boys nudged each other and gaped at Sally. She
swayed up to them and looked them over for a
moment. Grubby, yes. Rough, yes. But they had big
hands, strong arms, and pent-up energy like young
bulls pawing the ground. The sun was warm on her
head and there was an animal aroma to the mud
around her. She started to feel wickedly dirty. She
licked her lips, took another swig of her drink, and
turned round slowly so that she had her back to them,
her thighs right against their knees. Then she started

to bend at the waist, sticking her bottom out so that her little skirt rode right up between her arse-cheeks. She nudged herself in between the boys and they had to shuffle up on the wall to make room for her.

'I don't think so,' Maddock scoffed, putting his beer glass down on the ground. 'Look at you all. This ain't the bloody vicar's tea party. You wanted to congratulate me, right, miss?'

'That is absolutely right,' Sally breathed, crossing her leg and swinging one mule in the air. 'I've never seen anything so impressive. And I don't just mean your fists.'

Maddock strolled over to Sally. He took the glass out of her hand, placed it on the ground beside his, then yanked her up so that she was now standing on the wall. The lads turned silently to look up at her.

'I think we all need to let off a little steam after that fight,' he muttered. 'I reckon these boys deserve a treat after their disappointment in there. They saw something in the old barn the other day, too, which got them going. Your friend, stretched out on her back while Farmer Jack gave her one on an old hay bale. That's why you've been fighting over the barmaid, isn't it, lads? You need to get your rocks off.'

The lads nodded. They looked hungrily at Sally; every exposed inch of her.

'Time for you to find out what these town girls are like under all that slap.'

Sally grinned. Whether it was the sight of Maddock and his muscles sorting out the fight between the much younger men, or the vodka, she didn't know, but she felt the old Sally returning, literally pumping through her veins again as the three men ogled her. She raised her arms in the air as if on stage.

'Come and get it, boys!' she breathed, Marilyn

Monroe again, and parted her legs slightly, calves taut in the high heels, skirt riding right up over the golden triangle of hair that nestled over her pussy. One of the boys gulped and started stroking his hand up her leg. The other closed his hand over his own groin.

Maddock glanced at them both and was about to kick them, but when his pale eyes came back to Sally she could see the hunger light up in him. He rolled his sleeves up over his bulging biceps and stepped up to her, pushing the skirt up round her waist so that her bare pussy was revealed. Sally wriggled with pleasure, and put her hands on the boys' shoulders to keep her balance. Maddock ran his hands up the inside of her thighs and without further ado inserted several fingers into her; she softly parted in welcome beneath the yellow curls. Sally's knees shook at the feel of the gnarled fingers probing, not gently, inside her tender flesh. Then her throat swelled with a muffled moan as he slid his hands round to grab her buttocks and then pulled her down and pressed her groin into his face. His nose and his chin ground against her, bristles rubbing on the soft skin of her pussy. Then his fingers roughly parted the lips and she looked down to see his long, thick tongue, curling at the end, following his fingers up and down the crack. With each lap of his tongue she felt warmth seep through that part of her, hotting up her cunt like a furnace while she gripped the lads' shoulders harder for fear of tumbling off the wall.

Maddock's head rummaged against her for a moment longer, teeth and tongue nibbling at her, and then he withdrew his face, which gleamed with her juices. He licked his mouth then drew the back of his hand across it.

'She's warmed up for you, boys,' he said, stepping

back. Sally saw the outline of Maddock's cock inside his trousers, and wanted it badly, but he picked up his beer glass and leaned against a beer barrel.

The lads lifted Sally down so that she was sitting between them again. They each hooked an ankle round one of hers so that her legs remained apart and she couldn't get up or walk away – not that she wanted to. She caught her breath as one of the boys started to pull her vest up over her head so that her pert tits dropped out into the open. The vest was still on when the other boy grabbed her tits greedily and started to fondle them with his big rough hands, squeezing them hard and running the callused palms of his hands flat against the nipples so that they swiftly hardened into points against the bumpy friction. The other boy pulled the vest right off and started to suck on Sally's neck. He bit down to her shoulder, before grabbing the breast on his side and caressing it as well.

Sally thought she would go mad with the twin sensations of the boys working on her breasts, keeping her legs yanked apart, two sets of young hands kneading at her, and Maddock watching with his huge hard-on bulging in his pants. Then, oh, God, they both leaned across her and clamped their mouths over her nipples, pulling them out and biting them hard. She had always concentrated on her pussy and all its sensitive parts as her primary erogenous zone, and hadn't given much thought to her tits before. They had always acted as more of a fun accessory than the gateway to pleasure. But just looking down at the two nuzzling heads that pulled at them caused fiery ripples of desire to accelerate through her insides. She dug her nails into the boys' shoulders, squashing them against her, and allowed her head to fall back so that she could feel their lapping all the more keenly.

187

Then she felt something hard push against her stomach, circle there then move down to the soft point just above her pubic bone where her bladder was. It pushed in hard there, and Sally squealed with the urge to pee. Just then the bell inside the pub went for last orders, and the lads lifted their heads like a pair of foxhounds.

'Don't even think about it,' growled Maddock. He was now standing in front of Sally with his dick out. It looked even thicker than before, and he was holding it firmly against her stomach. The boys had lost their stroke momentarily and, along with Sally, they gaped at Maddock's cock, which he lunged at them like a spear before aiming it at Sally's pussy. Her breath rattled hoarsely in her throat as she chuckled with laughter and anticipation, and the boys' hands paused over her aching tits as they nervously watched what would happen next. The long muscled shaft seemed to have a life of its own, lifting blindly out of Maddock's hand and edging itself into the moist crack in Sally's bush – which was more than ready for him. She wriggled forwards on the stone surface of the wall, thrusting her pussy towards it to engulf it, but Maddock merely held his cock a little away from her, and the boys kept her ankles locked into place with theirs so that she couldn't move. They started to suck her nipples again while she felt herself struggling with the opposing forces of pleasure and pain, mixed with the renewed urge to pee. As they sucked they started to rub their crotches up and down against her hips and, as she answered them with a dance of bumping and grinding, she could feel the bulge of their youthful erections growing with each thrust.

Maddock was having trouble containing himself, she could see, and Sally flung herself backwards without warning so that her pussy was splayed out in front of him, filled now with a wild heat that needed satisfying. The mouths and hands of the boys were less fumbling and more confident now, and her whole body was alive with jangled nerves and sensations. As if reading her mind, the boys each took hold of a leg, which they pulled further apart so that they could all hear the wet kiss of parting pussy-lips, and they twisted their heads away from her tits to look over at what Maddock would do.

He bent his knees slightly so as to angle his cock directly at her. The boys helped by lifting Sally forwards so that her wet entrance met his determined knob and, without further ado, Maddock slid his length inside her until she was flat up against him. She wanted to wrap her thighs round his waist, but the boys still had her legs splayed out on either side of Maddock, her ankles locked on to the ground. She was unable to close herself around him, and that meant that the entire area of her sex was open to him, outside and in. Not just the sensitive inner core but her arse, her buttocks, the soft skin at the very top of her thighs. She let herself relax against the boys as Maddock started pumping hard, moving her back and forth up his penis until it nearly came out of her completely, then shoving it back in. After a couple more thrusts she saw veins like blue ropes standing along his muscled length, and he was shuddering. His thick neck twisted as he let out a shout of climax and the boys kept a tight hold of her until Maddock was ready to pull himself out and stagger sideways. He turned his back on them to pack his prick away inside his trousers.

'I'm not done!' Sally squealed, her splayed legs twitching with frustration as her inner muscles still tried to grab at the vanished prick.

'No problem,' murmured the thinner of the two boys. He pushed her down onto her back on the wall. The other boy swore and shifted out of the way, and somewhere out the front of the pub they could hear the main door closing and being bolted. Sally lay back and closed her eyes again. She wondered briefly what had happened to Janie, and then hoped she wouldn't show up right now. This was Sally's scene. She didn't want Janie to have any part of it. This was Sally and the locals, going for it hammer and tongs. And right now she was concentrating on showing this young blood what life was about.

'Three for the price of one,' she chuckled to herself, lifting her knees, feeling the gravelly surface of the wall scraping her back and buttocks. The other lad hadn't even bothered to support her head, just left her lying like a sacrifice on the top of the wall. She didn't know where he was, or where Maddock was. She heard the zipper go down on the taller boy's fly, a gasp and a pause, and then he started to fuck her. She stifled a giggle. It was very slender and seemed to be bending, not yet stiff enough. She reached round under herself and found his soft balls. She tickled her finger across them and the boy yelped, the young cock stiffened up, and she realised that although it was slender, it was long. It unfurled inside her like an eager snake, until she felt it nudge her back wall and the boy started to hump madly, grunting and groaning. He quickened his pace, holding onto her bottom and raising it to get a better angle as he whipped in and out of her faster than she thought possible. Meanwhile the other boy took both breasts in his hands again and twisted her hard nipples, and she felt an answering rolling of gathering ecstasy in her belly. The first boy flicked his hips wildly back and forth, faster and faster, then he yanked Sally up and off the wall so that her skin scraped across it and he shuddered his rapid climax into her, and started to subside gratefully down on top of her.

Sally tried to grab hold of his penis to keep it inside her, but she could feel it softening and slithering. Her excitement was turning into fury. She pushed the boy off her, and he sank to his knees in the mud, holding onto his soft cock, gazing at it as if the batteries had run out prematurely.

'Don't worry, lass, I'll get you there,' said the other boy who was now homing in on her clit. He rubbed it expertly considering he was so naïve. He must have read all about it in a porn mag, thought Sally, and by the looks of these two, and their voyeuristic little pastimes, they probably both did a fair bit of poring over X-rated magazines.

The second boy then kicked his mate aside and started to undo his trousers. Sally realised that her irritation was partly due to the now virtually uncontrollable urge to go to the loo, and her muscles were singing and stinging, closing frantically to keep her from pissing all over the ground. She sat up and pressed her knees together, then jumped down off the wall, hopping from foot to foot and trying to push the younger boy away with one hand while grabbing herself with the other.

'Time's up, boys. I need to go,' she squeaked.

But Maddock and the other boy were finishing their pints, and the younger boy just laughed, grabbed her, spun her round and bent her over the wall.

'I don't care about that,' he said. 'You act like that and then want to stop when you feel like it. I ain't about to let that happen,' he drawled in his thick Devon accent. 'I'm gonna takes what I want.'

He pressed his hands round her hips and deliberately flattened them against her stomach, so that she yelped. Then he spread the cheeks of her arse, wrapped them round his own shaft, which was short and very fat, and, tilting himself over her, he rammed it up her from behind. All pretence of catering to her pleasure was left aside as he served to satisfy his own needs. He bent her double so that her bare breasts scraped and squashed across the stone wall, and his thick, strong cock thrust up inside her, faster and faster towards his climax.

All at once there was a great rushing and building sensation inside her which made her teeth jangle and, as the boy started to shout with triumph as he was coming, she felt a dribble then a splash between her legs as her bladder opened beneath his weight and a golden shower cascaded down her legs. As she felt the release, a glorious satisfaction poured out as well. The boy brought his fingers down to be covered by the shower, and he laughed out loud. Sally laughed as well, and pushed back against him, rubbing her clit furiously as he called her a dirty bitch, and then her muscles quivered and she sank down beneath his weight, shuddering until her own climax subsided to a halt.

She shifted round on the wall and pulled her skirt down, feeling for her shoes. She grabbed for some tissues in her pocket and wiped herself as best she could while the boys gawped at her.

'There more where you came from?' the younger boy asked, shuffling beside her as they all tottered out to the front of the pub, which was shuttered now and silent for the afternoon. Sally was about to say no, there was only her, but Maddock came over and hoiked the lad away by his elbow.

'Back to work, you,' he ordered, shoving the boy

towards his Land Rover where the other boy already sat, his head lolled forwards, sated with beer and lust. 'We've all had our fun.'

He glanced over at Sally and winked at her, and as he jumped up into his car the old Saab came screaming round the corner and Janie honked the horn. Sally didn't move for a moment. She didn't trust her legs to work, for one thing. She just stared after the Land Rover, watching the blue exhaust belch out the back as it barely missed Janie's car and rattled off. She could hardly believe what had just happened; what she had just allowed those country ruffians to do to her.

'Who were they?' Janie asked, watching them in the rear-view mirror. 'The Three Little Pigs?'

Sally leaned against the car and wiped the sweat off her face. 'What happened to you?' she asked weakly.

'Well, I got waylaid – no, not like that, unfortunately. The car wouldn't start, and while I was struggling with it your Jonathan pitched up, to say goodbye.'

Sally straightened and held fast to the door handle. 'Oh?'

'He said he thought you were on your way back to London, but when I said you were thinking of staying on for a while, he seemed to change his mind, and said perhaps he didn't have to pack up the house after all.'

'That was a pretty swift change of agenda, wasn't it?'

Janie shrugged and waggled the gear stick.

'He's determined to talk to you. He was even waving his laptop about. Spoke to me all polite, as if I'd never put on your white negligee and climbed on top of him to exchange bodily fluids on the sofa a few days ago. Perhaps he's forgotten that I know how big that cock is!'

Sally tossed her head.

'He's got another think coming, if he thinks I'll crawl back to him so easily. It's not as if I need him for sex, is it? Sex grows on trees around here.'

She stared at the muddy tyre tracks left by Maddock's Land Rover.

'Oh, get into the car, woman. If we can't get any joy from the pub, we'll just have to make a picnic and take it down to the beach. You look like you could use some sustenance.'

Sally opened the car door obediently. The juices from Maddock and his merry men oozed down her legs onto the worn seat as she sat down, smirking. The car bucked, and moved off down the deserted village street.

'Oh, and by the way,' remarked Janie, indicating to go back towards the cottage. 'To celebrate the fact that we're all staying on for an elongated summer, Jonathan has asked us round to his grand place on the cliffs next week for a barbie.'

9

The time had come to dress up again.

'Only this time it's not fancy dress. It's to be serious *femme fatale* stuff,' decided Janie, as she rifled through Sally's tiny dresses and skirts. The warm afternoon hummed through the attic window, and Sally was peering through the telescope.

'There's nothing interesting to see out there.'

'All the interesting people will be at Jonathan's, that's why,' Janie told her, holding up a gauzy pale-pink slip-dress with slashed sleeves and hem. I hope that will include Jack, she thought. 'Now, this little number will be perfect. Makes you look like Tinkerbell.'

Sally took the dress and held it up in front of the mirror. 'I wore this in Paris.'

'Just the job, then.'

'I told you –'

'*I'm not crawling after him!*' Janie mimicked, getting up off the bed. 'Change the record. Think of him as a business proposition. You need a job. I can't keep you here indefinitely, fun though that would be. I'll have to move on myself, come September. Ben will be back, and I've got to go to Spain, to source some tiles.'

'So what you're saying is just use him for the business angle. Forget any other sort of relationship with him?'

'Who? Ben?'

'No, silly. Jonathan.'

'Rare for you to ask my advice,' said Janie, 'but, yes.

Any other kind of relationship with him would be dynamite. You'd only get burned. Just talk terms – tough terms. Lots of money, company car, your own office, working from home if you want to, as little contact with him as possible – you don't need me to tell you, Sal!'

But Sally was twirling slowly in front of the mirror, and didn't hear her.

Janie walked down to her own room, where she had already laid out a few items on her bed. She felt excited about the party, or whatever it was going to be, at Jonathan's house. Much as she loved Sally, she reckoned they both needed to get out of the cottage and dilute the atmosphere with some male company. She was constantly horny now. Every time she had felt a man's cock making itself at home inside her – and what a variety there had been in just a few days – she wanted more of it, like you could never have enough chocolate. But most of all she wanted Jack. She wanted to take things up where they had left off. She had gone up to the farmyard several times to try to find him, but he was never there; the place hadn't been touched since her log-hunt. Maddock would know where Jack was, but he was always at the other end of a ploughed field or halfway up a tree, and she wasn't inclined to chase after him. She knew Sally had been borrowing the car and trawling the countryside for Maddock as well. Mostly she had failed to pin him down, but once or twice she had come back scratched and bruised and Janie hadn't asked questions.

Janie slipped into her own choice for the evening, which was a long see-through, leaf-green Ghost dress. She pinned her hair up in a loose knot and let tendrils trail down her neck. She burned with hope that Jack would be there tonight. She wanted to erase the signs and smells of Sally from his warm body, just as she suspected Sally wanted to wipe the traces of her off Jonathan. Oh, the competition element made it all the more fun, especially as they had never before been in a situation where they had screwed the same men; but then, being closeted with Sally over the last few days had surprised Janie in lots of ways. She had shed her city brashness and become almost timid. Perhaps it was the flu she'd just had, but Janie quite liked this development as it had enabled her to grow more confident, and less reliant on Sally's opinion. Janie had practically swaggered into town to get paints and swatches. She had run about on the beach, aware all the time now of men's eyes on her tanning body, filling with desire when she looked back at them, tossing her hair and imagining wrapping her legs around a hunky stranger and forcing his cock up into her.

She held a hand against her breast and felt her heart pounding at the thought. How her mind had learned to lead her, even when there was nothing physically happening. She took a deep breath, sprayed Eternity all over herself, and walked out onto the landing.

'We need to get your lady editor back here for the "after" pictures,' she yelled up the stairs, running her fingers along the stripped banisters. There were still splinters to be smoothed out. 'And I don't just mean pictures of the house. Before, naked strumpets; after, ladies of the night.'

She heard a chortle from above. When they weren't talking about sex, she and Sally had worked hard on the cottage. With Sally working to Janie's orders – another about-turn in their normal roles – they had transformed it from a cute but tired house, stripping off all the old chintz to unearth a modern yet rustic look; stripped the wallpaper and colour-washed the walls. They'd thrown out the sofa covers and replaced them with plain linens, but kept the rugs and colourful cushions to add brightness to the pale, woody interior.

'Yeah, and let's get the little photographer back here as well!' Sally shouted.

Janie laughed then frowned. She glanced out of the tiny landing window at the road that wound away from the cottage.

'After that I must start selling my wares,' she said. 'I'm supposed to be persuading people like Jonathan and Jack that their houses need redecorating.'

Sally bounced out of her bedroom and down the winding attic stairs. She had tamed and curled her blonde hair so that it flew round her face, and wore the wispy dress with some Gina silver sandals. She looked like the old Sally – a demented angel.

'What are we waiting for, then,' she whooped, jumping down the last stair into Janie's arms. 'Let's hit the town!'

Jonathan's house was a white Art Deco affair perched on the edge of a cliff, and at first the place looked deserted. The sun was just beginning to set over the sea, bathing the house in an orange glow. One or two lights had been lit inside the house, but there was no one in the drive to greet them. Sally and Janie walked round to the garden. There was a circular swimming pool at one end, already floodlit from under the blue water, and in front of them two rows of iron braziers had been lit, the flames standing straight up and barely flickering in the balmy air, making a fiery path across the lawn towards a little gate which was propped open.

'So much for being *femmes fatales*,' muttered Sally, untying her sandals. 'Look how steep this path is!'

They clambered barefoot down the sandy path

towards the sound of rushing waves and low voices, and tumbled out into a tiny cove. Jonathan was standing behind a vast barbeque, which was laden with steaks and virtually hidden by the aromatic smoke. Behind another table heaped with salads and bread were Sam and Tom, both tipping beer down their throats from chilled cans. They wore pristine white shirts unbuttoned to their brown waists, and baggy surfer jeans.

'Gimme, gimme,' breathed Sally, fluffing up her curls and stepping over the sand towards them. The boys nodded politely at her as she approached them, but they both looked over her head towards Janie. She smiled, a knot of remembered pleasure forming in her stomach, but they were not who she was looking for just then. She basked for a moment in their admiration, and then Sally must have said something outrageous, for they both grinned down at her and started fighting over who was going to ladle the salad onto her plate.

'Good evening, Jonathan,' Janie said, holding out a plate for some sausages and glancing around restlessly. 'Beautiful place you have here. Shame it's only rented.'

'That was a lie, actually,' he replied, plonking sausages and a juicy steak on her plate, as her stomach rumbled. She was constantly hungry when she was down here by the sea. She picked up a sausage and started chewing the end of it.

'A lie?'

He was also restless, and he glowered at Sally flirting with his sons.

'Didn't want Sally to think I was too keen,' he confessed. 'I wanted to make it sound temporary. I love the way you do that, by the way.'

She raised her eyebrows, the sausage wedged into her cheek.

'Gobble that sausage, I mean.' He dolloped some mayonnaise onto her plate then looked up at the rocky cliff. 'It isn't rented at all. This is my own. I've just bought it.'

'But Tom and Sam said –'

'My sons said a lot of things. Mostly extremely complimentary about you, I may say, although I had to tick them off for rampaging through the local fauna and flora the minute they came off the M5.'

Jonathan walked across to another table and handed her a glass of champagne. Janie sipped greedily, the bubbles popping on her tongue and going straight to her head.

'No ticking off necessary, I can assure you. I can't remember when I ever had such a good time,' she remarked, adopting his formal tone. 'They are a credit to you.'

They both laughed in low, dirty chuckles, and clinked their glasses.

'But they seemed to think the house was rented, too,' Janie went on.

'Well, it *was* rented, but it's come up for sale while I've been here,' Jonathan explained. 'Jack and I had a tussle over it but I won. It's back to the drawing board at that old wreck of a farm for him.'

'Jack.' Her stomach gave a flutter. 'Is he here?'

'Not tonight. He was called back to London. Some medical emergency at his practice, but he'll be back in a day or two.'

'Oh, thank goodness,' she said, but still her stomach plunged with disappointment.

'Old love, is he? Asked Jonathan. 'That's the impression he gave me.'

Janie eyed her host, remembering Sally's harsh

words about him. It was so easy to be charmed into opening up to him. She decided to play it cool.

'No, childhood playmates, that's all. I just wanted to talk to him about renovating the farm. It's what I do.'

'No need for any of that here, is there, Jono? This place is like a new pin.'

Janie felt something soft pressing up against her arm and looked down to see a very large round breast encased in scarlet lace nudging at the crook of her elbow. Her eyes travelled upwards to see the olive skin and flashing black eyes of a woman she hadn't seen before. She looked exotic and dangerous as she stood on the beach in her scarlet lace mini-dress. Next to her Janie suddenly felt, in her long floaty dress, too demure and dreary.

'Mimi! I don't recall inviting you!' Jonathan exclaimed, looking flustered. He glanced across the gathering at Sally, who was glaring over at them from between the two golden boys. One of them raised a curl of hair that was stuck behind her ear and whispered something. Sally's mouth crinkled into a smile, though her eyes remained fixed on Janie's group. The brothers nudged each other and pulled Sally further along the beach.

'No offence taken,' Mimi replied, then took a champagne glass out of his hand and drained it. Her voice was gravelly, the result of several cigarettes a day, Janie reckoned. 'I rarely get invited to posh do's like this. Maddock hates them, but you're glad I pitched up, aren't you? Admit it. You're always glad to see me.'

'Jane, this is Mimi,' Jonathan explained. 'The local barmaid.'

Jonathan walked off abruptly to talk to another group of guests who were dressed as if they'd just climbed down the rigging of their boats. They made Sally, Janie and this Mimi look like dogs' dinners, Janie thought. Over by the water's edge Sally turned her back to the crowd, lifted her little pink dress right up to her bum, and started paddling.

'What's his problem? You don't look like a barmaid,' Janie remarked, nearly choking on her sausage as the dark woman watched her. 'Except for the impressive cleavage of course.'

She had no idea why she had said that, apart from the fact that she couldn't take her eyes off the tits spilling out of the lace. Mimi was standing close enough for them still to be touching Janie's arm; almost nudging her own breasts, in fact. Her stomach tightened as she saw how close both pairs were, the exposed nut-brown pair and her own pale ones, the dark valley between them visible beneath the thin fabric of her dress.

Mimi tipped her long neck back and laughed, and everyone turned to watch her, except Sally, who had waded into the water up to her thighs and was holding her dress right above her waist, oblivious to the party and deafened by the rushing of the waves. The two boys stood on the beach and watched her.

'You're right there. They're my best feature, I reckon, and get me jobs you wouldn't dream of.' She draped an arm round Janie's neck and pressed her mouth against her ear. 'My name's not really Mimi. It's Mary, but that's too ... well, prim, don't you think? Doesn't suit. And I'm only a *barmaid* –' she mimicked Jonathan's scathing tones '– for the summer. Jonathan likes to emphasise that as if it's an insult. His problem is, he fucked me last week and now he's embarrassed about it. I guess he thinks I'm beneath him. He's a mummy's boy. No balls, these city types.'

Janie felt a heat spread across her cheek where Mimi's lips still rested.

'You're only a barmaid in the summer, you said? What do you do in the winter, then?'

Mimi took another glass from the tray and wound her arm around Janie's waist. They started walking on bare feet towards the rocky steps. It was dark now, and a stiff breeze was coming off the water. Quite a few of the guests had already gone up to the house, and Jonathan had also disappeared.

'Darling, your pretty hair would curl if I told you,' she said, somewhat theatrically. 'Let's go up to the pool.' Mimi laughed, pulling Janie after her. 'Jono won't mind. I've been coming up here quite a lot to cool off. Can't stand all that salt water. Your friend OK back there?'

Halfway up the steep path they turned. In the twilight the tips of the waves gave off flashes of foamy white light, and Sally was pulling off her dress as she waded back to the shore. The boys darted forward and lifted her out of the water. The three of them looked like triplets in this light, tousled yellow heads laughing together, but where the boys were tanned golden, Sally's petite body was pale as it dangled between them. They carried her like a doll over to a bonfire they had made, and tried to sit her down in the flickering light, but Sally wouldn't stay still. She was crawling across the sand, pulling at the buttons on the shirt of the older brother. Behind her, the younger brother already had his shirt off and was frantically unbuttoning his soaked jeans.

'That's Tom, I think,' remarked Mimi. 'Or Sam. Can't tell the difference, though they're both equally tasty. You have to take the youngsters for a ride, don't you, just to see what they're like?'

She turned Janie's chin towards her, and Janie felt that weird heat flooding through her whole body this time, not just her face. She was glad the sun had set so no one could see her blushing.

'Want to join them down there? You look as if you're straining at the leash. Could be fun, I suppose.'

Janie turned back to look at the beach scene. Sally had undressed the older boy and pushed him onto his back. She continued crawling over him until she was poised over his face. The boy grabbed her buttocks and Sally hung over him, balancing on her hands and knees. Then, very slowly she lowered herself until her pussy was against his mouth, and rocked herself gently back and forth so that the soft curls were brushing against his lips. His head jerked up to try to lick her, and Janie could see that she was teasing him, but she'd be teasing herself more by holding herself away like that, and, sure enough, she sank down, tossing her head back with delight as he started to lick at her.

The younger boy scratched his head for a moment, and Janie really was tempted to run back down to the beach and give him something to do with the aching erection he held in his hands. She glanced at Mimi. Janie reckoned the pair of them could show him a thing or two. She felt a kick of desire in her and was about to suggest it when Mimi nudged her and pointed. The boy who Janie had straddled and suckled the other day was getting the idea, and he came and stood above his brother's hidden head, his knees slightly bent. The way Sally was kneeling, she was on a level with his young, erect penis. He thrust it towards her face, and she took it in one hand, balancing herself with the other on the ground, and guided the length towards her mouth.

'Been there, done that, haven't we? So perhaps we

should leave well alone tonight,' Mimi murmured, reading Janie's mind. Janie nodded. She and Sally had reached such an easy harmony over the last few days. She didn't want to rock the boat by muscling in on Sally's latest conquest. In any case, her encounter on the beach with those two was far more erotic than this. For a start, it had been lovely and warm out there, hidden amongst the dunes.

'You're right.' She chuckled quietly. 'Anyway, I'm afraid I have the satisfaction of knowing I got there first.'

'I know,' Mimi answered, equally quietly.

Janie allowed herself a delicious quiver as she remembered leaning over the younger boy's face and dangling her nipples into his eager mouth.

'Maybe we could join them – later,' she said quickly, pretending that it was the evening air that made her shiver. 'Let's go and find our host.'

'A swim, I think, in his lovely pool. You like swimming, don't you?' asked Mimi.

She walked ahead of Janie towards the little gate and the low hum of voices wafted across the lawn. Janie watched the barmaid's wide hips swaying, the tight red dress slipping higher up the brown legs with each upwards step.

'Yes,' she panted. She didn't realise she was so unfit. Why was she out of breath? 'But how do you know I like swimming? And come to think of it, how do you know I got there first with the two boys?'

Mimi waited for her at the gate.

'I saw you the other morning, in the sea. Wonderful body you have, Jane. I'd never have guessed you were a city girl. You look like you were born to frolic in the waves like some kind of goddess.'

Janie laughed and tried to push through the gate,

but Mimi laid her fingers lightly on Janie's arm, and her skin shivered again.

'Superb, I thought. You don't know how good you look, do you? One of my winter jobs is as a nude model. Artists' studios as well as magazines. I know a sensational body when I see one. I expect those boys thought all their Christmasses had come at once!'

Somehow, hearing this from a woman filled Janie with a startling, intense pleasure. Men could be relied on to admire anything with a pair of tits, within reason, and they showed their admiration not just by voicing it, but by displaying it with their dicks. She bit her lip as she thought of the various cocks she'd had in the last fortnight, the various ways she'd had them, and her cunt contracted sharply with remembered excitement. But the more adventures she had, the more she began to wonder if something was missing. She thought it was Jack. There was unfinished business with him going back years, not just weeks. But now there was the voluptuous Mimi, so up-front and sure of herself, filling Janie's head with sweet words and ideas, and refusing to go away.

'I'm flattered,' she murmured. 'You're pretty sensational yourself.'

'Come on.' Mimi's plump lips parted in a huge grin. Janie could imagine them wrapped around a giant penis, giving stupendous head. No doubt that's what every man thought when he looked at Mimi's mouth. 'I'll race you to the pool.'

Janie hesitated, then picked up her dress and dashed after Mimi's brown, toned legs. They pushed through a group of startled guests and reached the edge of the oval pool. It was enticing, the sparkling turquoise liquid illuminated by the underwater floodlights. The braziers flickered round the edge, and fairy lights were strung up along the front of the house. Loud music throbbed from inside the open-plan sitting room whose sliding glass doors were open to the terrace

'Terrible taste in music,' giggled Mimi, grabbing Janie's hand, and before Janie could take a breath she was pulled into the water with a shriek and a splash. The water was blood temperature. As she surfaced, Janie saw steam rise towards the already black sky. She swam to the shallow end. The water pushed at her gently as Mimi swam underneath and sprang up in front of her, black hair sleek against her scalp. It emphasised her enormous eyes and made her look even more mysterious.

'Best to take that lovely dress off. It will survive if it's not in the chlorine for too long. Can you unzip mine?'

She turned and lifted her long hair, and Janie unzipped the red lace dress. Mimi didn't move, so Janie pushed the dress off her shoulders with some difficulty. It was very tight, and stuck to her wet skin. She brought her hands round to the front of the dress and suddenly it slipped off, so that her fingers brushed against Mimi's breasts as she tried to catch hold of the dress. Mimi's head tipped back slightly. Janie knew that was the same movement *she* made when she was feeling aroused, and wondered if it was the same for Mimi. She felt the soft bouncing of feminine flesh against her hands, and Mimi's warm back and wet hair pressing back against her, and her breath caught in her throat. The other woman's big round breasts were just within her grasp and, instead of recoiling from the idea, Janie wanted to wrap her fingers round them. She had never been this close to a naked woman before, except probably Sally but, more amazingly, she had never wanted to touch another woman's body before.

Until now. There was a tense pause, then Mimi swished forwards so that her breasts were pressed right into Janie's hesitating hands. She wiggled them from side to side, teasing Janie, then suddenly she dodged sideways before Janie could catch hold of her, and pulled the red dress right off, tossing it out of the pool and onto a lounger.

Janie turned to pull her own dainty dress off, struggling in the water but not wanting to climb up on the steps in front of everyone. She wrung it out carefully and put it on the edge of the pool, doing everything slowly and deliberately to allow the moment of madness to pass. Mimi was just fun-loving, that was all. Of course she wasn't actually *flirting* with Janie. She loved men too much. And so did Janie, something she was still a novice at. But when she sank her shoulders back under the water and turned to see where Mimi had got to, the breath caught in her throat again, and the knocking of her heart grew rapidly. Mimi had swum back towards the deeper end and was leaning her head against the tiled side, arms outstretched along the edge, her tits bobbing like air-filled buoys on the surface of the water. Steam rose round them both. Her limbs were feathery as the water shifted, but her breasts were firm like fruit, growing out of the water.

The insistent knot of excitement tightened in Janie's belly, and she swam quickly over, not yet sure what she wanted to do. She glanced up at the other guests. Some of them were watching the girls cavorting in the pool, but chatting as they did so, not really paying much attention to a bit of horseplay that might be going on. Jonathan was by the house, deep in conversation, holding a plate of raspberries in his hand. Sally was engrossed down on the beach, and she already knew that Jack wouldn't be turning up tonight.

Janie glanced back at Mimi, who was looking straight at her, her lips parted, her tongue tucked into the corner of her mouth, her shoulders right out of the water so that her breasts were in full view. Janie's nipples hardened like nuts. Surprise washed over her as she realised she was aching to touch Mimi's glistening skin, and she swam right up to her. She bounced herself against her new friend, her own breasts brushing Mimi's arm. Still Mimi watched her, her tongue sliding slowly to the other corner of her mouth as if she was finishing a sugary doughnut. Janie floated round behind her, and hesitantly wrapped her arms around Mimi's tiny waist. For an awful second she felt Mimi stiffen, and Janie feared she had totally misread the scenario. But then she saw Mimi's cheekbones rise as she smiled. A crazy, untried thought occurred to Janie that, if this was the first time Mimi had responded like this to another woman, then it would be all the more special. But somehow she suspected this wasn't Mimi's first girlie experience. She looked as if she'd tried everything under the sun at least once.

Janie pushed them both away from the wall so that they floated on their backs, Janie beneath and slightly to one side of Mimi. She kept her hands loosely on Mimi's wide hips, and Mimi spread her arms and legs out like a starfish. As she paddled her hands, her body swayed into Janie's and, to steady her, Janie slid her hands up over her ribcage. She could feel no bone, only soft, yielding flesh and, as Mimi's breasts bounced against Janie's palms, she closed around each big mound. Janie was astonished that the feel of Mimi's tits communicated directly to her own, startling her nipples again into stiffness as if they too were being fondled. She pinched Mimi's nipples between forefinger and thumb, knowing how good the feeling was, and felt them sharpen into long, strong points. As Janie started to tease each taut tip, Mimi arched her back so that both her boobs and Janie's fondling hands were visible above the water. Janie squeezed harder and her pussy brushed against Mimi's bottom. The ball of desire in her stomach started to burn. She kept herself afloat under Mimi's body and opened her legs a little so that she could rub against the round buttocks.

Mimi suddenly wriggled away from her and again Janie was appalled. Was this how it worked or not? She had never touched a woman like this before, never even wanted to, let alone made the first move. Had she overstepped the mark already?

'Into the middle, where it's warmer,' said Mimi.

They wafted together into the centre of the pool where they could just stand on their toes. Now they faced each other, and Mimi stared at Janie's panting mouth. The wicked expression in her eyes and the moist parting of her lips sent lightning through Janie's belly. She felt drunk with the novelty of it all, the warmth of the water, and the flashing of Mimi's eyes. Her eyelashes fluttered at Janie as if she were hooking a man. Janie pulled her shoulders towards her, and wound one leg round the back of her thighs to stop her floating away.

Her fingers made dents in Mimi's spine and her eyes closed as Janie dared herself to take the initiative, brushing her lips against Mimi's generous mouth, tickling her lips with the tip of her tongue, still expecting resistance, for Mimi to push away in disgust. But she bumped herself closer, wrapping her arms around Janie, and pressed her lips hard in response.

There was an electric shock as Mimi's lips opened further and Janie felt the wet tip of her tongue. Added to the thrill of the kiss was the extraordinary sensation of her soft breasts squashed against Janie's. Four breasts jostling for space, nestling, crowding into one another, the sharp surprise of a nipple scraping across a nipple. As the two women thrust their tongues fervently around each other's mouths, their hips started to jerk and writhe in a dance against each other. Janie kept her leg hooked around Mimi's, and her pussy-lips parted to let her tingling clit rub up and down whichever part of the other woman she could make contact with. She danced Mimi round in a circle to get the full force of the friction and the full sensation of squeezing herself, breast on breast, as they kissed passionately in the steaming water.

As they came full circle there was a big splash at the other end of the pool. They pulled away from each other, but slowly, allowing their tongues to linger in a little slick of saliva, before they opened their eyes and turned lazily to see what the noise was.

Jonathan was swimming across the pool, already naked. They glanced round, and saw that now all the other guests were already ringed around the pool, sitting on loungers or standing, intrigued by the pool show.

'Where's Sally?' he asked, coming up behind Mimi. Janie felt a jolt of fury as her interrupted excitement started to ebb away.

'Who? You're interrupting, Jono. Go away,' Mimi snapped, then winked at Janie and pressed herself up close again. But Janie was distracted by the question.

'Sally's on the beach, seducing your sons.'

'We last saw them humping by the light of the silvery moon,' added Mimi, not looking at him but flicking her tongue out at Janie and making her head swim with the renewed Sapphic promise. 'Better get your big stick out, Jono, and stop them.'

'My big stick is already out, Mimi. Better watch out.'

Jonathan was just behind her, and Janie saw the inevitable desire leap in Mimi's eyes.

'I thought you weren't going there again?' taunted Mimi. 'After all, I'm *only* a barmaid.'

But the attraction between Jonathan and Mimi only made Janie all the more determined to carry on what she had started, and under the cover of the water she edged her hand towards Mimi's black bush, parting the soft lips with her fingers. Gasping with surprise, Mimi fell back against Jonathan, hooking her ankles loosely round Janie's thighs, her body rising to the surface again so that her breasts lay invitingly there.

'I'll have trouble choosing between the two of you, actually,' Jonathan replied, floating casually behind Mimi. All the guests craned forwards to see what would happen, and one of the yachties pulled his shorts and Breton jersey off and jumped into the pool to applause from the others. He swam up beside Jonathan, pushed him aside, and snaked his hands up over Mimi's breasts, squeezing them together so that the nipples stood up, dark and hard. Janie felt the fight increase in her. She didn't want to lose the chance to taste something of Mimi's body, now that she had tried it. She pulled Mimi closer into her own body, leaned over her stomach and nuzzled up until her lips brushed the curve of her breasts. She swiped her tongue up and nibbled at one taut nipple. The bud entered her mouth, thrusting up against her teeth, and Janie sucked hard on it, astounded by the wicked excitement that soared through her. As she did so there was an answering pull on her fingers, and Janie realised that she had been groping up through Mimi's moist crevice while she licked her tits. Strong spasms tightened and loosened round her fingertips as Mimi started to thrash about in the water. Janie gave her own little shriek of triumph, sucking hard on the tight nipples, ramming her fingers further up Mimi's tight pussy while it pulled frantically at her fingers. Janie rubbed at what she hoped was Mimi's clit, unsure of what she was doing, feeling her way by intuition. Then, suddenly, Mimi came, unmistakably, moaning loudly. Her head splashed back in the water, and everyone on the edge of the pool started clapping.

All of a sudden the clapping stopped, and through the haze of her excitement Janie thought she could hear someone shouting hers or Mimi's name. But Mimi's ears were under the water, and Jonathan and the other man were pulling her and Janie through the pool. The shallower it got, the higher their torsos rose from the water, until Jonathan's magnificent prick shot to the surface as if it had been fired from a cannon, and banged against Mimi's face. At the same time there was another splash. Someone else had jumped into the pool, but this time they were swimming up behind Janie, because she felt big hands landing on her hips. She didn't want to look round. Jonathan and the other man glanced at whoever had just dived in. The other two men placed their hands on their lips, for silence. Mimi's eyes were still closed and her chest heaved. Then Jonathan cradled Mimi's head carefully and, standing to one side of her, he inserted the swollen tip of his cock into the corner of her mouth.

For a moment Mimi was motionless, as if she had passed out, then her mouth opened slowly. Her tongue came out and welcomed the round knob, its slit glistening in the floodlights, before it slithered into her mouth. Mimi's lips, that were made for blow jobs, started drawing and pulling on Jonathan's length, her cheeks caving in with the strength of her sucking. Not even an expert mouth like hers could take in the entire length without choking, and the sight of at least a third of his long shaft sliding in and out of Mimi's mouth turned Janie's legs to jelly as she absently stroked Mimi's legs.

Suddenly Mimi was pulled away as the yachtie swam round the other side and stepped in between the barmaid's legs. She was still sucking on Jonathan's cock, but at the same time her knees jerked up and grasped the yachtie's hips. His penis was already upright and quivering, and he pushed it under the water, angled his hips and, with no more introduction, jammed it into Mimi just beneath the pool's surface, his buttocks clenching as he pummelled into her.

Janie was literally at sea for a moment. She had lost Mimi's lovely body to the two men and she felt cheated. Her own pleasure wasn't complete. She was certain there would never be another chance to taste more of Mimi, or to have Mimi fondle her. She wanted to be out of the pool, on a big warm bed away from everybody, rolling her body and fitting it with all Mimi's curves and crevices. She wanted to abandon herself to the experience of feeling Mimi's big lips kissing her again, going down on her snatch, nibbling her clitoris, tonguing her pussy – she wanted it all.

She had to laugh inwardly at herself and what was happening to her. A month ago the sight of her new friend being fucked right in front of her by not one, but two guys, would have shocked her to the core. But now she wasn't shocked at all. She was aroused by it, and by what the two women had started, and that was what was getting to her. She was aroused, and she was jealous, and Jonathan had barely even looked at her, let alone pulled her into the group.

Janie started to swim to the edge, but she had

forgotten the unseen man lurking behind her. He wedged himself to block her escape. Keeping her close to the threesome, he brought his hands down over her stomach and into her pubes, and pulled them roughly apart, rubbing over the tender insides that were still throbbing with unquenched lust. She kept her eyes wide open, focusing on Mimi's rapt face, but now Janie was losing control. She was going limp as her aroused body responded to the man's brutal stimulation. His big fingers under the water somehow muffled the roughness, but still a fierce renewed desire started kicking inside her.

Sensing her weakness, the man tilted her suddenly forwards so that the only thing she could grasp for balance was the thrusting hips of the man fucking Mimi, and as she grabbed him she was knocked right off her feet. Her buttocks tipped upwards and the man behind her grasped them for his own balance. He started to slam himself hard into her from behind, scraping past the sensitive labia and burying himself right inside. She didn't know who he was, but she was wet and ready, inside and out. Strong hands began rocking her violently back and forth as the penis thrust hard and fast, and Janie could hear Mimi's moans, muffled by Jonathan's massive cock in her mouth.

'She's always a few steps ahead,' the man growled in Janie's ear, and she caught a familiar whiff of tobacco breath. She had no strength to think further than the cock filling her, though, and she let the thick pole rock her with fierce, determined thrusts, pushing her forwards so that her face ground into the crack of the other man's buttocks. She pulled at them, feeling him pause fractionally in his fucking of Mimi to absorb the addition of Janie's fingernails and face up against his backside. She allowed herself to weaken, still holding onto the man in front of her but letting the man behind her shove her so that she was halfway up the other man's back and out of the water. Her breasts rubbed against his spine as it bent and stretched to aid his thrusting into Mimi. Janie forgot how many of them were in the water, joined in a sexual chain, forming a novel variation of a line dance.

As the man in front of her continued to slam into Mimi, making almighty splashes, the man behind Janie continued to slide his fat prick into her as she rubbed her clit under the water with her right hand. Then, at last, Mimi led the way, opening her mouth as Jonathan spurted into it, so that she could swallow his come but scream out at the same time. It was this that caused Janie to climb the pole of her own climax, catching up with Mimi and sparking a chain reaction. With a couple of fast jerks the man behind Janie growled and lifted her right out of the water with the force of his own orgasm.

There was a silence apart from the panting of the five participants and the lapping of the water against the edge of the pool. Then the laughter and clapping started again. The three men swam silently to the edge, shaking the water from their hair. Janie edged herself round to Mimi, unable to keep her hands off her, and pulled her to the edge of the pool as other people started ripping their clothes off and jumping into the warm water.

'Jane, that was beautiful, or it could have been. We should have been alone,' Mimi murmured, snaking her arm around Janie's waist and pulling her close. 'Why do men always think that the only sort of pleasure we can get is when they come barging in?'

'Maybe because night after night you're on your knees, begging for it, that's why.'

The tobacco breath was back – it was Maddock. He pulled Mimi roughly sideways and out of Janie's grasp, then wound her long black hair round his hand and pinned her up against the wall.

'Let her go, Maddock!' Janie cried.

He glared round at her. 'You don't have a clue. This filthy whore loves it any which way. The rougher the better. She may look like a countess, but she's no better than I am. You should ask her what else she does for a living.'

Mimi raised her chin and spat full into Maddock's face, but she was perfectly calm.

'You're the one who has no idea, Maddock,' she hissed. 'I've taught you everything, but you don't know who I am. Just you wait and see.'

He swept one rough hand down to her breasts, half-submerged under the water, and squeezed hard.

'Home – now.'

Then he hoisted himself out of the pool. But Mimi lingered, floating back towards Janie, and the two of them couldn't help admiring his muscled buttocks and swinging bollocks as he strutted over to a chair to get his clothes.

'She'll never truly be yours, Maddock,' Jonathan remarked from one of the sun loungers, where he was taking a towel from an admiring female guest and rubbing himself deliberately slowly so that everyone could see the magnificence of his member. 'This one's a free spirit. She'll be off come the winter.'

'Don't go with Maddock. Stay here. You were going to tell me,' Janie said quietly, as the other guests started caressing each other. 'What other jobs you do in the winter?'

Mimi smiled and kissed Janie lightly on the lips. Out of the corner of her eye Janie saw Sally arriving at the pool's edge, and she stiffened, but Mimi was pulling her head hard and had pushed her tongue between Janie's lips and into her welcoming mouth. Janie closed her eyes, shutting out Sally and all the other guests, and savoured Mimi's sweet tongue. Then Mimi pulled away again.

'Maddock is right in some ways. He likes to think I'm like him, moving round in circles, never venturing out of my pigpen, and that's fine for now. But what he doesn't know is that when I leave here I'll leave no trace. I'll go to the city, far away from these fields and hedges, far away from the sea, even, and he'll never find me. I'll massage, I'll model, I'll strip, I'll accompany people who need a companion, I'll sing – then I'll move on again.'

'I want to know more,' Janie pleaded, tugging at Mimi as she started to swish towards the steps to climb out. 'Come and see me at the cottage, and we can –'

'One day, maybe. But the piece missing from your life is not me,' Mimi said, squeezing her then letting her go. She climbed up the steps and padded naked across the terrace as the other guests parted to let her pick up her wet dress. Then she crouched down on the edge to whisper. 'It'll be some man or other that you'll want. But it was fun, Jane. We both learned something fun, didn't we?'

Janie opened her mouth to reply, but couldn't think what to say. Mimi straightened slowly, letting Janie see one last glimpse of her jet-black pussy before the dress went on.

'And here was me thinking you'd only just acquired the taste for cock,' hissed Sally in her ear. Janie wasn't listening. She wanted to say something to Mimi, but she was already walking across to where Maddock stood with his arms folded. They stamped off across the lawn and were swallowed up by the darkness, arguing furiously. 'I thought you were biding your time till Jack the Lad came back on the scene. Never had you down as a lezzie.'

'I'm not a lezzie,' Janie retorted, glancing at her friend and at Sam and Tom, still hovering close, their blond heads tousled and smelling of wood smoke, their boyish torsos gleaming in the floodlight. 'It just happened. And I think it was just the once.' She pulled herself out of the pool.

'Not jealous, are you, Sally?' asked the older boy. 'It looked like pretty convincing girl action to me. And very horny.'

'Yeah,' said his brother. 'I've never seen a girl pulling a girl before. Better than any movie!'

They laughed with adolescent cackles.

'You mean you don't fancy your mate?' the older boy asked Sally, snatching the towel his father had just been using and draping it round Janie's shoulders. He kept his hands on her, and she realised she'd been shivering.

'She's my oldest friend,' Sally answered crossly, 'and I love her to bits, but I don't fancy her, for God's sake!'

'Well, more fool you,' the boys chorused, roaring with laughter again. 'We think she's sex on legs!'

'What's going on here? Some sort of tiff? Have we all displeased you in some way, Sally?'

'Fuck off, Jonathan.' Sally tossed her head. Even the boys were stunned into silence.

'You forget whose house this is,' Jonathan said coldly. 'You know who it is who should be *fucking off*, as you so maturely put it. And boys, behave.'

Janie shrugged apologetically at him, and he turned

on his heel, instantly switching on the host's charm to a couple who, drenched and giggling from cavorting in the pool, were asking him for their clothes. She could see Sally regretted her outburst, but Janie had had enough.

'Sally, behaving like a sulky kid does nothing but get people's backs up. How could you be so rude? Honestly, I can't get it right, can I? If I leave you alone to get on with whatever you want to do, you complain; if I come and join in with you, you complain. What is it that you want? To be the centre of attention? You're pissed off that we all trooped up here and didn't stay to watch your acrobatics down on the beach.'

'No.' Sally reached out and held onto Janie's arm. Her fingers were cold. 'You're wrong, it's not that. There's only one thing bugging me, no matter what I do to take my mind off it, and he knows perfectly well what it is.'

'Well, you're not going to impress him with that little show. I can't help you with this particular battle.' Janie sighed, and started to make for the house, where she could see a silver tray set with full glasses of champagne.

'Oh, no you don't,' said the older boy, swerving up behind her and scooping her up in his arms so that her towel fell off, while his younger brother scooped Sally up just as Jonathan was turning back to say something.

'Oi!' Jonathan shouted, as the boys started running round the pool. Sally couldn't stay pissed off for long, and started kicking her arms and legs in a pretend bid to escape. 'There are some girls here your own age, you know!'

A gaggle of fair-haired jailbait in tennis shorts and designer T-shirts stood shyly at the corner of the terrace, wondering what kind of orgy they had happened upon. The boys glanced across at them, waved coolly, then stuck their tongues out at their father.

'Let the party begin!' they yelled, and plunged, with their arms full of real woman, into the steaming swimming pool.

10

The afternoon sun made diamond shapes on the grass as it seared through the leaves. Janie and Sally reclined on their sun-beds, sunglasses firmly on their noses and tall glasses of Sea Breeze cocktails clamped firmly in their hands.

'Does he have to keep clicking like that? It sounds like a swarm of crickets,' Sally complained, raising herself up on her elbow.

'That's great, stay like that. Wow, this is going to make me a fortune!'

The photographer dipped and wheeled across the grass towards them. Sally raised one knee and pushed it sideways, cupping her pussy with her free hand, and he dropped to his knees to finish his film.

'Derek, isn't Shona Shaw waiting for you down in the village?' Janie asked. 'She's finished her write-up. She only let you stay on this morning because we said we had a job for you.'

Sally chortled. 'And have you finished what we asked you to do?'

'Yes, it's all built,' Derek squeaked. 'Come round the side of the cottage, and I'll show you.'

'I daresay she's expecting you to escort her back to London,' Janie chided. She stood up and stretched, gloriously aware of the way her breasts lifted and then bounced down. She and Sally had the tiniest of bikini bottoms on and nothing else.

'Let her wait.' Derek puffed out his chest. 'I want to stay here with you. My portfolio will be enormous.'

'That's not all that's enormous about you, darling, but really, it's time to scoot.' Janie smiled at him. 'Apart from anything else, you've worn us out.'

Janie strolled slowly into the cottage, enjoying the slavering looks of the young man. At the door she turned and saw him pleading desperately with Sally to be allowed to stay, but she was being equally heartless. She pinched his face in her hand, gave him a long, slow kiss, then pointed over to his car. They had enjoyed their morning with him after Shona had gone, letting him take photographs of them in the cool shade of the willow tree, but now it was time for some serious sunbathing.

'Here,' she said, handing Sally another drink. 'This is what this holiday was meant to be all about.'

'Yes, and only today have we achieved it.'

Sally bit the straw and sucked her cocktail as Derek crunched at the gears in the vain hope that they would relent and summon him back to perform some more tasks.

'But think what else we've done! A sparkling new cottage –'

'Hope Ben will approve.'

'And at least one new sex slave!'

They laughed. Derek's van jerked reluctantly up the drive and started to turn into the road. All at once there was a cacophony of squealing brakes and beeping horns.

'Honestly. It sounds like the Cromwell Road out here!' grumbled Sally as she and Janie wandered to the fence to investigate.

'He'll do anything to stay here at the cottage, the scallywag,' she chortled. 'Even engineer a car crash!'

'You know, I'd do anything to be able to stay on. I've already been here a week longer than I intended.' Sally sounded serious for a moment, and Janie looked at her. 'I know it's taken me a while to settle down, and I've been a grumpy mare at times, but my cold's quite gone and I feel really at home here.'

Janie felt the sun's warmth seeping into her back along with a sense of satisfaction and peace. She nodded.

'Well, I have to say, against all the odds you actually look like you belong in the wilds of Devon. And I'm used to having you here.'

Sally beamed. 'So right now the thought of either of us going back to London seems like utter madness – oh, God, who's that?'

The gutteral roar of the car which had been arguing with Derek's at the little junction hadn't receded. In fact, it was getting louder, crunching up their drive and materialising into the shape of a shiny Mercedes with blacked-out windows.

'Looks like your ride back to London,' Janie tried to joke, but her heart sank. Jonathan was throwing up dry stones in an unnecessarily violent parking manoeuvre, and the expression on Sally's face was already changing into the mixture of petulance and desire that overcame her every time Jonathan was mentioned.

'Nonsense,' she murmured weakly. 'He hasn't been in touch since that party, so he can go to hell.' She trotted towards the gate. 'I ain't going nowhere.'

Janie remained where she was, staring over the fence at the fields. The peaceful afternoon was already fragmenting. She certainly didn't want to stick around while those two spent the rest of the day either bonking or fighting. Perhaps she'd go to the beach, she thought. She glanced over at the car. Jonathan and Sally were in their customary pose, one on either side of the gate, squaring up to each other, though it was difficult for Sally to be convincingly aggressive wearing nothing but a pink thong.

As they started to argue, someone else suddenly got out of the car and Sally's head snapped round furiously. It was Mimi. She was wearing a white trouser suit with nothing underneath the loosely buttoned jacket, and her wild hair was swept up into an elegant coil. Janie's stomach contracted with the memory of caressing the other woman's dark skin in the floodlit swimming pool ten days or so ago. She didn't move, but folded her arms across her chest.

Mimi pushed Jonathan out of the way with an impatient comment, opened the gate which he had still not entered, and laid a friendly hand on Sally's arm. But it was Janie she was aiming for, and both Jonathan and Sally stopped bickering and stared as she stalked across the dry grass.

'Hi, Jane,' she breathed, and Janie's heart started pounding. 'Don't look so afraid!'

She took Janie's wrists and forced them away from their defensive posture across her bare front. The sun was full on Janie, shining on her lightly-tanned breasts. The nipples perked up eagerly as Mimi looked her up and down.

'I'm not afraid. I'm pleased to see you,' Janie said, and meant it. She gestured towards the table and umbrella where the ice was just about melting in the cocktail jug. 'I haven't been back to the pub, though I meant to come and find you –'

'You wouldn't have found me. I haven't been back to work there since I last saw you. Our brief conversation at Jonathan's party got my feet itching again.'

Mimi kept hold of one wrist as they sat down under the umbrella, but shook her head when Janie offered her a drink.

'I can tell from the outfit that you haven't just come from filling the optics,' Janie said. 'You look sensational: like a fashion editor, or a rock star. But what does Maddock make of it?'

Mimi tossed her head, forgetting that she was looking sleek, and one thick tendril of hair dropped out of her hairpins and brushed her hot cheek.

'Maddock? He has no say in what I do. He tried to order me back behind the bar when I told him I was quitting. He thinks that's all I'm good for. That, and opening my mouth and legs.' She sniggered, but her face softened a little. 'I mean, that *is* one of the things I'm good for, but not the only one. To prove it, I gave him and his merry men the seeing-to of their lives last night. But he didn't know it was the last time. He doesn't know I'm going away. He doesn't know he's just been something to play with while I've been killing time down here. I always wondered what a *real* country boyo would be like under all that straw and mud and thick accent, and now I know. Anyway, he needs to pick on someone his own size, if you know what I mean.'

'Yeah, chalk and cheese doesn't begin to cover it when it comes to you and Maddock. Beauty and the beast, more like. But it's not the winter!' Janie's voice rose embarrassingly, and Mimi chuckled her deep, smoker's chuckle. 'The summer's only half done. You said you'd be going in the winter.'

'I know,' grinned Mimi, 'but I rustled up a couple of contacts and I've landed an offer I can't refuse. I'm going to LA to work on a film.'

'Wow! I didn't know you were an actress as well.'

Janie knew she sounded star-struck, but she couldn't help it.

'I'm not. At least, not exactly. I'm going to be what they call a stand-in. There are various stars who I can double for. Catherine Zeta-Jones, maybe –'

'Wow,' Janie said again. 'That's so glamorous.'

Mimi shrugged and glanced over her white linen shoulder. Jonathan and Sally had sat down, one on each sun-lounger, but they were barely talking. They looked more interested in what was going on under the umbrella. Mimi rubbed finger and thumb together like a gangster.

'Money, darling. It's good money. And it will lead to other things. Or maybe I'll be back by Christmas. In London. Or Devon.'

Her black eyes burned into Janie's, and Janie's stomach gave an excited lurch. She wanted Mimi to come back to Devon, but she couldn't help wondering if she ought to get real. Mimi was like a glittering, exotic bird about to flap away into the blinding sky, and yet two weeks ago she'd been pulling pints in the Honey Pot Inn. Why on earth would she come back, now that her transformation was complete? Janie returned Mimi's wide smile, then started to laugh.

'Anything can happen, can't it?' she replied, and Mimi nodded, taking Janie's hands. She stroked the inside of her wrists suggestively and Janie sat very still, marvelling at the strange reaction shivering under the surface of her skin.

'Take my card. You could come out there with me, see what's there for you.'

Janie looked at the card where it lay between them on the table. *Mimi Breeze*, various telephone numbers, and an email address. Somehow she knew she'd be seeing this woman again.

Mimi leaned across the wooden table, the lapels of the white jacket falling open to reveal her plump brown breasts. Janie stared at them, then back at her face. Mimi's red-painted lips parted, drew nearer, and then she pressed them onto Janie's mouth. They radiated heat, and her tongue came out and slicked round to find Janie's. There was the merest flutter of its tip against Janie's lips, and Janie needed to respond, her tongue sliding warmly out to meet Mimi's. The world stopped as their mouths locked hard onto each other, tongues flickering a delicate dance while their lips closed and sucked. But as Janie started to fidget on her chair, wanting to touch Mimi's breasts again, Mimi suddenly withdrew, released Janie's hands and stood up. Jonathan jumped to attention as if he were her servant.

'I have to go. I'll see you,' Mimi whispered huskily. She ran one long red fingernail down between her breasts, then raised it quickly and tucked it between her lips for a moment. Janie did the same with her own finger. Then Mimi walked away with Jonathan to the garden gate.

'Amazing what a decent outfit can do to transform a person, isn't it?' muttered Sally, sauntering up to the table, and trying to look as if she didn't care. 'She was the local bike until yesterday. Now she looks as if she owns the place.'

Janie just nodded blankly, still in her chair.

'And what's Jonathan doing bowing and scraping like that?' Sally demanded. 'Have they been – has something been going on? He's surely not driving her off somewhere? Oh man, I haven't even *started* with him!'

Sally hopped from foot to foot, itching to cross the grass and listen to what they were saying, ready to jump if he threatened to climb back into her car. But then the sleek nose of another car appeared at the small junction, and a mellow hooter sounded, shocking some sleepy birds into flight. Mimi turned, waggled her fingers at Janie and Sally, and walked off down the bumpy drive. The car inched forward, and they saw that it was a white limousine. A chauffeur got out and held the door open for her, and Mimi got in. For a moment she, the car and the chauffeur wavered in the heat-haze just like a mirage before the car slid silently away behind the hedge and was gone.

'This place becomes more like fantasy-land every day,' Jonathan remarked casually, as he strolled back towards the girls, sat down and helped himself to the jug of cocktails. 'But it won't do. It's time we all got back to real life.'

'Meaning?' Janie tore her attention back to him.

'Why should we get back to real life?' Sally butted in, pouring herself a drink as well. 'We're having a blissful time down here. Looks like you and that barmaid have had a pretty blissful time of it – why spoil it with talk of "real life"?'

'Because we have to get back to work,' Jonathan answered. 'And you're coming with me.'

Janie decided to sit tight and hear what he had to say.

'In a way he's right, Sally. We can't loll around in the sunshine forever.'

'Who's side are you on?' Sally snapped, banging her glass down.

'It's not a question of sides,' Janie sighed. 'It's a question of getting real, earning money, having one's own place to live. After all, this is only meant to be a holiday.'

'But you've managed to get some work done while

we've been here – with my help!' retorted Sally. 'And maybe you'll even get noticed, if that article gets a good response.'

'And I intend to follow it up, if it happens, once I'm done down here. But I'm not the restless career girl, Sally. You are.'

'That's right,' said Jonathan. 'If you come with me, you could have all this kind of luxury, and so much more, whenever you liked. As well as the use of my place, of course.' He leaned back in his chair and wiped a large white handkerchief round his neck. 'With all the money you'll earn working for me and my new business partner.'

Sally leaned her chin on her hand.

'And who is he, this new business partner? What kind of business?'

'Catering, clubs, entertainment. We need a PR whiz kid, with a head for business, the ultimate front woman, in fact.'

Janie and Sally raised their eyebrows at each other, interest simmering.

'And that's me?'

'Of course.'

'And the new partner?'

Jonathan took a swig of his drink.

'His name's Mastov.'

Sally and Janie gasped. Jonathan looked at them both as if he'd just delivered the crown jewels. Janie looked at Sally, and then flicked her arm in the air as if cracking a whip, at which Sally started to giggle.

'You mean Mastov of Holland Park?'

'Yes, but how did you know –?'

Sally stood up, kicked Jonathan's feet out from under the table so that his legs were sideways. She stuck her bottom out, her pert cheeks divided by the strip of pink thong, and Jonathan took hold of her hips. Then she lowered herself down onto his knee and started to rock her crotch up and down his chinos.

'Because, King Dong, I've screwed him. I've been tied to his Chinese lacquer bed in his mansion, and I've seen the extent of his portfolio –'

'You little trollop!' Jonathan feigned horror. 'So much for mooning round after me!'

'I have to keep myself entertained, Jono. You know I need it day and night. I can't just sit around waiting for the likes of you to come to your senses, for months on end. Not until you prove to me that the only way forwards is for me to come back to London with you, on my terms, and in my own time.'

'Don't flatter yourself.'

Jonathan tried to shove her off his knees, but she spread her legs wider across his thighs and lifted herself on tiptoe so as to push her bottom right back into his groin. She tilted her hips so that she caught his hidden penis with her pubic bone, and Jonathan slumped back in the chair.

'There is one condition that I would like to make if we are going to work together. To be together,' he said, his voice serious. Sally stopped wriggling.

'Can't promise, won't promise.'

'You have to promise this one thing, Sally. Don't pout like that. It's very easy.'

She tried to distract him by licking at his ear. He pulled her back, and made her look at him.

'You have to promise that you will not shag my sons again. It's far too sensitive, too close to home. You can't go there. Not if this is going to work.' Jonathan's voice cracked. 'I nearly went spare when I saw you with them on the beach at my party.'

'Good. That was the intention,' Sally flashed back.

There was a pause. Both Janie and Sally flushed. Sally tossed her head, knowing she was beaten on this one.

Janie turned away to hide her own lascivious smile. Didn't stop *her* going there for seconds, did it? she thought.

'OK,' said Sally. 'They're dead tasty, but – they're your little boys, and I'll leave them alone. I promise.'

'Good girl.'

Jonathan's hands slid round to the front of Sally's belly and inched under the thin fabric of her thong, and Sally winked at Janie. She was once more in control. Janie winked back and walked to the other end of the lawn.

Sally might be finding her old self, but Janie was all at sea. That Mimi had *breezed*, literally, into her life, turning part of it upside down, and now she was gone again. God knew what she'd done to Maddock and the other locals while she was here. They would never have encountered anyone like her. She had shocked Janie with the electric attraction she had ignited – the only time she'd felt that for a woman. Those breasts, big and round like her own, bulging with sensuality and invitation, just like her own. No wonder she hadn't been able to resist touching. Her own tits were tingling again, and she felt hollow with longing. She needed filling. She looked up and down the empty road, the heat-haze still wavering over the silent hedges. She feared Jack had been put off coming near her after seeing her straddling Jonathan that first morning in the cottage. He'd probably heard who else she'd been straddling, too. Having come so close to rekindling their childhood friendship, she would probably never see him again.

She got up and went back to the sun-lounger, lay

down and closed her eyes. The sun was hot on her body. Her arms and legs felt heavy. Her breasts seemed to swell, though, rising like dough to greet the sun, and the more she thought about them and compared them with Mimi's, recalled them floating like buoys in the swimming pool, the harder her nipples grew and the more empty she felt.

This is the end of my adventure, she thought mournfully, and felt the dozy approach of sleep washing through her.

But there was to be no peace, because over by the umbrella Sally was starting to squeal, and not trying to contain the noise. Janie opened one eye, and saw that Sally was lying on her front across the table, the strip of her pink thong hooked over to one side. Jonathan was standing behind her, stroking her buttocks, slowly unzipping his flies, then stroking her some more. He tipped cold liquid from the jug over her bare back so that she shrieked and wriggled, and then he leaned over her and licked it off her spine, keeping his pelvis well away from her buttocks. Sally twisted round and tried to grab at him, but he took her wrists and spread her arms back down on the table so that she was spread-eagled in front of him, face down in the shade of the umbrella. Janie could see the affection in his eyes as they lingered on Sally, and she wished her friend could see it, but Sally was in her element anyway. She rose on tiptoes again, her strong dancer's calves and legs lifting her bum towards him, and he took her arse-cheeks and spread them open, then slid both his thumbs up and down her dark crack. He sat back down on his chair and buried his face between her buttocks, lifting her higher so that he could lick down towards her pussy, while his thumbs circled the tiny hole of her arse. Janie's cunt contracted violently as she watched, and she wanted to shut her eyes, but she was aching to be touched, and she wanted to watch. Watching made it worse and made it better at the same time. She licked her dry lips, which had the faint trace of Mimi's lipstick on them. She remembered Mimi's warm tongue slicking round hers, then she pressed her hand over her pussy like she had started to do when she was on her own on the beach. But then she remembered further back as if it was months rather than weeks ago; remembered that first stormy night, the first time for years that her pussy had been probed and entered, lying back as she was now, but on the scratchy hay bale. Lying in the warm sun, it seemed bizarre to think that only a couple of weeks ago she had been wearing a heavy jumper, coat and trousers and that it had been cold and raining. She started to touch herself, tangling her fingers in the tight auburn curls of her bush, and tried to recall Jack's shadowy face in the gloomy barn. Her head turned to watch Sally and Jonathan, wanting in her desperation to run up to them and take his cock out from his trousers and stuff it in to *her*, but wanting them to have their moment.

'They're at it like rabbits, aren't they?'

Janie had been so busy watching them she'd not seen him coming across the lawn, and for a daft second she thought she had, after all, fallen asleep. But the noises Sally was making were real enough, and so was the figure of Jack, appearing from behind her lounger.

'They're talking business,' she explained, and he laughed loudly.

'Is that what they call it. Actually, I came here to talk business, too.'

'It must be the country air,' she said, in shock that

her fantasy man was now standing in front of her. 'Look at them.'

She sat up and wrapped her arms around her knees to hide herself, but he hadn't once looked at her tits. He was standing rather formally a few feet away.

'I don't want to look at them,' he said. 'I want to look at you. Who'd have thought it? I've been trying to reconcile that wild woman in the barn with little cousin Janie. But every time I've seen you you've been wearing fewer and fewer clothes, and that sweet Janie has vanished little by little.'

'You've only seen me twice since that night in the barn,' Janie pointed out, feeling stupid as she said it. 'You've been gone virtually the whole time.'

'Miss me?'

He sat down on the grass, and she felt hope unfurling in her heart.

'Yes. No. Stupid question. I wanted to see you, that's all,' she said. 'To explain –'

'About what? Stealing my logs? Stealing my honour in the barn?'

'Yes. No. Bloody hell, Jack, you always used to do this!'

'What?'

'Confuse me, interrupt me – tease me.'

'Not enough, I now realise. I should have teased you to breaking point. What fun that would have been. I'm sorry, Janie, you were saying. Explain what?'

She sighed crossly. He was wearing another old T-shirt, long khaki shorts and had bare feet, and though he was dressed like a scruff he was no longer the dog-eared schoolboy who'd tormented her back then. He was chewing a piece of grass and looking over at Sally and Jonathan. His hair was longer and curlier than a month ago, and she wanted to wrench his glasses off.

'About what I was doing with Jonathan that day you came over,' she said awkwardly. 'I wish you hadn't seen that. It wasn't how it looked.'

'It looked pretty sensational from where I was standing. You're going to tell me you were simply borrowing him, I suppose,' Jack muttered, half turning back to Janie, but with his eyes still glued to Jonathan and Sally. 'Although, maybe it wasn't just the once. Is this what goes on all the time when Ben's back is turned?'

Sally was still flat on her front, gripping the edges of the table. Jonathan had stopped tonguing her and Janie looked up in time to see him slowly feeding the incredible length of his penis into her from behind; he pushed her a little way across the table with every inch that went in and made the jug and glasses rattle. Janie pressed her legs together as she watched, remembering the feel of that extraordinary length of gristle when she had pole-danced up and down on it.

'No. Yes. We've been a little crazy this summer,' she stammered, trying to get his attention. 'But you weren't around, Jack.'

'More's the pity.'

He grinned up at her from his place on the grass, and she spread her hands helplessly.

'What do you mean?' she demanded. 'I thought I was getting a telling off! I thought you were going to run off and tell cousin Ben.'

Jack unfolded his legs and stood up. 'Do you think it's safe to grab a drink?'

She slapped him on the leg and he tiptoed up to the table, reached round the rutting pair to swipe the jug and glasses, and ran back to her.

They chinked glasses, and knocked back the strong cocktail as if it was lemonade. Janie felt woozy, and she lay back with another sigh on the lounger, hesitated for a moment, then lowered her knees and stretched herself out. Jack wasn't quick enough to hide the lust gleaming in his eyes as she wriggled into a comfortable position with her long legs slightly parted and her breasts bouncing softly with each judder of her heart. There was a silence between them, while at the far side of the lawn the table creaked desperately.

'You're wrong, and you're right,' he said.

Janie frowned, and closed her eyes.

'Riddles, as usual. What are you talking about?'

She felt the end of her lounger give as he sat down on it, but she kept her eyes closed. A warm sense of contentment was coming to life in her toes and starting to work up her body.

'I mean, you're wrong about me telling you off,' he explained. 'I'm not. You can do what you like. I'm jealous as hell, that's all. I should have been here. I should have been the one to have you. Not all these others – and especially not Maddock.'

Janie let out a snuffle of laughter, but he didn't laugh back. She held her breath, still stretched out, still heavy with anticipated pleasure.

'There's a lot more to Maddock than muddy boots and Land Rovers, you know,' she started to tell him. 'A real son of the soil. I mean, he uses it like a battering ram –'

'Shut it, Janie. Doesn't suit you being so crude. I thought you were more civilised that that, even if you are a thief.'

She giggled, and wriggled again. The sun was losing its ferocity, but was still just warm enough to make Janie want to fall asleep.

'But you were right about my running off to tell Ben,' he added.

She was befuddled, now. She'd forgotten how his

mind worked, always darting about. She raised her glass and took another long drink.

'I mean. I did tell him. He knows everything.'

Janie sat up sharply, spilling her drink over herself just as the wooden table scraped across the terrace. Jonathan was crouched over Sally, thrusting himself violently into her, and she was shouting out, and then they were yelling out together before he slumped down onto her back. But Jack wasn't looking at them now. He had sat down closer to Janie than he realised, and he was watching as the cold drink dripped off her nipples.

Janie looked down. The cold had hardened them again. The effect was more startling than simply exposing them to the open air. They were singing and burning like little beacons, hot with desire, and their sharpness was accentuated by the swell of her breasts. Her breath caught in her throat as the constant flutter in her stomach sped up. She sat still for a moment, attempting to make sense of what Jack had just said, but all she could think about was his eyes on her tits and the shifting, fidgeting arousal deep between her legs. She shuffled on the lounger towards him until she was right in front of him, then lifted one of his legs across the seat so that he was astride the lounger, and therefore facing her.

'Lick it off,' she said, and her heart gave a leap of surprise at herself. He carried on looking at her nipples. Only the jumping of his pulse in his muscular neck showed any sign of life. She whipped his glasses off and put them on the grass behind her.

'I said, lick it off. You'll do as I say, Jack. We're not children any more, and it's not me who's taking the orders.'

She reached out and grabbed his curls, tangled her

fingers through them and dragged his head towards her. He pulled away for a moment, and she wondered if she was making an idiot of herself, but then he groaned, a cracked, genuine groan as if to give up any more resistance, and she kneeled up so that his dark head was on a level with her breasts. She cradled him, pushing him into the dark, inviting cleavage.

'They were covered before in all those layers,' he murmured. 'In the barn. I felt them, but I had no idea how luscious they've grown.'

Jack's voice was muffled up against her skin, and she shifted closer still on her knees until she was straddling his legs. She locked her knees behind his back so that he was trapped in front of her. Her mind wouldn't keep still. Now she was thinking of the blond boy on the beach, taking her breasts in hesitant, clumsy fingers and wondering what to do with them until she showed him. But as the warm tip of Jack's tongue started to trail across one breast, into the sweaty valley between, and up the other hillock, she knew this was different. This was a man at work. She stopped moving and let his tongue do the talking. It came back over the bulge of one breast, stopped short of the bursting nipple, and started to circle it. It took all her willpower to avoid thrusting the nipple into his mouth as she had done with the blond boy. To stop herself she looked over at the garden table, but Sally and Jonathan had disappeared, leaving the pink thong discarded on the terrace.

Jack's tongue was flickering like a lizard's over Janie's nipple now. She could feel the nipple sticking out almost an inch away from its base, so that every touch of his tongue was close yet distant, not touching the flesh of her breast at all. She shifted very slightly on her buttocks so that she was able to press her aching crotch against his. Her bikini-bottoms were soaking, and they stuck to her pussy-lips as they shifted. The electric shocks of sensation were seared all over her, from her nipples down to her navel, from the outer layers of her fanny to the cavern of her anus, and she started, very slightly so that her thighs ached, to rise up and down to find a way to answer the clamouring of her body.

One of Jack's hands was pressing a breast, but the other came round and rested on the small of her back, pushing her harder against him, and she laughed softly as her wet bikini made contact with the buttons of his shorts. They would be leaving a damp patch there, she thought, sliding her hands away from his head and down his warm torso to his waist. She started to undo his shorts, and suddenly he took the tortured nipple into his mouth and started sucking hard, biting it, then leaving it, cold with his saliva, and turning to the other one while his fingers took over the teasing and pinching of whichever nipple was free.

'I want this to go on forever,' she murmured, pushing his shorts down over his hips. His head jerked back as he looked at her.

'Is that an order?'

In answer she wriggled backwards, letting her breasts drop heavily down in front of her, so that she could pull his shorts off. He wore nothing underneath, and her tongue came out and slid across her lips as she saw the firm erection rising out of his groin.

'It was covered in all those layers. In the barn –' she chuckled softly, taking it in both her hands and rubbing them up and down so that it grew longer as she fondled it '– I felt it, but I had no idea how luscious it had grown.'

'Are you taking the piss?' breathed Jack.

She chuckled again, pulling hard at him, measuring his weight in her hands. Then, still holding him, she crawled off the lounger and onto the grass, then tugged him down on top of her. For a moment he was on all fours above her, still wearing his T-shirt, his cock stiff in her hands and dangling over her stomach, then she spun round onto her knees and pushed him down onto his back as he had pushed her onto the hay bale.

'No, my darling, Jack. I'm taking the penis.'

She knew she couldn't hold out much longer. She realised this was what, in the back of her mind, she had been working towards all summer. The variety of her sexual experiences had been stunning, and she was anxious to repeat them, even with Mimi, but Jack had been the one initially to arouse her. They had awoken each other in the barn during that storm. He was the one she had wanted to find again, whom she wanted to go even further with, if he would let her. Now that she had tried new things, new positions, new people, she wanted to try it all over again with him. She suspected that was what, for all her brazen talk, Sally wanted with her Jonathan Dart.

'Fuck me, Jack,' she said loudly, not caring who might hear or about sounding 'crude'. She yanked her bikini-bottom aside to show him her pussy, feeling it was more sexy to keep it half on. He smiled a lazy smile, halfway to a laugh, his dark-brown eyes gleaming at her from under his long eyelashes. She felt a frisson of amusement at the unaccustomed beauty of his eyes. It had been too dark to see them properly in the barn. He had never once removed his glasses when they were kids. Now he was naked and vulnerable before her. But he was still stronger than her. She tried to lower herself onto his rearing, ready cock, but he gripped her hips and stopped her just as the rounded tip of it brushed her pubes and sent tiny trickles of desire across her sex. She waited, her legs shaking with the effort, and then he let her drop far enough down for the tip to burrow in, to get just short of her burning clitoris, before stopping again.

'Not totally in charge, Janie,' he gasped. Then he yanked her down onto him so her crotch was against his and she shrieked out loud with the brutal impact of his cock jammed right up inside her. Then they were humping like crazy, making up for lost time, no longer caring about control. She stretched herself out on top of him, squashing her breasts against his chest, her mouth slicking across his, her legs stretched out flat between his. She let his hips take their weight, lift them both off the ground and down again as her inner muscles gripped and pulled him further and further in. Then she was up again, knees bent on the grass, bouncing up and down on him, hearing herself yell and scream with the release of tension, then lying down again to try to slow the rising tide of climax. But it wouldn't turn back, and she let him rock her, simply moved with him, as she pressed her ear to his chest and heard his growls of ecstasy. She felt his cock juddering and hardening still more inside her and the lusciousness of the sensation unlocked any remnants of control. The orgasm flooded through her, warm and wet and long-awaited. It kept on shaking her until all she could do was roll with him sideways onto the grass and trap him with her legs until it had all faded away.

'You really didn't know who I was in the barn?' he asked after a moment.

'No. You just popped up at the right time, when I needed someone to remind me how good sex was. I really needed to fuck.'

'Are you serious? I thought you were such a sweet girl, Janie Flower. At least, you used to be. I'm shocked.'

She laughed and sniffed the sweat on his skin.

'Don't give me sweet. You and that foul cousin of mine bullied me mercilessly for years. Either that or you just left me out of all your games. You couldn't stand me. No wonder I didn't recognise you the other night. Although I suppose I should have clocked the glasses.'

'You're so wrong. We both fancied you, even then. We had wet dreams about you. We used to fight over you.'

'You were always so horrible to me! And anyway, Ben's my cousin; he couldn't fancy me.'

'That's what he thought, until I stupidly pointed out to him that you were only second cousins, or something, and anyway, it's not illegal.' He reached for his glasses. 'We fell out for years because of you.'

Janie pulled the tangled hair off her face. 'Don't believe you. Ben's never mentioned it.'

'He wouldn't – too proud. But you can ask him when he gets here. When we were last all together, we were growing up too fast. Not kids any more.'

'I was fifteen, and you were both sixteen.' She twisted her hair into a plait and let it drop down her back.

'And all the games were over.'

'You were taking pot shots at me with an air rifle!' screamed Janie.

'No, I was aiming for seagulls, and trying to impress you!' Jack shook his head. 'I was going to ask you for a date, but then you just vanished, the summer was over, and so was our childhood.'

'Sentimental tosh.'

'Ask him.'

She punched him playfully and looked around the garden. They can't have been lying there for long, but the sun had started to creep behind the row of tall trees bordering Jack's farm, and the air was definitely cooler. There was still no sign of Jonathan or Sally. The approaching dusk suddenly jogged an old memory.

'There was a moment, now you mention it,' she murmured. 'You and I, alone in – was it that barn, or another one? Somewhere filled with straw.'

'We were playing hide-and-seek with some younger cousins of yours. It was a hay rick out in one of the fields. We were the wrong age to be playing games like that, but the right age to be so totally sex-obsessed. But we were – or I was – whenever you were around. You and I fetched up hiding right inside the hay bales. I was so close to you. I wanted to kiss you. I don't know how I got it so wrong, but instead of melting into my arms, you scrambled out of our hideout, screeching!'

Janie laughed. 'All I remember is seeing my reflection in your glasses as you bent closer and closer to me.'

They were silent for a few moments.

'He'll be here soon,' Jack murmured, as if to himself. Janie edged herself off him, feeling his still firm penis sliding slowly between her wet lips and thumping down onto his leg. She lay on her back for a while, looking at the sky which was very pale with the approaching sunset.

'Who?' she asked dopily when he didn't say anything more.

'Ben. Cousin Ben. I told you, he knows everything.'

'And he's coming here?'

'Hot foot! Amsterdam is like a rest-home compared with what's been going on in this place!'

He pulled her back towards him, holding her against his firm body, and she felt a fresh stirring of desire inside. She hooked her leg over his, realising that the burgeoning excitement wasn't only reserved for the new, grown-up Jack. It was the thought of Ben fancying her all those years ago. Handsome, aloof Ben, who she was scared of, even now, and only ever spoke to on the phone.

'Come on, let's go see what those other sex fiends are up to.'

She flipped away from him, suddenly restless. He groaned and put his arm across his eyes. Janie jumped up, pulled on his shorts and her broderie anglaise gypsy top; most of the buttons were missing. She walked round the corner of the cottage. Of course – there it was, just as she had envisaged the first night she and Sally were there. They had cajoled poor Derek into constructing it before he left, and there it stood. The wigwam.

Sally bounded out of the kitchen door as Janie approached. She was carrying cushions and rugs.

'We thought we could have our supper in here, but there isn't room,' she chirped. 'Jono and I tried it out just now,' she said, with a wink, 'if you know what I mean. There's only room for two people to do it doggy style. But you can have too much of a good thing. Even I know that! We'll have it out here on the lawn,' she whooped, her face flushed with sex and triumph. 'Supper, that is!'

Jonathan followed her with a crate of champagne and a shining new barbeque set which he'd produced from the boot of his car. Like Janie they had pulled on any old thing to wear. She giggled to see Jonathan sporting the famous pinafore. Sally had on his polo-shirt, which reached to her knees.

'Guess what,' Janie started to say, bending to go inside the wigwam and grinning with pleasure at its blood-red interior, illuminated by the setting sun. 'Guess who's coming to the cottage?'

'What was that? We've got to tell you something, too.' Sally dropped the cushions onto the grass outside. 'Jonathan and I are going back to London.'

Janie frowned. 'You can't. The summer isn't over yet.'

'I don't mean immediately. But in the next few days. We've got a business to set up.'

Janie's limbs were heavy with a new contentment. She had no energy to argue or worry.

'Whatever makes you happy, doll. Think you'll find it hard to leave, though.'

Sally rested her head on Janie's arm for a moment.

'You're right. It's been a tonic for me, coming here. I never dreamed it would be so good. You're the best, Janie. And who would have thought that the icing on the cake would be that king of bastards following me down here and gulping down humble pie and a lot more besides?'

'Who would have thought it?'

'And who would have thought you would turn into the local nympho? You almost put me in the shade. I said *almost*.' Sally laughed. Jonathan yelled something, and she turned to go out. 'By the way, what were you going to tell us?'

'Nothing. Nothing.'

Janie stood in the middle of the wigwam, where the fire would be if they lit one, and stared up to the pointed, twiggy ceiling just above her head. It was just right; Derek had done well. He'd probably had a wigwam when he was a kid. But it was too small. They were adults now. It was just an illusion that they could all have played in here. She felt a slight plunge of disappointment in her chest, and as she wrapped her arms round herself something told her to keep Ben's impending arrival to herself.

Local nympho – daft description, but she liked it. And Sally was right. Everywhere she looked, Janie saw sex. Everyone she looked at. She stretched her aching back. She'd got the man she wanted. She was beginning to like the new Janie.

An unexpected breeze tugged at the sheet that Derek had folded back to form the entrance to the wigwam, and someone else crept inside. Her body relaxed in the knowledge that any second now Jack's medical hands would start to caress her again, and she knew how they would feel on her, and she would show him some more tricks. She didn't turn round. The hairs on her neck rose as he paused behind her. She could hear him open his mouth to say something, but then she could just hear his breathing. She closed her eyes. Sally was right. There was just enough room for two in here. Somehow that had the effect of muffling the garden outside, as well. Somewhere she could hear Sally and Jonathan arguing about the food, but in here all was quiet and dark.

At last his hands came round to her front, very slowly stroking her stomach. Hesitantly, she thought, smiling. As if he'd never touched her before. She leaned back against him, and felt him stagger slightly at her sudden relaxed weight. She took his hands and pushed them up from her waist, up over the little blouse until they rested on her breasts. She felt him stiffen with desire behind her. His fingers trod over the broderie anglaise fabric in search of buttons, and found the couple that were still straining to keep it fastened over her breasts. She kept her fingers lightly on his wrists and stopped him from flipping the buttons undone. She wanted to relish the feeling of her breasts being covered, but only just. Her tits were swelling with excitement, threatening to burst the buttons anyway. She smiled to herself, stifling excited laughter. Now she really would look like a ravished milkmaid, her little blouse sliding off her shoulders. No more sweaters, coats, baggy shirts – she hadn't even worn a bra for a week. Her breasts pushed forwards heavily and eagerly into his hands and her laughter turned into a soft moan. He was breathing hard into her neck now, pressing himself up against her.

'Hold it right there,' Janie said into the steamy silence. 'This is my wigwam. This is my fantasy. In here, you do as I tell you.'

Jack paused, then drew back from her. The flap of the wigwam dropped down, enclosing them in a blood-red cocoon.

'Kneel down,' she ordered, and saw him do so. Slowly she started to undo one tiny button, revealing the deep cleft of her cleavage, the rounded shapes of her breasts illuminated by the light outside. Then she undid the other button, held the blouse closed for a moment, then opened it, and slid it off by wriggling her shoulders as she'd seen Sally do when she was doing her Kicker Girls striptease. Janie let her breasts drop heavily forwards in the light.

As if on cue some music started up inside the house – slow, jazzy tunes. Janie took her breasts in her hands and started to knead them, gently at first, then more firmly. This was going to be her own floor show. She couldn't dance, but she knew enough now about pleasure to do it to herself. She couldn't see Jack's face clearly, but she knew he was wearing a lustful expression. She could also imagine Ben's face, kneeling beside his friend, watching her as well.

A great surge of hot lust pounded through her as she stepped further into her fantasy. The music pounded with it, and she caressed her breasts more passionately, swaying and letting her hair swing down her back. She let herself relax, knowing those eyes were on her, knowing that those boys would be getting hard watching her and watching each other. The heat curled up from her cunt, through her body and right into her head. She was delirious with the excitement of what she was doing, and who she was with.

She curled one arm under her breasts to keep them raised, her hand fondling and squeezing the yielding flesh, and with the other hand she pushed the shorts down and let them fall to the ground. Then she stepped across to Jack, and placed one foot on either side of him so that her crotch was up against his face. His hands stroked up the back of her legs, tickling the skin behind her knees so that they nearly buckled. She pushed her soft bush aggressively against his face and felt his breath blow across her pubes. She started to sway her hips, into him and away, unable to stop herself moving in a way that matched the ripples of desire that were already pulsating through her. He grasped her buttocks, digging his fingers into them, and pulled her pussy against his mouth. She was so horny already that when his tongue snaked out and touched her clitoris she let out a loud groan, ground herself against his face, then with superhuman effort she stepped away again. It wasn't time yet. She swayed round to face the imaginary Ben. He would be up on all fours like a dog, right behind her, virtually snarling, his face nuzzling up against her thigh. She swung round again to Jack, spread her legs on either side of his head and rested her pussy against his face. He opened her sex-lips with his fingers, held them wide apart, and gently nibbled into her.

Janie smiled to herself and felt her legs give way as Jack's teeth worked her into a frenzy. She was surprised at how harsh he was being. She liked it. She could imagine Ben nipping and biting like that, but she had turned herself on so much just by imagining them both watching that she feared she would come quickly if she wasn't careful. Time to slow down.

She stepped away from Jack's busy mouth, and heard him curse under his breath. She kept one hand on her tits and the other cupped over her bush and, forcing herself to keep her fingers still in case she flicked the button way too early, she crossed her ankles and lowered herself to the ground, just like a squaw. Then she spread her arms in a welcoming, permissive gesture, and lay back on the rug.

Jack was crawling all over her at once, stroking and kissing up and down her prone body, pulling her legs apart, bringing her hands up over her head, and again Janie imagined that it was two of them. She rolled and twisted as Jack pulled her hair out of the way, then moved down towards her breasts and heaved them up so that her taut nipples were offered to the warm air. She wriggled and squealed, already twitching with her approaching climax, imagining herself floating above, watching the fantasy. She wondered how long she could hold on for.

'I want to feel you inside me – now.'

Janie opened her eyes and felt the familiar warmth of Jack's body as he lay down on top of her. He pressed his mouth onto hers and kissed her long and hard, then he pushed her legs further apart, and eased his throbbing dick inside her. She knew that if she let herself go she would climax wildly with the pleasure of knowing Jack was hers once more. She could hardly picture Ben any more. This was Jack's story. She wondered what Ben would think of her now, closeted inside this wigwam, his old friend's cock buried deep inside her, her tits bare and swollen, her mouth open with ecstasy. She hoped he'd be impressed, but then again – what did it matter?

'Janie! Jack! Someone here to see you! And the barbie's nearly ready!'

Sally's voice sliced through the sound of their heavy breathing, and Janie and Jack smothered their laughter.

'Just a little bit more,' Janie breathed. 'Do it, Jack.'

She was wet and welcoming, and Jack was fired up, and she wrapped her legs round his waist as he started to thrust himself into her. She kept her mind on Jack, her thoughts trained on that first time, in the barn, with those lads watching through the door; kept her mind on it as if it was a film; heard herself at last calling Jack's name. This was where she wanted to be. She let the waves of her own climax break as Jack thrust harder and harder to reach his goal. His buttocks slammed against her as he gave in, kissing her neck as he groaned her name in response and filled her with his spunk.

They could hear giggles and shouts coming from somewhere near the barbeque. Jonathan would be there in the pinafore, tossing his sausages.

Janie sat up, drew her knees up to her chest, feeling the sticky fluid slicking across her thighs and over her stomach. There was a chinking of glasses outside as Sally bustled noisily out onto the terrace, and the smell of charcoal heating up on the barbecue. Out on the big lawn Jonathan was noisily trying to erect the old swing seat.

'Come on, let's eat.'

'Is that another order?' Jack chuckled, as he fumbled with the wigwam doorway.

Janie laughed. The wigwam shook precariously as they struggled to get out. It started to lurch to one side, and then Derek's flimsy structure toppled right over, its bamboo legs in the air, the material falling gently in on itself like a collapsed parachute, leaving the two of them staggering about naked and blinking at the light.

'So you found her, Jack.'

They spun round, clutching scraps of red material round them. Jack looked like an Indian brave in a loincloth.

Ben was standing on the grass, looking hot and incongruous in a grey business suit. He looked around his own garden as if he'd just landed from Mars. Janie remembered that slightly defensive stance. When Ben was a boy he would plant his feet in that exact fashion, slightly apart, when he was faced with an argument. Except usually he would be brandishing a bow and arrow, as well, to emphasise his superiority.

'Ben!' cried Jack, trying to greet him amid a clatter of bamboo twigs. 'Good to see you! How was Amsterdam? I wasn't sure exactly when –'

'Look at you; the pair of you. Can't trust you for a second. I thought you were supposed to be looking after the place, Janie?'

'Ben! I – I have been. I mean, I am. You can see. All new.'

Janie bit her lip, furious at the way he made her feel eight years old again. Jack put his arm round her.

'And I thought you were over that crush of yours, Jack? I didn't expect to see you both rolling about in my garden when I got back from yet another tough, exhausting business trip. Amsterdam was tough and exhausting, thanks for asking.'

'It's hard to take a telling-off when you're butt-naked. Sorry, Ben,' Jack pointed out. 'And I refuse to believe that you haven't been up to some pretty racy things yourself while you've been over there. I mean, Amsterdam's your home from home, isn't it? Tough and exhausting? I don't think so. All those canals, those bridges, those rickety gables, those doe-eyed girls, creatures of the night sitting cross-legged in the ultraviolet light of their windows, beckoning –'

Ben started to laugh. He took his jacket off and threw it across the back of one of the terrace chairs.

'Someone's got to be grafting away to keep you lot in cottages and barbecues! I'm only kidding. It's great to see that you've finally got it together. You always had the hots for Janie, even when we were all beating the shit out of each other.'

'I had the hots for you, too,' Janie blurted out.

'Ah, she speaks! Well, my timing this time was cock-eyed yet again, wasn't it? And the best man won.'

Janie glanced at Jack. 'Yes, he did.'

'Now then, now then, what's going on here? You all look far too serious,' chirruped Sally, bustling across the lawn and brandishing a pair of tongs. 'If you two have stopped shagging in the – in what's left of the wigwam, it's time to tuck in.'

'Is that what it is? A wigwam?' Ben snorted.

'Don't you snort, young man,' Sally chided. 'That's Janie's fantasy, that is. You don't know the half of it.' She waved the tongs at Janie. 'You've come a long way, girl. I never thought we'd get further than talking about it in front of the fire and now look. You've shagged yourself senseless in there. Just one member of the cast missing, wasn't there?'

'What are you on about?' asked Ben, undoing his collar and flipping his tie undone.

'We're talking about fantasies, cousin Ben,' Sally said, as she picked up some more cushions and rugs and dropped them in an inviting pile near the barbecue. 'This cottage of yours is enchanted. All sorts of things happen here. And how beautifully your little cousin Janie has grown up, wouldn't you agree?'

'Yes, definitely. Her friend isn't so bad, either.'

Sally slapped him on the arm. Jonathan turned from the barbecue to see what was going on, and they all laughed at him.

'He can't tell me off for flirting,' chortled Sally. 'Not when he looks like the cover of a raunchy cookery book! Now, Ben, you're wearing too many clothes. Why not start with the trousers? You need to take these trousers off. Come on, there's a good boy.'

She started to undo his belt buckle, and slipped it expertly out from around his waist. Ben held his hands up in surrender.

'It's difficult to tell who's in charge,' he yelped, as Sally advanced on him again, snapping her tongs.

'Sally, I need a hand here!' shouted Jonathan. There was a clanking of metal as the swing seat conspired to fall apart again.

'Let's eat!' Ben pleaded, backing away from Sally towards the food.

'Let's help Jonathan,' Jack said, then kissed Janie and followed Ben across the grass. 'And I'll try to explain about who exactly is in charge.'

'Yes, would you do that? For some reason I thought

I'd left Maddock in charge of my property while I was away, but I see no sign of him.'

'I get the feeling he was made to feel, how shall we say, redundant. Janie did all the work on the cottage. He came round once or twice, I believe.'

Jack and Ben sat down on the rug and watched Janie tossing the salad and Sally taking a hefty bite out of a sausage.

'I bet he did,' murmured Ben. 'Must have scared the living daylights out of them, if I know anything about his tactics!'

'They gave as good as they got,' Jack replied, but Janie shot him a look. She knew he wasn't comfortable with that particular anecdote.

'Maddock's used to being king of the heap around here, isn't he?' she remarked, handing them two heaped plates.

'And a very good king he makes, too, in a caveman kind of way,' Sally added with her mouth full, 'but he's had some knocks this summer. Even the barmaid dumped him.'

Jonathan had given up trying to assemble the swing seat and had pulled his trousers back on. He thumped a tray of bottles and glasses down on the grass. The twilight had dropped over the garden, and a riotous full moon was floating in the navy-blue sky.

'I wouldn't worry about Maddock,' Ben said, and they all looked at him. 'He looked happy as a pig in shit when I dropped in at the Honey Pot earlier. There's a new bird behind the bar already, and she looked right up his alley.'

'A proper country wench, you mean?' Janie asked, winking at Jack.

'We're just tourists,' Ben answered. 'Look at us,

partying up here in our cute cottage. Down there, in the Honey Pot, they're the real thing. She'll do for Maddock, all right. Lots of blonde curls, big tits and haunches, sturdy legs, strong arms that could swing a couple of heifers. Think I'll make my way down there myself later on!'

LOOK OUT FOR THE ALL-NEW BLACK LACE BOOKS – AVAILABLE NOW!

All books priced £6.99 in the UK. Please note publication dates apply to the UK only. For other territories, please contact your retailer.

DRIVEN BY DESIRE
Savannah Smythe
ISBN 0 352 33799 0

When Rachel's husband abandons both her and his taxi-cab business and flees the country, she is left to pick up the pieces. However, this is a blessing in disguise as Rachel, along with her friend Sharma, transforms his business into an exclusive chauffeur service for discerning gentlemen – with all the perks that offers. What Rachel doesn't know is that two of her regular clients are jewel thieves with exotic tastes in sexual experimentation. As Rachel is lured into an underworld lifestyle of champagne, diamonds and lustful indulgence, she finds a familiar face is involved in some very shady activity! **Another cracking story of strong women and sexy double dealing from Savannah Smythe.**

FIGHTING OVER YOU
Laura Hamilton
ISBN 0 352 33795 8

Yasmin and U seem like the perfect couple. She's a scriptwriter and he's a magazine editor who has a knack for tapping into the latest trends. One evening, however, U confesses to Yasmin that he's 'having a thing' with a nineteen-year-old violinist – the precocious niece of Yasmin and U's old boss, the formidable Pandora Fairchild. Amelia, the violinist, turns out to be a catalyst for a whole series of erotic experiments that even Yasmin finds intriguing. In a haze of absinthe, lust and wild abandon, all parties find answers to questions about their sexuality they were once too afraid to ask. **Contemporary erotica at its best from the author of the bestselling *Fire and Ice*.**

THE LION LOVER
Mercedes Kelly
ISBN O 352 33162 3

Settling into life in 1930s Kenya, Mathilde Valentine finds herself sent to a harem where the Sultan, his sadistic brother and adolescent son all make sexual demands on her. Meanwhile, Olensky – the rugged game hunter and 'lion lover' – plots her escape, but will she want to be rescued? **A wonderful exploration of 'White Mischief' goings on in 1930s Africa.**

Coming in July

THE RELUCTANT PRINCESS
Patty Glenn
ISBN O 532 33809 O

Martha's a rich valley girl who's living on the wrong side of the tracks and hanging out with Hollywood hustlers. Things were OK when her bodyguard Gus was looking after her, but now he's in hospital Martha's gone back to her bad old ways. When she meets mean, moody and magnificent private investigator Joaquin Lee, the sexual attraction between them is instant and intense. If Martha can keep herself on the straight and narrow for a year, her family will let her have access to her inheritance. Lee reckons he can help out while pocketing a cut for himself. **A dynamic battle of wills between two very stubborn, very sexy characters.**

ARIA APPASSIONATA
Juliet Hastings
ISBN O 352 33056 2

Tess Challoner has made it. She is going to play Carmen in a new production of the opera that promises to be as raunchy and explicit as it is intelligent. But Tess needs to learn a lot about passion and desire before the opening night. Tony Varguez, the handsome but jealous Spanish tenor, takes on the task of her education. When Tess finds herself drawn to a desirable new member of the cast, she knows she's playing with fire. **Life imitating art – with dramatically sexual consequences.**

Coming in August

WILD IN THE COUNTRY
Monica Belle
ISBN O 352 33824 5

When Juliet Eden is sacked for having sex with a sous-chef, she leaves the prestigious London kitchen where she's been working and heads for the country. Alone in her inherited cottage, boredom soon sets in – until she discovers the rural delights of poaching, and of the muscular young gamekeeper who works the estate. When the local landowner falls for her, things are looking better still, but threaten to turn sour when her ex-boss, Gabriel, makes an unexpected appearance. **City vs country in Monica Belle's latest story of rustic retreats and sumptuous feasts!**

THE TUTOR
Portia Da Costa
ISBN O 352 32946 7

When Rosalind Howard becomes Julian Hadey's private librarian, she soon finds herself attracted by his persuasive charms and distinguished appearance. He is an unashamed sensualist who, together with his wife, Celeste, has hatched an intriguing challenge for their new employee. As well as cataloguing their collection of erotica, Rosie is expected to educate Celeste's young and beautiful cousin David in the arts of erotic love. **A long-overdue reprint of this arousing tale of erotic initiation written by a pioneer of women's sex fiction.**

Black Lace Booklist

Information is correct at time of printing. To avoid disappointment check availability before ordering. Go to www.blacklace-books.co.uk. All books are priced £6.99 unless another price is given.

BLACK LACE BOOKS WITH A CONTEMPORARY SETTING

☐ IN THE FLESH Emma Holly   ISBN 0 352 33498 3 £5.99
☐ A PRIVATE VIEW Crystalle Valentino   ISBN 0 352 33308 1 £5.99
☐ SHAMELESS Stella Black   ISBN 0 352 33485 1 £5.99
☐ INTENSE BLUE Lyn Wood   ISBN 0 352 33496 7 £5.99
☐ THE NAKED TRUTH Natasha Rostova   ISBN 0 352 33497 5 £5.99
☐ A SPORTING CHANCE Susie Raymond   ISBN 0 352 33501 7 £5.99
☐ TAKING LIBERTIES Susie Raymond   ISBN 0 352 33357 X £5.99
☐ A SCANDALOUS AFFAIR Holly Graham   ISBN 0 352 33523 8 £5.99
☐ THE NAKED FLAME Crystalle Valentino   ISBN 0 352 33528 9 £5.99
☐ ON THE EDGE Laura Hamilton   ISBN 0 352 33534 3 £5.99
☐ LURED BY LUST Tania Picarda   ISBN 0 352 33533 5 £5.99
☐ THE HOTTEST PLACE Tabitha Flyte   ISBN 0 352 33536 X £5.99
☐ THE NINETY DAYS OF GENEVIEVE Lucinda   ISBN 0 352 33070 8 £5.99
        Carrington
☐ DREAMING SPIRES Juliet Hastings   ISBN 0 352 33584 X
☐ THE TRANSFORMATION Natasha Rostova   ISBN 0 352 33311 1
☐ SIN.NET Helena Ravenscroft   ISBN 0 352 33598 X
☐ TWO WEEKS IN TANGIER Annabel Lee   ISBN 0 352 33599 8
☐ HIGHLAND FLING Jane Justine   ISBN 0 352 33616 1
☐ PLAYING HARD Tina Troy   ISBN 0 352 33617 X
☐ SYMPHONY X Jasmine Stone   ISBN 0 352 33629 3
☐ STRICTLY CONFIDENTIAL Alison Tyler   ISBN 0 352 33624 2
☐ SUMMER FEVER Anna Ricci   ISBN 0 352 33625 0
☐ CONTINUUM Portia Da Costa   ISBN 0 352 33120 8
☐ OPENING ACTS Suki Cunningham   ISBN 0 352 33630 7
☐ FULL STEAM AHEAD Tabitha Flyte   ISBN 0 352 33637 4
☐ A SECRET PLACE Ella Broussard   ISBN 0 352 33307 3
☐ GAME FOR ANYTHING Lyn Wood   ISBN 0 352 33639 0

☐ FORBIDDEN FRUIT Susie Raymond   ISBN 0 352 33306 5
☐ CHEAP TRICK Astrid Fox   ISBN 0 352 33640 4
☐ ALL THE TRIMMINGS Tesni Morgan   ISBN 0 352 33641 3
☐ PLAYING WITH STARS Jan Hunter   ISBN 0 352 33653 6
☐ THE GIFT OF SHAME Sara Hope-Walker   ISBN 0 352 32935 1
☐ COMING UP ROSES Crystalle Valentino   ISBN 0 352 33658 7
☐ GOING TOO FAR Laura Hamilton   ISBN 0 352 33657 9
☐ THE STALLION Georgina Brown   ISBN 0 352 33005 8
☐ DOWN UNDER Juliet Hastings   ISBN 0 352 33663 3
☐ THE BITCH AND THE BASTARD Wendy Harris   ISBN 0 352 33664 1
☐ ODALISQUE Fleur Reynolds   ISBN 0 352 32887 8
☐ SWEET THING Alison Tyler   ISBN 0 352 33682 X
☐ TIGER LILY Kimberley Dean   ISBN 0 352 33685 4
☐ COOKING UP A STORM Emma Holly   ISBN 0 352 33686 2
☐ RELEASE ME Suki Cunningham   ISBN 0 352 33671 4
☐ KING'S PAWN Ruth Fox   ISBN 0 352 33684 6
☐ FULL EXPOSURE Robyn Russell   ISBN 0 352 33688 9
☐ SLAVE TO SUCCESS Kimberley Raines   ISBN 0 352 33687 0
☐ STRIPPED TO THE BONE Jasmine Stone   ISBN 0 352 33463 0
☐ HARD CORPS Claire Thompson   ISBN 0 352 33491 6
☐ MANHATTAN PASSION Antoinette Powell   ISBN 0 352 33691 9
☐ CABIN FEVER Emma Donaldson   ISBN 0 352 33692 7
☐ WOLF AT THE DOOR Savannah Smythe   ISBN 0 352 33693 5
☐ SHADOWPLAY Portia Da Costa   ISBN 0 352 33313 8
☐ I KNOW YOU, JOANNA Ruth Fox   ISBN 0 352 33727 3
☐ SNOW BLONDE Astrid Fox   ISBN 0 352 33732 X
☐ QUEEN OF THE ROAD Lois Pheonix   ISBN 0 352 33131 1
☐ THE HOUSE IN NEW ORLEANS Fleur Reynolds ISBN 0 352 32951 3
☐ HEAT OF THE MOMENT Tesni Morgan   ISBN 0 352 33742 7
☐ STORMY HAVEN Savannah Smythe   ISBN 0 352 33757 5
☐ STICKY FINGERS Alison Tyler   ISBN 0 352 33756 7
☐ THE WICKED STEPDAUGHTER Wendy Harris   ISBN 0 352 33777 X
☐ DRAWN TOGETHER Robyn Russell   ISBN 0 352 33269 7
☐ LEARNING THE HARD WAY Jasmine Archer   ISBN 0 352 33782 6
☐ VALENTINA'S RULES Monica Belle   ISBN 0 352 33788 5
☐ VELVET GLOVE Emma Holly   ISBN 0 352 33448 7

☐ VIRTUOSO Katrina Vincenzi-Thyre   ISBN 0 352 32907 6

☐ FIGHTING OVER YOU Laura Hamilton   ISBN 0 352 33795 8

☐ COUNTRY PLEASURES Primula Bond   ISBN 0 352 33810 5

☐ THE RELUCTANT PRINCESS Patty Glenn   ISBN 0 352 33809 1

BLACK LACE BOOKS WITH AN HISTORICAL SETTING

☐ PRIMAL SKIN Leona Benkt Rhys   ISBN 0 352 33500 9   £5.99

☐ DEVIL'S FIRE Melissa MacNeal   ISBN 0 352 33527 0   £5.99

☐ DARKER THAN LOVE Kristina Lloyd   ISBN 0 352 33279 4

☐ STAND AND DELIVER Helena Ravenscroft   ISBN 0 352 33340 5   £5.99

☐ THE CAPTIVATION Natasha Rostova   ISBN 0 352 33234 4

☐ MINX Megan Blythe   ISBN 0 352 33638 2

☐ JULIET RISING Cleo Cordell   ISBN 0 352 32938 6

☐ DEMON'S DARE Melissa MacNeal   ISBN 0 352 33683 8

☐ DIVINE TORMENT Janine Ashbless   ISBN 0 352 33719 2

☐ SATAN'S ANGEL Melissa MacNeal   ISBN 0 352 33726 5

☐ THE INTIMATE EYE Georgia Angelis   ISBN 0 352 33004 X

☐ OPAL DARKNESS Cleo Cordell   ISBN 0 352 33033 3

☐ SILKEN CHAINS Jodi Nicol   ISBN 0 352 33143 7

☐ EVIL'S NIECE Melissa MacNeal   ISBN 0 352 33781 8

☐ ACE OF HEARTS Lisette Allen   ISBN 0 352 33059 7

☐ A GENTLEMAN'S WAGER Madelynne Ellis   ISBN 0 352 33800 8

☐ THE LION LOVER Mercedes Kelly   ISBN 0 352 33162 3

BLACK LACE ANTHOLOGIES

☐ WICKED WORDS 5 Various   ISBN 0 352 33642 0

☐ WICKED WORDS 6 Various   ISBN 0 352 33590 0

☐ WICKED WORDS 7 Various   ISBN 0 352 33743 5

☐ WICKED WORDS 8 Various   ISBN 0 352 33787 7

☐ THE BEST OF BLACK LACE 2 Various   ISBN 0 352 33718 4

BLACK LACE NON-FICTION

☐ THE BLACK LACE BOOK OF WOMEN'S SEXUAL   ISBN 0 352 33793 1   £6.99
     FANTASIES Ed. Kerri Sharp

To find out the latest information about Black Lace titles, check out the website: www.blacklace-books.co.uk or send for a booklist with complete synopses by writing to:

Black Lace Booklist, Virgin Books Ltd
Thames Wharf Studios
Rainville Road
London W6 9HA

Please include an SAE of decent size. Please note only British stamps are valid.

Our privacy policy
We will not disclose information you supply us to any other parties.
We will not disclose any information which identifies you personally to any person without your express consent.

From time to time we may send out information about Black Lace books and special offers. Please tick here if you do <u>not</u> wish to receive Black Lace information. ❏

Please send me the books I have ticked above.

Name ....

Address ....

....

....

....

Post Code ....

Send to: Cash Sales, Black Lace Books, Thames Wharf Studios, Rainville Road, London W6 9HA.

US customers: for prices and details of how to order books for delivery by mail, call 1-800-343-4499.

Please enclose a cheque or postal order, made payable to Virgin Books Ltd, to the value of the books you have ordered plus postage and packing costs as follows:

UK and BFPO – £1.00 for the first book, 50p for each subsequent book.

Overseas (including Republic of Ireland) – £2.00 for the first book, £1.00 for each subsequent book.

If you would prefer to pay by VISA, ACCESS/MASTERCARD, DINERS CLUB, AMEX or SWITCH, please write your card number and expiry date here:

....

Signature ....

Please allow up to 28 days for delivery.